HUW the BARD

CONNIE J. JASPERSON

ISBN-13 - 978-1-939296-04-7

ISBN-10 - 1939296048

Riff on a Burne-Jones Window by C.L. Johnson
PD|CC-SA-3.0-AT
Maps © Connie J. Jasperson
Edited by Eagle Eye Editors
www.eagleyeeditors.me

Myrddin Publishing Group
Contact us at - www.myrddinpublishing.com

Contact us at: www.myrddinpublishing.com

This book is dedicated to Irene Roth Luvaul, who pulled it from my head, to Carlie M.A. Cullen who spent endless hours helping craft it and Maria V.A. Johnson who put the final polish on it. The three of you made Huw live—without you wonderful, cruel ladies, I couldn't have made it to the finish!

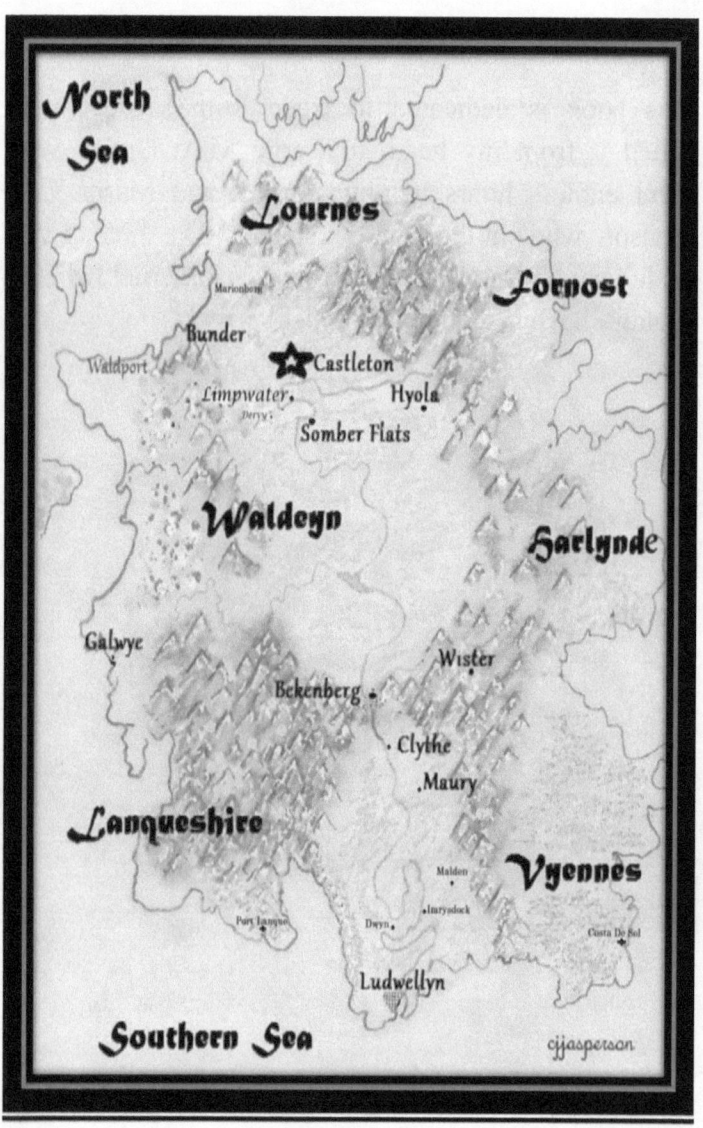

TABLE OF CONTENTS

Clythe

Maury

Maldon

Imrysdock
Dunmorra

Emmerton

Moireton

Dwyn.

Lumley

Davey

Pyndrys

Shandy Town

Ludwellyn

map of Eynier Valley by cjjasp

Chapter 1 Murder in Ludwellyn

The Sailor's Rest was a modest inn, known in a certain strata of society for its good food, decent ale and clean rooms, despite its location down on the seedy docks of Ludwellyn. The outside was carefully maintained to appear less inviting than it was in an effort to discourage visits by the upper nobility, as it was regularly frequented by tinkers and traveling folk when they had business in town. No one wanted to draw attention to that.

In a room on the third floor, Huw Owyn stood as still as he could while his betrothed, a dark haired beauty named Sinean, put the finishing touches on his disguise. "Hold still or it'll be uneven," she admonished, both giggling madly at his predicament. "This is serious, Huw!" She liberally powdered his hair, turning his black curls white.

At least, he *thought* she was his betrothed. With Sinean it was hard to tell.

"Aye, ma'am! Standing as still as I can. Oh, that tickles…Oh, no…." Abruptly he sneezed as a puff of powder went up his nose. They both giggled again as she struggled to disguise him as quickly as she could.

An independent woman and free spirit, Sinean was captain of a mercenary crew. Her lads worked as guards on many of the local merchants' ships as a cover for their clandestine activities, and they frequently set sail out of town. In a moment of passion, she'd agreed to marry him someday and Huw intended to be there when the day arrived.

Fortunately, Huw had no problem with Sinean's chosen profession. He was a fully-trained bard, an occupation that didn't really encourage marital fidelity in the lives of its members. Both professions frequently kept them apart; at times the distance and loneliness were hard to bear. 'Temporary infidelity' happened. In much the same way as mercenaries, bards were notoriously unfaithful spouses. In Huw's opinion, a mercenary would be the perfect match for him, as she wouldn't expect more fidelity from him than she'd be able to offer in return.

The way he saw it, the only thing standing in the way of their eternal bliss was her passionate devotion to the cause of bringing down the powerful Clan Grefyn. Huw secretly feared Sinean's revolution meant more to her than he did. He didn't know half of what she and her crew were involved in, and it worried him. But when they were together, none of it mattered and he was sure their love would be strong enough to make a good marriage.

Sinean drew the bonnet down over his once black curls. She tucked most of them up underneath the lacy bonnet, leaving a few loose in the style of ladies of the older generation. Next she carefully applied her precious stock of face paint to his eyes and lips, drawing lines to age him and adding a small beauty patch to his smooth cheek. "Your eyebrows...those are definitely not a woman's! Hold still," she commanded. "Let me do something about them." With that, she briskly plucked them, causing him to swear under his breath, but he stood still until he could take it no more.

"Ow! How do you women do this to yourselves? Ow! Stop! I'm an old dowager, and believe me, Sinean, no man looks at a dowager's eyebrows!" Huw sighed in relief as she, at last, let go of his face and turned to fastening his dress. He sucked his breath in as she frantically tried to hook the dress closed behind him. All the while, the Grand Duke's men pounded on doors down the hall, loud voices occasionally demanding they be let in to search for traitors. With each passing moment the hammering drew closer.

"It won't close, Huw! You'll have to keep the shawl on, or they'll be slitting your golden throat, my songbird." Giggling, Sinean pulled him to sit at her dressing table and pressed a book into his hands.

The long-abused chair gave out under him, all the years of rough handling by indifferent lodgers having finally taken their toll. The startled look on Huw's face would have been priceless under any circumstances, but he looked so like an affronted old fishwife Sinean could hardly contain her laughter.

"Oh, good grief, don't make me laugh, girl," Huw said, with a tinge of hysteria. "I won't be able to quit!" He struggled to get up, his legs tangled in his skirts.

"You make a large woman, love, far too tall and healthy. At least try to *look* like you might be my sickly aunt." Pulling him to his feet, Sinean straightened his clothes again. "Thank God you still have your pretty-boy face—you make a comely old dame." She rearranged her own dress, exposing more of her shoulders than was strictly necessary in Huw's opinion. "I much prefer your chin without the manly beard." She kissed his powdered cheek. "You don't need a patch of ratty fur to prove you're a man, Huw. You have all the right equipment under your dress!"

"But I look like a girl without it," he said, his vanity stung to the core. It had taken him a year to grow, and now it was a 'ratty' thing?

"It's no great loss, love. I like the new you. Besides, no one will recognize you without it. Maybe not even me, but I *would* pinch your fine, manly arse." They laughed and kissed, hands hungry for each other. They quickly broke apart as the pounding came closer.

Huw pushed the remains of the broken chair behind the bed with his foot. "It's fortunate

you're a tall woman, Sinean love. But, I'll slouch a bit." He stooped over and asked, "How's this for a dowager's hump?"

Sinean giggled as she saw Huw transformed before her eyes into an elderly widow, stooped and infirm.

A heavy fist beat on her door. "Open up for the Grand Duke Grefyn! Open up, I say! We come in search of traitors."

Sinean opened the door, saying irritably, "Give over, you lot. There are decent women in here, and you're lowering the tone of this establishment! I vow I'll never stay in this place again—my aunt is of the same opinion, aren't you, Aunty?"

"Absolutely," warbled Huw in a credible falsetto. "I won't stay in a place that harbors traitors or thugs!" He slapped the shoulder of the startled soldier with his folded fan and minced over to the window. He stood glaring out at the street, fanning himself and dabbing at his eyes with a lace handkerchief.

The large thug with the crooked nose intoned, "We're looking for He-e-w, the Bard. He's a wanted man, a traitor to Eyn. Do ye have knowledge of any bards? Speak now or face the Grand Duke Grefyn's wrath." With his Lanque accent proclaiming his origin, the bully held out the paper for Sinean to read. Indeed it did read, 'H-e-w, the Bard,' neatly misspelled.

"There's no man named 'Hew' in this room,

so shove off," replied Sinean, her voice dripping with scorn. She thrust the paper back at them.

The men drew their swords, pointing them straight at her, and she gave a little scream, jumping back.

"We're decent women. What would we be doing with a bard in our room?" Her voice was now terrified, and it was not entirely an act. "Put up your weapons!"

"Ohhh...." Huw's wail was enough to shred the wallpaper. "They've drawn steel in our room!" he moaned. "Help! Constable! Rape! 'Tis a disgrace, a black disgrace.... Don't let these thugs harm us!"

"There now, you've upset my aunty! Now go and harass some other elderly woman." Sinean ran over and put her arms around Huw's shoulders saying, "Sit down Aunty—the bad men are leaving!" Glaring at them, she led Huw to the good chair, surreptitiously nudging the remains of the broken one further behind the bed.

Suddenly noticing Huw's manly fingers, heavily calloused from both harp and lute, she quickly thrust some needlework at him, saying, "Here, Aunty, this will calm you." He took it, wondering what he was supposed to do with it.

As soon as Huw took the mending, Sinean went back to the door. Scolding and shooing the Duke's ruffians, she pushed them out and slammed the door behind them. She turned the key in the lock and, leaning against the door, looked at Huw with an impish grin on her face.

Huw grinned back. "It seems we're stuck in this room for a while with nothing to occupy us. Why don't I show you what's under my dress?" He winked at her, laughing. They fell to the bed, kissing. Huw had his hand down her bodice, and she had her hand up his dress when another knock sounded on the door. Hastily standing up, Huw warbled, "Who is it?" Shaking his skirts back down, he pulled Sinean to her feet and she quickly smoothed the bed.

"It's me, Waite." The innkeeper's voice sounded from the hall.

Quickly they let him in and locked the door again. The innkeeper brushed his thick hair back from his flustered, worried face. "Huw, you have to go north, tonight. If you don't, the Crows will surely kill you! And...I've bad news for you." His grim face and the tone of his voice emphasized his words. "I just heard the Crows finally caught Balen and Loris. They hanged them in the street. Their bodies still dangle there as a warning to all!"

Huw's face drained of all its color. "My father... no... no, it can't be true!"

Waite's normally jolly face was serious, dark with worry and fear. "There's worse news. When they'd done with Balen and Loris, the Crows marched to Bards' Street and torched the guild hall. All who escaped the thugs in the streets were gathered there, thinking themselves safe! But they weren't, were they? There's no one left, Huw. The whole street is ablaze. There are fears the fires will take the whole city if they can't get it under control! I've got my boys up on the roof, wetting it down. If the storm lurking on the horizon comes in, we'll be safe enough down here, I think. Thank God for the endless rain!"

Huw's knees gave out and he sat on the bed, stunned by the enormity of what Waite had so bluntly told him. "It's the spring conclave! Of course they were all there, awarding pins to the journeymen. I should have been there too but for Sinean."

Waite's voice continued, saying words Huw struggled to comprehend through his shock and disbelief. "Clan Grefyn is paying two golds for every bard, and believe me, there are plenty of folk willing to take it. They're all dead, Huw, and you'll soon join them. You must get out of here! Don't stay and tempt fate, man. I can smuggle you out in the empty kegs. Joss will be coming for them tonight. It'll get you as far as Shandytown. From there you'll have to make your own way. Keep going north and don't stop until you get beyond the Bekenberg Pass. You'll be free of Grefyn's reach there."

"Balen is dead?" Bewildered, Huw asked, "How could it be? He's the guild master. Even the Grand Duke Anvel Grefyn can't just murder the guild master!" Huw sat clutching his stomach, feeling the nausea rising. "My father! Oh, God, no. No!"

"Apparently he can, Huw, and he did! My boy, Bili, saw it." Waite's sharp blue eyes looked at him with pity. "You're all that's left of your guild. The old man's arm is long, and he's unforgiving. These Crows wanted your guild silenced, and they're not the only ones. Many others in high places of both clans have long felt the guild reached too high. Balen's indiscretion in telling that old tale over Yule at House Corlyn did your guild no favors. The Grefyn's men now go to every tap room and tavern in every town in the Eynier Valley, and no one dares stand in their way. The Crows who're scouring the streets now are promising murder to any casual entertainer caught in possession of a harp, pipe or lute in an effort to be rid of your sort."

"No…No…. This is madness! What sort of man is this full of vengeance?" Huw's face blanched white under the powder and paint and he wrapped his arms about himself, rocking back and forth.

"They came and pressed me hard, but I stuck to my story." Only then did Huw see the bruises on Waite's face, feeling a shock of horror. "I told them the last I saw, you were on your way to the guild hall and must have died in the fire with the rest of them." Waite shook his head, his face full of woe. "Balen should never have told Henri's new governor *The Tale of the Grefyn's Bones,* knowing Lord St. John would understand exactly what he was referring to and would do some investigating. Especially not at House Corlyn—

Grete Corlyn is the Grefyn's wife, for the love of God! Corlyn is as loyal to Grefyn as is House Lyndys. It was the apple that tipped over the cart!"

Huw's voice dripped with scorn. "It's no secret! King Henri had to be warned. The Grefyn's gold is ill-gotten. His treasury is once again full of Lanqueshire's golden Bones, just like the bad old days. His thugs speak with their harsh sounds." Huw was livid, his blue eyes sparking as he said, "The oh-so-wily pirate-king of the Lanques is once again using the greed of the Black Grefyns to get their foot in the door here. And Anvel Lyndys, Grand Duke Grefyn, in his senility is allowing it to happen!"

He looked up and met Waite's gaze. "They might be pirates, but they aren't stupid! First Lanqueshire will own the Black Grefyn Clan and then they'll rule the valley just as they did three hundred years ago. They'll make us nothing but a province of theirs, forcing us to till our own soil as serfs, under their lash, just like in the old days before we joined with Wald."

The gold coins of Lanqueshire were stamped with a ship on one side and a pair of crossed oars on the other. Someone once said they may as well have stamped a skull-and-crossbones on them; thus they were called 'bones.'

His face contorted with wrath, Huw continued, "Anvel Grefyn would be the puppet king of Eyn, which could never stand against Lanqueshire. How can any reasonable person support such a thing? Wald and Eyn must stand united. It's only King Henri's knights and the fact we're one country, Waldeyn, that keeps us free." As he warmed to his subject, his low tones filled with intensity. "So what if King Henri's men put a stop to Lanque ships docking in Ludwellyn until they apologize for meddling in our politics? They *should* apologize! They offer us little enough besides their thugs and criminals in exchange for our land and wealth. The Grefyn's loss of a few golden bones is no reason to murder an entire craft!" Huw managed to keep his voice low despite his outrage.

Waite's disgust was evident in his sharp manner. "Well, your father stopped Grefyn's plans for the moment, but he gave his life for it! Don't be a fool, Huw. Take the road north!" Waite bent down, and picked up a bundle. "You're all that's left of the guild your grandfather conceived and Balen built. You must see to rebuilding it. Think of the tinkers, lad! We're depending on you—don't throw your life away. You're our people's only hope. Without the bards, we've no hope of regaining acceptance, ever."

Huw nodded, too overwhelmed to speak any further.

"I'll come for you when your ride to freedom gets here. Joss has agreed, but I'll have to load the wagon myself. When he arrives back at the brewery in Shandytown, he'll leave his barn door unlatched. You'll be away safe, but you must stay low, at least until you get to Bekenberg." Waite tossed the bundle onto the bed. "These clothes are all I have to spare, nothing fancy, but you must wear them. Leave your bard's finery behind. You're only a tinker-lad now. You'll never wear those robes again."

"Oh, God, Waite. You've been so good to me, when you didn't have to." Huw shuddered. "You took a beating for me—why you'd stand up for me, I don't know. You deserve better than this."

"You're our people's last hope, lad." Waite's voice softened as he said, "It's a long walk, Huw. You're looking at two-months just to Clythe. Stay low and stay safe!"

Waite let himself out of the room, and Sinean locked it behind him. Huw put his head in his hands, trying to absorb the magnitude of his loss. "This is madness! How could this be?"

"I don't know, Huw, but it happened, and you must flee or you'll surely die!"

Consoling him as best she could, Sinean's mind quickly ran through all the possibilities, settling on the only one she could live with. "You must seek out the Bear when you get to Clythe." Her uncle liked Huw and would help him. "I fear we're going to be parted forever now." Tears ran unheeded down her cheeks. "I'll not let this go unpunished. I swear it to you!" Sinean knelt in front of him and rested her head on his knee.

Looking up at him with her dark eyes full of

tears, she said, "I vow my crew and I will avenge your father as I avenge my own. Balen will not be forgotten! I swear I won't rest until the Crows are all dead—the Grefyn and every one of his brutish creatures who sow his poisoned words among the people. How I despise him! I'll not surrender until we're free of his iron fist!"

Slowly, trying to speak through his shock and misery, Huw touched her hair. "You are lovely, Sinean." Tears welled in his eyes at the realization of what she was telling him. "So lovely and so dear to me. But I understand your words." He heaved a sigh, feeling one more slab of misery piled on top of the rest. "You're telling me you'll not be going with me. You're saying I'm going north alone. You won't give up the cause no matter how hopeless it is, will you? Your uncle warned me it would end this way. He knew all along, but I didn't want to believe him." His eyes filled with tears again, and he said, "I set you free of our contract, and hope...." Huw's voice broke as the enormity of what had happened became clear to him.

She held him, and his shoulders shook as he cried for his father, Balen, and for his oldest friend, Loris. He wept for all the bards whose tales and ballads were once the glory of the Eynier Valley and whose songs and stories wouldn't be heard again for many years, even if he could somehow rebuild the guild. He wept for the wedding he'd never have and the woman who loved him, but not enough to give up her revolution.

When Huw had cried himself dry of tears, Sinean washed the powder out of his hair and removed the paint and patches from his face, turning him back into the man he was. Then they drew the drapes and made love until it was time for him to pack up his kit and leave behind the only life he'd ever known, each one loath to lose the other.

He hid his small bowed-lute in his kit, wrapped in a wool scarf. He left the bow behind as it wouldn't fit in the pack Waite had found for him. The lute could be played like a regular one, and he could make a bow for it later; it would be easy to do. Atop that, he placed his uilleann pipes, broken down and also swathed in a scarf. He thought perhaps when he made it to the North, he could earn his way as a casual entertainer; tinkers often did.

There was nothing else to put in his kit. He was leaving with only the few precious instruments he could hide. He had no money. All his gold was in the exchequer in Ludwellyn, so he wouldn't be able to get it unless he made it all the way to Castleton. He had no food and no clothes but those on his back. He dared not be seen in his elaborate bard's robes. He didn't even have a bedroll because the inn was full to bursting with people hiding from the rioters, and there were no blankets to spare, although he did have a cloak that would suffice.

With the uprising, Waite had nothing to spare

from his kitchen. The meal they had for dinner was a watery soup and small slices of bread. Waite thought he could get by for a week if he was careful with what he had, but the tap room was closed until the markets could reopen.

Huw was forced to leave behind 'My Lady,' his priceless harp, concealed under their bed. There was no way he could stay hidden while carrying such a large instrument on his back. "I give My Lady to you, love. I'm glad now I taught you. You play her well, and sing like an angel. Think of me whenever you play her, my lady-love, for I'll surely be thinking of you!" His voice caught. "I crafted her for my master's piece and was given my master's pin for her." His heart was leaden at the thought of all he was leaving behind. He said in as cheery a way as he could muster, "I'll make another when I get to where I'm going."

"I'll care for her forever, Huw. Oh, love, I'll miss you!" Waite arrived, and leaning against the door jamb, Sinean wept, watching as he silently led Huw away, down the back stairs, and out of her life.

Already Sinean had begun to plan her next move against the Grefyn. She loved Huw and would miss him desperately, but the bitter truth was she never intended to marry him, no matter what she'd agreed to in a moment of weakness.

And Huw the Bard was a terrible weakness, one that could be used against her.

Sinean had far too many secrets to keep. Several in the rebel underground felt her relationship with the bard endangered their own security. These men and women would not be sad the guild had met such a terrible end. The Bards' Guild had been impartial in the gathering and dissemination of information Balen Owyn believed posed a threat to peace in the Long Valley.

Lately she'd grown ever more terrified someone would decide that, alive, her handsome lad was too much of a danger to them. His position was so perilous, she'd made up her mind to leave him when her crew next shipped out, but she wouldn't have been able to tell him why. Because of her secrets, he had no idea how close to the knife's edge he walked.

Relief flooded through her as she realized Huw was effectively dead and there would be no danger to him from her 'friends.' Now he was safe! She greatly needed those people if her plans were to succeed, but revolutionaries could be so reactionary at times, especially when their lives were at stake.

I love you too much for your own good, Huw Owyn. God help me, I love you! The tears flowed down her cheeks as she tried vainly to sleep. *At least now you'll be safe. Your life was in danger from all sides, and I couldn't protect you!*

Unable to rest, dawn found her seated by the window, staring at the banked fire. When she closed her eyes, all she could see was the shock and despair on her lover's face when he realized she'd abandoned him. *How could I be so cruel? But this way, at least, you'll live.*

Chapter 2 The Long Road North

Throughout the Eynier Valley, the man who was the titular head of Clan Grefyn was known as *the* Grefyn, the absolute ruler of his small Duchy. Nothing happened in the far south of the Long Valley he didn't have a hand in. Further north, the depredations of the Crows of Clan Grefyn were somewhat constrained by the Dragons of Clan Weyllyn, and the Crown soldiery usually kept the peace. Now, working frantically, the Crown soldiers helped to control the fires and quell the rioting.

Unfortunately, as the conflagration spread beyond the artists' quarter, the port's fire-watch was too poorly manned to adequately contain it. They were overwhelmed by the chaos of the burning city, despite the many brave souls who fought desperately by their side and lost their lives. As the fires raged out of control, pandemonium ruled the streets. Ludwellyn teemed with people fleeing the burning city. In the dark alleys and tinder-dry tenements of the poorer sections of town, panic and confusion led to many fatalities that could have been avoided had calmer heads prevailed. For those unlucky denizens who couldn't escape, it was as if they'd not yet died but had still gone to hell.

The air was filled with smoke and myriad other unpleasant scents. Adding to the misery, the wind carried burning brands over great distances, starting new fires and expanding the confusion. The Crown soldiers had long since lost control of the situation. Several times, Joss was forced to use his whip to beat the desperate refugees off his wagon, though he didn't want to. He felt terribly sorry for them, but was already courting more danger than he'd bargained for in his cartload of kegs. Still, sometimes a man had to take a stand when the great houses ran roughshod over the common people. In some way, this cargo was his small rebellion.

Huw huddled in an empty ale keg, more miserable and terrified than he'd ever been. All his admittedly young life, he'd been the darling of the nobility. His love songs and epic tales entertained them; his harp provided the backdrop to their lives. Because Huw was discreet, the highest among them employed him to set the scene for their carefully choreographed trysts and assignations, as well as their parties and fetes. His tales and comic songs entertained their children for birthdays and holidays. The noble houses vied with each other for his services and paid him handsomely to make their events the important parties to be seen at during the social season.

Yet those very nobles turned on the guild, deliberately murdering his father, hanging him like a common criminal. Those same lords then slaughtered his entire craft, fifty men and boys, all of them the highest, most well-regarded musicians and storytellers in the Eynier Valley. The murders had been planned for months; the very timing convinced Huw. It was the only week of the year the bards would all be under one roof, when their complete destruction could be guaranteed.

How did we not know what they were planning? We guested in their homes, shared all the news and gossip freely with them regardless of which house they'd sworn allegiance to.

Why? Huw's mind ran in circles, unable to comprehend the depth of hatred that had been lurking under the surface of polite society for those of his craft. That the animosity was there all along was apparent in both the speed with which everything had happened and the fact no one seemed to care that a guild master and fifty men and boys were murdered and the city set ablaze in the process. They'd do worse to him if he were caught. Waite had been very clear on that.

Huw's thoughts spun, turning the same morbid visions over and over, leaving him alternately weeping and raging impotently. *How could they have done such a heinous thing? Why? Only last week Grand Duchess Grete Grefyn had her spring fete. Balen, Destin, Brent and I—we played our most difficult pieces, and her husband's fawning toadies were lavish in their praise. Of course, they were green with jealousy that of all the noble houses, she alone managed to have all four masters perform in concert for her fete.*

Our performance, followed by the best journeymen in the guild playing the dance music for the grand ball, made her fete the most outstanding success of the season. And this was our reward? Does the Grand Duchess Grete know what the beast she's married to has done?

It took a long while to get out of the city due to many stops and starts. At last, the noise of the tumult began to dwindle; the wagon left the cobbles and the city behind, passing through the North Gate to the country. Once the paved streets ended, the cart swayed and bumped, lurching down the muddy, rutted road to Shandytown. The motion soon had Huw swallowing against his mounting nausea, making his imprisonment more miserable.

He had little room to move, and the stifling smell of the keg was nearly overwhelming. Between the stink of stale ale, the claustrophobic confinement of the cask, and the interminable swaying of the cart, Huw's stomach finally rebelled violently, adding the odor of vomit to the general stench of the barrel. Clutching his kit to his chest, he prayed for deliverance. Not normally a religious man, Huw fervently begged Almighty God to get him safely out of the wretched prison and into whatever nightmare awaited him on his mad flight north.

After several hours of utter misery, the echoes of the horses' shod hooves clip-clopping penetrated Huw's consciousness. By the sound of it, they'd entered a cobbled lane, so were nearing their destination. Finally the cart stopped. After a few moments, Huw heard a gate opening and felt a jerk forward. Again they stopped and Huw heard Joss close the gate behind them. The cart jolted again and this time rolled until, with a lurch, it stopped once and for all. He heard Joss set the brake and felt the wagon rock as the caskman climbed down.

Young voices drifted to Huw's ears, saying, "Do you need help with the kegs, Da?"

Joss's gruff voice replied, "Nah. You boys get back to bed, or you won't be worth anything come dawn. Tomorrow will be soon enough to off-load the cart. Was a hell of a trip, lads."

One of the older boys asked something Huw didn't quite hear, but Joss replied, "Yes, there's trouble in Ludwellyn, and it won't be settled soon, I promise you. I'll tell you about it tomorrow."

Joss unhitched the horses, getting them curried and settled down. "Long day, fellas, but you did well," he said to the beasts. There was a slight clink as Joss shut the gate on a stall. "Rest up!" The muted sounds of the caskman patting one of the horses, who whickered in answer, penetrated Huw's prison. At last, Huw heard Joss walk past the cart. Finally he heard the slightest squeak and groan of hinges and doors opening and closing.

After waiting for what felt like forever to be sure he was alone, he prepared to climb out of his uncomfortable hiding place. *I never imagined a stable could smell so sweet,* he thought as he lifted the lid, sliding it over the top of the next keg. Gripping the rim and using his arms as levers, he pulled himself to a standing position, inhaling deeply. The cool, fresh air was a reprieve, somewhat dispelling the stinks of vomit and stale beer. His legs were useless, numb from the cramped position. As they gave out under him, Huw held himself upright by leaning on the rim of the barrel. Moments later, he found himself clinging to the edge of the keg in excruciating pain as the feeling returned to his extremities.

"Oh God…." Clutching the rim, Huw pressed his face to the crook of his arm, smothering the groans he couldn't hold back as the blood rushed to his feet. Tears ran down his face as every blood-vessel and nerve in his legs and feet screamed their agony from the pain of a thousand needles. After many long moments the torture subsided and he was able to stand unassisted. *God in heaven, thank you, a thousand times thank you! How long was I trapped in this thing?*

Slinging his kit over his shoulders, Huw crept out of the stable and lowered the bar on the door. Silently as he was able, he strapped his scabbard on, fumbling with the buckle. Huw was a poor swordsman, so the blade was for appearances. Waite had insisted he wear it, despite the fact Huw was worse than useless. When forcing it on him, Waite's words were, "Did you never listen to Balen? Learn to use it, you fool. If you appear to be unarmed, you'll be a target for thieves and highwaymen."

He checked his sleeves and boots, making sure he could access his knives with an economy of motion. Huw might be a terrible swordsman, but with those blades he'd always been deadly. However, the tooled leather sheaths were crafted to be worn under a bard's robes and wide loosely-gathered sleeves. The harness was cumbersome, though he was used to wearing it.

The trouble he had now was the shirts of a common working man were made closer fitting, as cloth was expensive and no laborer could afford to waste it on something like big loose sleeves just for fashion. Despite his concern, the straps that ran up his arms and crossed his chest, keeping the specially crafted sheaths in place when he drew them, didn't show at all above the rawhide laces at his throat. They remained hidden even though the shirt laced lower than his old ones had. With a small amount of adjustment at the cuffs, the knives were as handy as possible and wouldn't show no matter how he raised his arms. Now he'd have to get used to throwing them without giving himself away, as he didn't have the robes to disguise his movements.

He'd refused to wear Waite's proffered boots as his were specially made with his blades in mind. *I'm going to have to alter these breeches so they don't catch when I unsheathe my boot-knives in a hurry.* Huw's were smaller than most standard defensive knives, thinner and razor sharp. They were extremely effective and were one of the secrets of the Bards' Guild that had died with Balen and the others—unless Huw was fortunate enough to survive the next few weeks. *Two months until I make it to Clythe…I'll probably starve to death if I don't get caught first.*

The brewery yard was dark with no moon, and the air was cold and clear. He paused briefly at the rain barrel to wash the worst of the mess off him, feeling better as the stinking evidence of his weakness was washed away. Try as he might, the stains remained; he'd never washed his own clothes before. *I wonder where I can find soap. I'm going to have to get some if I don't want to smell like a vagrant.* Moving quickly, he slipped through the darkened streets of Shandytown and emerged into the wild country.

Running through the dark, Huw had no idea how far he traveled or where he was, except he followed the muddy, rutted high road north. Still too devastated to sleep despite his exhaustion, Huw alternately ran and walked until he'd put a good distance between himself and Shandytown.

Once the eastern sky grew light, he began to walk like any other laborer on the road looking for work, making every effort not to look over his shoulder, or behave in a guilty fashion. The last thing he wanted was to be mistaken for a thief. Hunger set in, but still he continued until, in a garden at the back of a still-dark cottage, he found a thick plot of tiny new carrots in need of thinning, the first sprouts of the new spring. Carefully, he liberated them from the neat row they were trapped in, tangled closely together. *This is the first breakfast I've ever missed,* he thought, as he plucked the tiny vegetables, thinning the row in such a way the gardener would never miss them. *No eggs and bacon or buttery toast for you today, Huw. You're a wanted man.*

Rinsing the carrots off in a water trough behind the tiny sheep byre, he took his scant meal into the woods, where he ate it slowly and rested a brief moment. His nerves overcame his fatigue, and trying to remain hidden from view of the cottage, he emerged from the thicket near the road and turned north. Huw continued walking as quickly as he was able, though he was now footsore and still hungry.

The sky lightened, but the sun remained shrouded by a strange haze which he soon realized was the smoke of the burning city.

Toward noon, the storm Waite had prayed for the day before came rolling in. The heavy clouds were strangely colored from the smoke, and the wind blowing in off the sea brought the reeking scent of the distant fire, causing Huw to hurry. His thin cloak didn't protect him much as he struggled to keep warm despite the chill wind. Trying to keep his mind off his misery, he wondered how much of the city had burned thanks to the Grefyn's madness. He shuddered, thinking, *How many innocents have died in that mess? How does a man sleep at night with the weight of all those lives on his conscience?*

The torrential rain was filthy and the color of ashes, but toward evening it fell clean again, rinsing his cloak as it drenched him. Once it grew dark enough for him to slip in unseen, he took shelter in a barn from the relentless storm. He found some withered windfall apples from the previous autumn's harvest that had been set aside for the oxen. Careful not to give himself dysentery, Huw only ate two of the better ones, ignoring the bad spots and putting a couple more in his pocket for later. Spreading his cloak out to dry, he slept lightly, and was awake and gone well before first light. He knew a farmer would soon be coming out to do whatever farmers did so early in the morning, and he had to be on his way before he was caught.

Two long, wretched days later found Huw huddling under his cloak, hidden in a large hedge that ran along the high road, trying to get some rest. Sleep eluded him for a long while. For meals, only the few apples he'd found in the first barn and a handful of early carrots and onions he'd been able to steal from the dark gardens of the local farms sustained him.

Huw had no idea how to hunt the small game he frequently saw. Only the evening before, he'd lain in wait for hours, tempting a fat rabbit, throwing his knife as quickly as he could. His movement startled the rabbit and Huw's dinner escaped unscathed. The streams were full of fish, but he had no way to catch them even if he'd known how. He tried scooping one out as he'd read bears did, but was unsuccessful; he was sure there were fat trout lurking there, laughing at his inept attempt to catch them.

"Two things you need, Huw, the means and ability to catch and kill your own food." His sense of failure was complete as he heard himself repeating his father's admonitions aloud.

Balen had often tried to interest him in hunting and fishing, but Huw was stubbornly indifferent to those occupations. "You never know when you'll need to live off the land, lad! You're riding high now. The great houses welcome and feed you, but what happens if you fall from grace? How will you feed yourself?" Balen's words echoed in his head.

Speaking sternly to himself to break the lonely silence, Huw muttered, "You're in a fine jam now, lad. You never took Balen's attempts at fatherhood seriously and now you'll die from your ignorance." He hated the sound of self-pity in his voice, but he couldn't get past his misery. "He tried to teach you how to live, but you thought he was worrying about nothing. You believed the fame and glory would last forever."

Dark thoughts ate at him. In the space of only a few days, he'd lost his innocent pretty-boy looks. Now he wore the face of a man who'd seen too much, and the change made him even more handsome, though he didn't know it.

Huw was unable to shake the memory of Sinean choosing to stay in Ludwellyn. Her abandonment was sharp in his mind, at times consuming him. Along with the increasing pains of hunger, a pall of bitterness settled into his heart, making him more despondent than he'd ever believed possible.

Sinean's casual betrayal of his love cut like a knife. When he thought of what he'd given up to follow her, he felt like the fool his father had accused him of being. "The position of bard to House Weyllyn comes only once, Huw. There will always be women." Even dead, Balen's words stung him.

His old friend, Loris, had accepted the position, and now he was dead, hung beside Balen with less regard than a common criminal.

The guild, begun by his grandfather and nurtured by his father to become a true voice for the people, was wiped away as if it had never been. Balen had begun the practice of training apprentices and awarding the hardworking journeymen unique pins and positions in the best noble houses. As they gained in wisdom and discretion they became masters. The Bards' Guild had established high standards and was respected among the artisans' community. Talented entertainers were everywhere; nearly everyone in the Eynier Valley could sing or play a flute and frequently did. But it was the rare, gifted ones who had both perfect pitch and an eidetic memory.

Only a few had the ability to memorize the epic tales that were the oral history of the Eynier people and could unfailingly tell them with the right cadence and timbre of voice. Only the gifted had the power to draw the audience into the stories and songs, bringing a moment of complete wonder and escape into the listener's life. Those rare men had entry into places very few common people would ever see except as servants. Balen had charged Huw and the other masters with searching for those with the ability and bringing them into the guild.

All his life Balen had nurtured and built up the guild until it was comprised of fifty men and boys, trained to be so much more than simply entertainers. Bards kept the true history of the valley in their heads because books could be burned when people in high places disagreed with the way events had actually occurred. The bards of Balen's guild all took vows to speak the truth, no matter how hard, swearing on their lives and hopes of heaven. Impartiality had given them an immunity that had been the only restraint on the greed and harsh strictures of Clan Grefyn and, to a much lesser extent, Clan Weyllyn.

The Crows always considered the bards to be arrogant and traitorous since they refused to answer to one clan, the bards saying instead they were of the whole valley. The Dragons of Clan Weyllyn had never been overly fond of them for the same reason. Still, until now, no one dared to harm them because they'd needed the bards—at least Clan Weyllyn had. The truth usually worked in favor of Weyllyn, and bards were frequently welcomed in their homes. For the most part, they'd been accepted into the great Grefyn houses, but certain songs and tales were strictly forbidden.

The rumors Huw now heard from other travelers indicated the rural population didn't connect the fire that destroyed a quarter of the city and killed countless innocents to the murders of Balen and Loris. In a stroke of brilliance that appeared accidental, the old Grand Duke Grefyn had destroyed the life-work of three generations of Owyns. With the fires and riots, the public hangings of Balen and Loris had faded in importance. Since leaving Ludwellyn, Huw hadn't heard even one mention of it other than in passing, and the gossips had them dying in the fire along with the rest of the guild and most of the skilled artisans in the city.

Huw knew in his heart the murders would never be avenged because so few people knew what had really happened. Clan Grefyn had emerged the victors. There was no doubt about that.

Deeply entwined with and overlaying the despair he felt over the unforgivable slaughter of his father and dearest friends, Huw mourned the loss of Sinean as deeply as all the others.

Huddled in the dark, dry space under a hedge with his arms about his knees and his cloak wrapped tightly around him for warmth, Huw cried once again until he had no more tears. Only then was he able to fall into a fitful sleep.

Chapter 3 Jak the Whore

Waking stiff and sore a few short hours later, Huw peered out of the hedge, trying to gauge his surroundings. Laundry flapped on a line across the field. In the distance, a familiar-looking manor house shone in the damp sunshine. *Oh God. Of course! I've camped under a Grefyn hedge. Now what?* He thought carefully about his options while his stomach growled. *I might be able to earn a meal. Common laborers do it all the time. The last time I was here, I was with Dolan playing for the oldest daughter's coming out party.*

For a moment Huw thought longingly of his former finery. The colorful embroideries and intricate needlework depicting musical notes, stars, moons, and suns in gold thread had marked him most clearly as a master-bard. *The few servants who waited tables during the banquet would never recognize me dressed like this, without my beard. If I appear at the stable and offer to work for a meal, I won't be different from any other laborer looking for work.*

Having made his decision, Huw stood up and brushed himself down as best he could. Shaving in the cold waters of a nearby irrigation ditch with no soap was a challenge, but he bled only a little.

All he'd eaten in the days since leaving Ludwellyn were a few fruits and vegetables stolen in the dark. He'd never before felt such terrible hunger, and it was strong enough for him to abandon caution. He now pitied the beggars he'd seen starving on the streets in Ludwellyn more than ever, realizing with a pang he was no different.

The pain of hunger was indescribable. Before his flight from Ludwellyn, he'd frequently said he was starved when he'd missed a meal or been late to one, but now knew the difference between temporary deprivation and true starvation. There was no comparison. He'd reached the point where he'd do anything to fill his belly, recognizing the real possibility he could end his days as a beggar. *It's a measure of how far you've fallen, Huw. But you're not there yet— you still have something to offer! Your strong back has some work left in it! Use what you have!* He stowed his knives and sheathes in his kit, knowing he'd most likely have to take his shirt off to do any hard labor. No commoner would have weapons like his; they were too obviously unique and marked him as either a spy or a bard.

I need a new name, he thought, as he approached the kitchen door, *a common name, one every village has three of.*

That's how Huw the Bard found himself mucking out the stables at Earl Ardyce Pyndrys's country house and answering to the name "Jak." The earl was a distant cousin of the Grand Duke Anvel Grefyn himself. Apparently, he was away at sea on business for his cousin, and his lady wife and children were still at their townhouse in Ludwellyn. The social season wasn't yet over in the city, continuing without a pause despite the tragedy there, and Lady Pyndrys was making sure her children were seen by prospective spouses. The galas and fetes weren't nearly as grand as they'd once been— all the best musicians having died in the horrible fire that had consumed the city—but the nobles were nothing if not resilient. They made do with impromptu concerts by the musically inclined from within their own ranks. Thus, the country manor remained the domain of the servants for a while longer.

Having heard all the news he could glean, Huw set to work at his task of mucking out the stable with a will and an eye toward a good meal. Despite his shaking hands and weak legs, he put as much effort into his work as he could muster, earning an approving grin from the head-groom. Sure enough, at about noon, he was told to wash up at the pump and come in to have a bite. He made use of the soap that sat on a dish and then cleaned his boots carefully before entering the kitchen.

Seated at the table, somewhat squashed between the fat cook, Elise, and Davis, the head-groom, Huw enjoyed the excellent meal with the rest of the Pyndrys's servants. With their masters away, they were a jolly group, and if they were aware of the trouble in Ludwellyn beyond the general tragedy of the great fire, they didn't mention it. Huw was quiet, speaking little and forcing himself to eat his soup politely when his hunger was nearly unendurable. Eating slowly so his long-empty stomach wouldn't rebel and savoring each mouthful, Huw gave silent but fervent thanks for his food.

The camaraderie around the table made him feel homesick, but for what he didn't know; since being apprenticed, he'd never had a home life such as this.

The servants were a tight-knit group and they laughed and joked, Davis acting as the father and Elise, the over-plump cook, as the mother. "Jaky-lad, you're a good worker. We could find you a place here if you want it. There's always more work than there are hands to do it," Davis told him.

"I must see my ma afore she passes on," replied Huw, using the same slow, thick, low-country Eynier accent as the locals. "I were told by the dock-master my uncle is calling me home and I must hurry."

"Ah, well, you must travel on then. But if you should come back, just ask for Davis, and I'll see you have a place here." After thanking the cook for their fine meal, the stable hands and grooms all tramped out to return to their tasks while the serving girls began clearing up. Huw also thanked Elise for the fine meal and was about to stand and take his leave when a plump hand on his leg stopped him.

"Jaky, wait a moment, don't hurry off just yet. I'll gladly send you away with some bread and cheese," said Elise. She'd been eyeing him appreciatively through the meal, something Huw was accustomed to and didn't think much about. Women always eyed bards that way. However, this was different. Her eyes betrayed her intention as she looked pointedly at his crotch and ran her hand up his thigh. "You're such a handsome lad, and you look so hungry. I'll be happy to provide you with a bit for your journey after we have a nap. You must be very tired after all the work you did this morning. I usually rest a while in the afternoon, so I'll have plenty of time to comfort you. A little more work now, and you can travel faster, later."

Taken aback by the frankness of her intention, Huw blushed, not sure what to say. She repelled him somewhat, being a rather greedy-looking woman, although she was pleasant enough. Still, the memory of his terrible hunger was strong, and he knew he'd be hungry again once he left there. In the course of his work, he'd found himself servicing women he didn't particularly desire for a multitude of reasons. Balen always said, *"Bards need information, and women like to talk after a satisfying romp between the sheets, especially unhappily married women in high positions. They all want to be loved by pretty lads who sing them love songs, and you must be prepared to do what it takes to leave them happy and keep them always willing to confide in you. You must be their dirty little secret!"*

Huw found it to be true, and of course, he'd done what was necessary and even found enjoyment in some of his extra duties. But this...this was different. This wasn't offering a bored noblewoman a shoulder to cry on, followed perhaps by a discreet tumble to make her feel she was still young and desirable. This was selling his body for a crust of bread.

Thinking about the hunger he'd experienced in the days since leaving Ludwellyn, Huw's stomach overcame his scruples. *It's not so different and she'll give me food for my journey. I won't have the chance to eat tomorrow unless I can take some with me now. Just shut your eyes and do it, Huw! Besides, you like them plump. How hard can it be?*

Once in the dark confines of her stifling room in the servants' quarters, Elise proved to be a demanding connoisseur of men. Huw was forced to use every trick he'd ever known. Though he found it difficult at first, after a few moments of feeling completely out of his element, he was able to do what she wanted, bringing her to ecstasy several times. He did climax eventually, but there was little passion involved for him—it was purely mechanical, a physical response to certain stimuli. The amount of effort required to satisfy her lust negated any desire he might have felt. He found some enjoyment in it, but even in the heat of the moment he couldn't bring himself to kiss her mouth and wouldn't even consider kissing the secret place between her legs. Huw used his hands with as much creativity as he could to stir her to the peak of arousal, and entered her only once she was fully ready.

Unfortunately for Huw, once was not enough to please Elise, whose appetite for sex and pretty boys was as large as her appetite for sweets, and she intended to have her fill of handsome Jak. It wasn't until he'd given her three resounding moments of utter carnal delight she finally let him rest. When Huw was eventually allowed to leave her room, he was exhausted, though she'd fed him delicious chocolates from her secret stash as a reward. He left Elise tired, well-satisfied and smiling widely as she resumed her duties in the kitchen.

The stable hands apparently knew to what extent he'd had to work. They looked at him sympathetically as once again he bathed at the pump in the stable yard, taking the time to wash his clothes and soap his entire body in the icy water. No amount of lathering could make him feel clean.

He put the wet clothes back on, not caring he was freezing in the cool of the spring afternoon. Picking up his pack, he scarpered, nearly running down the lane to the high road. Sundown found Huw exhausted from his exertions and determined to put as much distance as possible between himself and Elise, who'd offered him her bed for the night. *Who'd believe a woman that size could be so nimble between the sheets? But she did give me two loaves, a chunk of cheese and another hot meal.* He laughed sardonically to himself, thinking of how hard he had to work for those gifts.

Four days ago you were the golden boy, poised at the top of the most powerful guild in the Long Valley, fully trained to take over when your father stepped down. His eyes felt the sting of bitter tears welling and resolutely he pushed them down. *Today you're less than nothing. You've sunk to a new low, Huw Owyn. Today you're nothing more than a starving gigolo! You'd better make your hard-earned bread last.* His guts twisted as he thought of how quickly he'd come to understand hunger, loss and desperation. *Four days without food is all it took to bring you to your knees. Wouldn't Balen be proud of you now? God knows what you'll have to do at the next kitchen you come to, just to earn a meal.*

Over the next few days, Huw slowly made his way north. He was forced to avoid the high road, as bands of thugs and highwaymen now patrolled great stretches of it, most of them proudly wearing the black cloaks of the soldiery of Clan Grefyn over their chainmail.

Though he tried to make his food last, within three days Huw once again suffered from hunger. Desperately he tried to avoid it, but was eventually forced to knock on backdoors and beg for work in exchange for a meal. He managed to find a bit of day-work here and there for an occasional night in a barn or a meal. Because he had to stick to the back roads, he was unable to inquire at the country manors, asking instead at small farms and cottages.

He managed to get a meal nearly every day but frequently, because of his youth, good looks and obviously precarious circumstances, was often pressured to do a little extra. Now he found himself in the business of selling his sexual services for the price of his meals, a circumstance that was terribly damaging to his pride. He struggled to find some joy in the act, and several times resorted to pretending his pleasure just to be done with it. *It's only a role, Huw. It's the lead role in the Epic Tragedy of a Life Gone to Hell. At least I'm able to bathe and use their soap afterward.* The irony of his new lot in life was not lost on him. *I wonder how many times I could have helped someone and I passed them by, all because they stank of misery and hunger and I didn't want it to rub off on me. God, what an arrogant prat I was.*

Once again shaving in the cracked mirror on a battered dresser in a lonely farmhouse, he faced his reality. This time it hadn't been a woman demanding his body in repayment for his meal. Now he understood why the beggars on the streets of Ludwellyn were so determined to ask for handouts in public, where the only indignities they'd be subjected to were the occasional kicks from passing strangers. *Now you truly are Jak the Whore,* he admitted to himself, shivering and unable to forget the coldness of the bed and the sleeping occupant, who'd treated Huw with thinly veiled disdain but used him anyway. *I'm not cut out to be a whore. The fact that it's work takes much of the joy out of it.* Now he found it hard to look himself in the eye. *What will I lower myself to next just to fill my belly?*

After leaving that farmhouse, he struggled to find work, in a desperate attempt to avoid being put in the position of having to choose between selling his body and starving. But he was unsuccessful and run off as a vagrant when he refused to trade sexual services. "The road's full of pretty lads with empty bellies, boy. You'll pay with what you have or you'll starve. Now get off my property or I'll turn my dogs on you." The woman's harsh voice followed him and he left as quickly as he could.

Anxious to escape being used again, he redoubled his efforts to try to feed himself, eating the tightly curled tips of fern fronds. They weren't terrible, but would have been better cooked in butter, which was not an option for him as he had no way of making a fire, and nothing to cook in. Butter was only a dream. He could find no berries; it was too early in the year. He'd yet to catch any sort of game, though had come close and still had no idea how to land a fish.

Huw bathed in the cold streams daily, but with no soap it was somewhat futile. Still, the act of bathing helped him maintain some dignity.

Three weeks passed. Once again, hunger overcame caution, and Huw resorted to knocking on the door of a very rural farmhouse, his starvation driving him to do whatever he had to for a crust of bread. A young, somewhat lonely-looking man opened the door, his somber expression not disguising the almost womanly beauty of his features. He was far and away the most beautiful man Huw had ever seen.

He said his name was Davey Llewellyn, and he kindly shared his simple but tasty meal. Afterwards he said, "Forgive me, but I'm wondering if perhaps you're a lad like me, a lad with a certain stigma."

Huw's heart sank. He'd heard this question before, introducing him to the underbelly of forbidden homosexuality that lay hidden below the surface of polite society among the nobility. Several prominent men had discreetly approached him despite the condemnation and abuse of lads who loved other lads, knowing he wouldn't speak of their secret any more than he would a lady's invitation. As Balen and the other masters had explained to him, he'd done what was needed to keep on the good side of that particular noble, and had even found pleasure in the act when the aristocrat was a good, decent man.

Huw wasn't really attracted to men, so the two occasions of having homosexual relations in exchange for food had been difficult for him. He'd gotten through it by keeping in mind it would soon be over, and he'd have a meal and a wash in hot water to show for his pains.

He slowly shook his head, plainly wondering if the man would demand his sexual services. Seeing the wary look in Huw's eyes, Davey sighed. "I thought perhaps you were on the run because you were like me, but at least you didn't attack me for it. Sometimes the stigma is hard to bear. It's why I'm living out here alone and on the Grefyn side of the river. I had to leave my family. My grandfather killed my lad, Wend, with his own hands when he found out Wend loved me. It was more than the old man could bear. He wanted me to marry, even had a bride picked out, but I couldn't, not after what he did to Wend. I had to leave home then because my family would have suffered from the stigma of having a son who loved a lad. I can't live the way they want me to. I don't know why."

The depth of sadness in Davey's eyes touched Huw deeply, and for once the bard was at a loss for words. Finally he said, "I never realized lads like you suffered from love the same way lads like me do. I'm embarrassed I was so ignorant, though my father often told me the heart is a willful thing and love blooms in unexpected places. I never understood what he meant until now. I'm terribly sorry for your loss. This valley is a cruel place to live. There's no tolerance here for anyone who may be different." He tried to think of something, anything that might give the despondent young man hope. "I've heard there's less concern over stigmas of any sort in the North, and lads like you are more readily accepted and not abused." Huw decided to confess his own situation. "Perhaps you should head that way. I'm going north because I'm a bard. I'm Huw Owyn, son of Balen Owyn. The Crows have decreed my kind will be murdered on sight, as will anyone who harbors a bard." Understanding dawned in his host's eyes, and Davey nodded when Huw added, "You mustn't even remember you've seen me—your life depends on this. So here we are, Davey, each of us with a stigma that could get us killed." He proceeded to describe the events in Ludwellyn and what he had frequently been forced to do since.

On hearing Huw's frank confession as to how low he had sunk, Davey said, "I can teach you how to live off the land, and I'll do it because no decent man should have to sell his body."

The very next morning he began by teaching Huw to fish for his breakfast and how to clean it. Then he showed him the easiest way to cook it over a campfire. As they roasted the first fish Huw had ever caught, he thanked Davey. Optimism he might really survive after all filled his heart. "You've saved my life. And I've discovered something I was too stubborn to learn before. Fishing is fun because your mind roams free while you're filling the pot, and you're not wasting time because you'll eat the rewards!"

Davey laughed, quoting the Eynierish proverb, "If you give a man a fish you've fed him for a day, but if you teach him how to fish you've fed him for a lifetime." Grinning he added, "Tomorrow you'll learn how to snare a rabbit or a fowl. A plump quail or pheasant makes a pleasant change from fish."

The next day, they rose early. They walked into the woods and Davey showed Huw how to find a game trail. It surprised Huw that he was able to see exactly what Davey meant when he pointed out the signs. "Why does that surprise you? You've been living wild for all this time, so you've begun to notice things, whether you realize it or not." Then Davey showed him the best spot for setting a snare on a game trail, and finally how to set the trap.

While they waited, Davey showed Huw several plants that grew wild and were not only edible, they were well-known herbs Huw had been eating all his life, but didn't recognize.

"This is rosemary, Huw. You can find it all year round." Davey pointed at an evergreen shrub that grew everywhere, and picking a frond he held it out to Huw. "Smell this—now do you recognize what it is?" Rosemary was one of Huw's favorite herbs. "You can keep some dried in a packet for seasoning your game. And here, this is burdock. If we don't eat too much it's good for us. This plant is chicory, and look! Here's dandelion, which I think tastes bitter and…aha! Fennel. We'll have a good salad, even if we don't snare anything today."

"I can eat these? I didn't know," replied Huw with some chagrin. "They're everywhere, and I didn't know they were food fit for humans." He was astonished at the quantity of edible plants flourishing with the onset of spring.

"This is the best time of year for wild greens and root vegetables if you must live by foraging. They're young and tender now." The two men walked, looking at various plants. "Oh, good! These are wild carrots," said Davey, stopping to dig. "Eat just the roots though. They're best right now when they're young, but even woody they go well in a stew and are better than going hungry." Davey found many roots and leaves for their dinner. Indeed, as the day wore on, Huw discovered he'd been starving in the midst of plenty.

Davey said, "You'll still go without occasionally. You can't hunt for game on any of the land this side of the river if it's attached to a noble house, but at least you won't starve. You can usually fish for anything but salmon with impunity, and the Crows won't shoot you full of arrows for picking greens. You may miss a few meals, but you should be able to get by now. It's a matter of getting used to the different flavors. They aren't what you're used to, but they'll keep you alive. Knowing how to forage for a wild stew or salad will keep you healthy until you get to the North."

That evening they dined on rabbit stew made from ingredients they had gathered. The process of skinning and gutting the rabbit was much less difficult than Huw imagined it would be, and the results were well worth the effort.

The next day Huw snared a pheasant. Davey showed him how to prepare the bird, gutting and plucking or "field-dressing" it. That, too, was much less trouble than Huw expected. "Some folks don't pluck the birds and simply skin them to save time, but I think they're better when they're plucked. It's not really that much more trouble," said Davey as he rapidly removed the feathers, starting at the chest. "Nip this little bit off with your knife…and singe these little pinfeathers off over the fire like this…and see? Now when I put a sprig of rosemary under the skin, this bird will make a fine dinner for us."

Huw stayed with Davey several days and learned how to field-dress a bird quite well. Before he left, Huw washed his clothes with soap and bathed properly. Davey let him sleep by the fire, asking nothing of him except conversation. The young man gave him a flint and steel for starting a campfire, a small pot to cook in, water bottle and a hook-and-line so he could fish for himself on his way north. Huw also had his snare in his pocket.

Davey warned Huw again about the water in the rivers and creeks. "You're fortunate you haven't gotten sick from the water. You should boil it before you drink it. If you don't like the flavor, put some mint in and when it cools a bit, pour the tea into your water bottle. You'll have a decent enough tea to drink cold. Dysentery can kill you." Davey apologized for the little he was able to outfit Huw with, regretting he had no extra soap to give, but Huw was immensely grateful for all he'd shared and told him so.

"You've done more for me than I can ever repay," Huw told him, clasping Davey's shoulder. "You saved my life and renewed my faith in humankind."

When Huw reluctantly left, Davey sent him off with as much food as he could spare. "You're right. I'll go north once I've settled my affairs here," he said as Huw waved goodbye. "Perhaps we'll meet again, but if we don't, God bless you and keep you safe. I'll never forget you were kind when another would have attacked me."

Chapter 4 Ilene

As Huw woke in the morning of what he thought might be his forty-eighth day on the road, hunger once again dominated his thoughts. He was still following the trade road, but now there were fewer streams to fish in. He had some success in snaring game when he couldn't fish, but he was still famished most of the time. The weather had turned sour as it often did in late April, and he rarely found dry shelter he didn't make from branches or find under a hedge. The woods were wet, and his campfires burned fitfully or not at all, but despite those hardships, he resolutely bathed in frigid creeks and washed his clothes as best he could.

I may be a beggar, but I don't have to look like one, he consoled himself as he tried to wash and shave.

Despite his best efforts, he'd become rather seedy-looking, and his clothes now sported stains he couldn't remove. Few people would give him work much less a meal, thinking him a ne'er-do-well who might rob them of their valuables.

At last, he managed to make his way to the town of Lumley, which marked the nearest border between the duchies of Grefyn and Weyllyn. *Lumley answers to the Grand Duke Weyllyn. I should be safe enough here,* he thought. But just as he was about to step out of the hedge and onto the high road, a troop of mail-clad Crows appeared riding down the road in the distance, all bravado and noise. *Ah. This is why game has been scarce the last week. The Grefyn saves his gold by making his Crows live off the land and the poor must starve. I remember hearing he makes them sleep in the stables when they come to an inn. They have to buy their own ale and because of his parsimony, they bully everyone and take what they want rather than pay for it.*

Settling back into his hedge, Huw waited until long after dark before finally making his way to the backdoor of the Spotted Dog, an inn where he'd spent many an evening with his harp while traveling from house to house in the old days as a journeyman. Knocking quietly, he waited in the dark, hoping Glyn had heard his tap.

When the door was opened, it was with shock he saw his host. Glyn's face bore many fresh bruises, and his left eye was swollen shut. "Who is it?" The cleaver in his hand gleamed in the light of the kitchen.

"It's me, Huw Owyn," Huw replied, horror tingeing his voice. Someone had beaten Glyn mercilessly.

Glyn's fist reached out and pulled him into the light. "You're not welcome here," he whispered, upon seeing it was truly Huw standing there. "There are Crows nesting in this town, looking for your sort, and they're not being gentle about it." Abruptly releasing him, Glyn said, "Wait a moment. I've a bite to spare for you." The man turned back to the kitchen and returned with something in his hand. Thrusting a trencher of bread filled with stew at Huw, Glyn firmly shut the door in his face.

Huw vanished into the darkness. Crouching under shrubs in the shadows outside the city walls, Huw said a quick prayer of thanks and a blessing for poor Glyn, who'd tried to help him despite the presence of Crows in his common room. Then he ate every last scrap, feeling the pain of hunger diminish with each mouthful. He'd never tasted anything so good in his life. When he finished, Huw ghosted among the piles of refuse and the privies in the alleys of Lumley, making his way out of town as silently as he was able.

Huw began to realize that some terrible thing, far beyond his personal tragedy in Ludwellyn, had happened to upset the balance of power between the ruling clans. Whatever it was had given the Grefyn the confidence to burn down a quarter of the port city and murder an entire craft in his efforts to gain control of the Long Valley, and then send his Crows into Weyllyn villages. Clearly, the Grefyn feared no retribution from Weyllyn or the Crown.

This meant something had weakened the elderly Grand Duke, Daffyd Weyllyn, because the Crows of Clan Grefyn were making themselves at home in his lands. The affiliations of these border villages were always contested between the two clans, but with Daffyd Weyllyn's ascension they'd known forty years of stability and had prospered. The man known as *the* Weyllyn was a sympathetic and just ruler. The people of his duchy had no fear of his men and knew their daughters were safe from their depredations.

How am I to get any news? I can't just knock on a door and ask, "Pardon me, but what's going on with the Weyllyn?" But I need to find out! Huw thought for a moment and then decided to risk crossing the farmlands between the road and the southern end of the River Limpwater, which cut a meandering path through the center of the valley. Once on the other side of the river, he could work his way north to Imrysdock, the hereditary seat of the Duchy of Weyllyn. Some information should be available there, something to tell him why everything in the Long Valley had gone to hell so abruptly.

With this in mind, at dawn Huw began crossing fields and woods. In the crisp morning light, he walked along the outside of a garden wall belonging to a fine country manor.

He'd just passed the end of the wall when an imperious voice commanded him to stop. With his heart pounding, Huw halted but did not turn around. A young-sounding lady's voice said, "Please look at me when I speak to you, sir!"

Reluctantly Huw did as she ordered and was quite surprised to see a very young, somewhat haughty lady wearing the garden attire currently favored by noblewomen. There were distinctly bitter tones to her voice as she said, "Where are you running off to? If I can't leave, why should you be allowed to go?" Suddenly, her haughty attitude changed. "Wait! You're far too young to be one of ours. Whose man are you?"

Huw feigned ignorance, trying to buy time. "Why, I'm my own man, my lady. I'm a tinker by trade." He saw her skepticism. "I'm on my way to Clythe to see my ailing mother, so if you'll excuse me, I'll trouble you no longer." He bowed and attempted to leave.

Again, her voice stopped him, this time full of sardonic humor. "You're trespassing on private lands. And the road is *that* way," she pointed the way he had come. "Why are you running to the river?"

"Ah, my lady, it's a long and boring story. I wish to get to the other side so as to avoid some unpleasantness. Several brothers are rather unhappy with me on this side of the river at the moment." Huw offered her his most charming smile. "They'd prefer I go to the other side, too."

"So you like the ladies then. Why else would these brothers be unhappy with you?" She looked him up and down. "Sit down and tell me all about it."

"Um…ahhh…a gentleman is always discreet, my lady. I'm sure my transgressions are of no interest to you." Despite the little voice inside his head that warned him to leave, he found himself admiring her charms and imagining what she might be like to kiss.

She abruptly sat on the grass where her book and parasol lay and patted the ground next to her. "My name is Ilene," she said, with a smile. "What are you calling yourself today?"

"Jak, my lady," he replied. Stretching out on the ground next to her, his mind sorted out exactly where he was and just whom he was imprudently dallying with. "Why are you interested in a fool like me? I'm fleeing from terrible danger, and am most likely running into worse. And if this is the house I think it must be, you're most definitely trouble for me." His smile charmed her completely. "You may be the daughter of an important person."

"If you're running from what I think you're running from, I truly *am* trouble for you," she replied. "But I'm not the daughter of this house. I suppose I'm the lady of the manor since I'm the wife of Earl Rann Dwyn. Sounds grand, doesn't it?"

Huw leaned on his elbow and looked up at her. She gazed into the distance, a hint of bitterness coloring the smile on her face. "What are you doing immured here in the country, Countess? Surely the social season is still in full swing in Ludwellyn. The last parties of spring are in preparation. Why are you not there?"

"And what would a tinker named Jak know about the social season in Ludwellyn?" she asked, looking at him out of the corner of her eye. "Besides, my lord doesn't need a wife dangling about his neck in Ludwellyn ruining his social life. He's been quite frank as to my station in his life."

"I know little of society, my lady, only that it exists," Huw replied, flashing his charming smile again. His eyes openly appraised the young woman, curious about her. "You don't seem old enough to be Earl Dwyn's wife. He's rather old, as I recall." This was said with the arrogance of youth. Rann Dwyn was only ten years older than Huw, but his gaunt face had already begun to show the signs of premature aging, which dissipation and lecherous behavior often led to.

"Yes, he's quite old," she agreed. "Though we've been married for nearly a year, I don't really know him very well," she said with some distaste. "But I do know he's not well acquainted with tinkers." She glanced at him. "He despises them actually."

"Sad, but true," Huw agreed. He shrugged with his impudent grin firmly in place. "I and my kind are most definitely not high on his list of friends." He rose and gathered his possessions. "And now, my lady, I shall take leave of you. I must get across the river today."

He had walked four steps when she spoke again.

"I hate my husband," she said. There was no trace of bitterness. It was just a simple statement.

Against his better judgment, Huw stopped and turned back to her. "But why?" He didn't know why he felt so compelled to ask her. "What causes you to despise him?"

"I didn't choose him. I was given to him like a prize heifer despite my earnest wish to the contrary." Ilene looked at Huw. "I'd hoped to fall in love one day. I thought my marriage would bring me that which the *bards* all sing of, true love between a man and a woman." Huw didn't miss the emphasis and winced. She'd recognized him, but he still couldn't place in which house he'd seen her. This meant she'd been very young, perhaps not yet out in society.

Huw sat back down next to her. "What did you get instead?"

"I got a husband twelve years my senior, a man who's rarely home, and when he *is* home, he's most ostentatiously drunk. I got a husband who ignores me, except to demand his rights for an hour or so before he goes into town to the tap room and his friends. My duty to him is to suffer through his clumsy attempt to disguise rape as my marital obligation."

"I'm sorry you've suffered, Ilene," Huw's words were sincere. He felt a need to comfort her, though he knew he should be on his way. "All men are not like him. I loved my lady very much. But now I'm a hunted man, and she chose not to come with me." He couldn't disguise his intense resentment at the memory. "I don't care for your husband either, if you want the truth. He's somewhat involved in my troubles."

"I know. He's actually the source of many of your troubles," replied Ilene, a look of pity crossing her face. "He mindlessly does whatever the Grefyn requires of him, the wretched toady. He hopes to be made heir, but everyone knows Amstyce is going to be my uncle's successor."

Huw looked at her questioningly.

"My brother, Amstyce. Duke Lyndys. He's my uncle's favorite and will surely be the next Grand Duke." She looked at Huw as if he should have known, and indeed he *should* have. But the girl had grown since he'd last seen her. "I recognized your voice when you spoke, even without your harp," she said. "You are ...." Hurriedly, Huw placed a finger over her lips. Smiling, she continued, saying, "You're a tinker named Jak."

"And you've grown both beautiful and witty since I last saw you, my lady. You're wasted on a dull stick like Dwyn. But as much as I would enjoy tarrying, I fear I must be on my way now. Birds of prey are looking for me as we speak."

"Yes, they're looking for your sort. I heard you were most definitely dead, along with your entire craft, in the guild hall disaster. I admit I wept for you." Her eyes conveyed the truth of her words. "But here, come back to my house with me. I'll feed you and let you bathe in a proper bath. I can also find you some clean clothes." She stood up with a fluid, graceful motion and tucked the book into her pocket. "My husband has more than enough to spare. He has rooms full of clothes he's never worn."

"No, my lady. I wouldn't compromise you in such a way. I don't want to be responsible for your death," Huw's tone was light, but his eyes were serious. "If you're caught sheltering me, your husband will have a reason to seek a new wife. You'll die young, just as the previous three countesses did." It was an oblique warning, but she knew what he spoke of. "He'll not be kind to you, should he find you harboring a traitor."

"He's not kind under the best of circumstances, and I'm likely to die young anyway." Her desolate expression said she fully believed it to be true, though she immediately tried to brighten up for Huw. "But don't worry. I'll see to it no one knows you're here. At House Dwyn the servants are few and very old. They pay little attention to me. They doubt I'll survive, you see. They don't want to become too attached. You're right, Tinker-named-Jak. My husband is rather hard on his brides." Her wry tones barely disguised her scorn. "At this time of day, the servants are busy. They are too few in number for the tasks they have to fulfill, so I try to take up as little of their attention as possible and only play lady-of-the-manor when my husband is home.

Tonight I'll dine in my rooms, as usual, and they'll overfeed me, also as usual. You'll share my dinner and we'll both be well fed!" She held her hand out to Huw. Reluctantly he grasped it and she pulled him to his feet. "Once you're fed and rested, you can be on your way. I owe you as much for the tales you...." She paused and grinned wickedly at his warning look, "...for the tales that must surely surround a pretty tinker-lad like you."

"Every instinct tells me to run now, as far and as fast as I can, my lady. You're a deadly danger to me—in more ways than just the obvious." His eyes openly betrayed his interest in her. "You were but a schoolgirl when last I saw you. Now you've grown into a beautiful woman."

"Come," she pulled him toward the manor house. "My husband has been away in the South for more than a week this time. I don't want to waste these golden hours of blissful solitude when he's absent, but I confess I'm lonely. Tell me what's been happening."

"What I could tell you would make a stone weep, my lady," Huw said, and his grief surfaced once again. "It's a long and sorrowful tale, one I'd rather not talk about just now. Suffice it to say, there's been an outbreak of death in Ludwellyn, and I fear it's only the beginning of something dire for the Eynier Valley. I'm sorry to have to tell you this, but your family is the source of it. I know all who answer to the Grefyn are not tied up in this. Some of you have no choice but to follow where the wind blows. Your uncle has all the power—indeed he's gone mad with it."

"Not only my uncle. My husband and brother are his creatures, too." Shaking her head sadly, Ilene led

Huw to the front of the house. She left him there, hidden in a small, overgrown private garden. His thoughts were chaotic, and he berated himself for not running while he had the chance. Before long, a tall window opened onto the garden, and she beckoned him to come in. In what seemed like no time, Huw found himself in the last place he imagined he'd ever be—in a Grefyn countess's private bath chamber.

It was an amazing room, with a deep tub into which the water poured from taps set into a beautifully tiled wall. All the hot water anyone could wish for was available at his fingertips. In a small closet to one side was a flushing toilet. No stinking chamberpots lingered malodorously in this country manor. The lady's private dressing room was through a curtained doorway.

"It's said King Henri Dragoran has installed this plumbing in his northern keep in Castleton," he said, as he watched the tub filling with steaming hot water. "How is it the water is hot when it emerges from the tap?"

Ilene grinned. "There are two large boilers in a room off the kitchen, and all four of the bathrooms are served by them. Not as many as the king's but more than any other noble house. It's why my husband was so intent on having it installed here," she replied, with the trace of bitterness that now lurked ever-present in her speech and mannerisms. "My husband spends little money except on his own comfort or to impress others. Having the most modern plumbing in the whole Eynier Valley impresses his friends." Her tone implied they were friends who found her husband's company convenient for the moment. "Even the Grefyn hasn't had his palace plumbed yet."

The tub was nearly full, and she turned to Huw, saying, "I'll leave you to bathe in peace. Here are some of my husband's clothes. He'll never miss them. He's only worn them once and will never wear them again, so they're perfectly good." She giggled and said, "I'll burn the poor things you're wearing after you've changed."

He set his kit and sword-belt on the floor in her dressing room and quickly disrobed, feeling a sense of disorientation. *This is a terrible idea. I could be caught naked in here, so why am I doing this? Am I an idiot? But, oh God, what a lovely bath this is.* Sinking down into the hot water was nearly more blissful than he could stand, and he found himself groaning with the sheer pleasure of it. Gradually the pains of the road soaked away, making him feel almost like his old self.

A bar of lavender-scented soap sat on a clean flannel, both waiting for him, and he made lavish use of them. After he'd washed his hair, he used the tortoiseshell comb she'd left, teasing out the snarls and knots he hadn't been able to get out with only his fingers. His dark curls then fell in ringlets over his shoulders to his waist. Shaving with warm water was a real treat, when he thought of all the icy streams and ponds he'd bathed in since leaving Ludwellyn.

Too soon the water had cooled, and he rinsed days of filth down the drain. Then he courteously washed the tub out, as one always did at a public bath. *Such luxury! You don't have to go to the well to refill the buckets here,* he marveled. *No kettle on the fire, everything right there waiting for the next lucky bather! A man could get used to this!*

At last, he stood dressed in clean clothes and felt very fine indeed. *I didn't realize how stained my clothes were*, he thought with some chagrin. She'd left him a plain white shirt with wide sleeves laced at the wrists and throat to wear over simple black breeches, clothing no different than that of many other men. He wouldn't stand out at all, as nearly every man of means in Waldeyn dressed in a similar fashion. It was no wonder the earl seldom wore them, as the man's taste ran to much gaudier clothing. He tended toward silks decorated with lace and embroideries, if Huw remembered him correctly.

Just as his hand touched the knob on the door, he heard voices in the lady's chamber. One belonged to an arrogant-sounding man. With his heart thumping, Huw silently picked up his possessions and retreated to Ilene's dressing room. He pulled the heavy curtain closed and sat on the cushioned bench. He looked about, making sure all his possessions were safely in there with him. With relief he saw nothing incriminating had been left behind to indicate his presence.

It soon became apparent the earl had returned unexpectedly and was demanding his conjugal rights. The sounds of a rather one-sided argument could be heard from his hiding place. Ilene protested she was unprepared for his visit. "If you'd given me more warning, my lord, I would have met you downstairs, as is your due. Please, allow me to set a proper meal before you and your men...."

Noises, as if the earl had struck Ilene and knocked her to the floor, gained Huw's attention. Rann Dwyn sounded rather inebriated as he loudly declared her preparations mattered not to him. He was only back long enough to pick up clean clothes and fresh horses. Then in the coarsest of terms, he insisted she give in to his wishes there and then, striking her several more times. Soon the regular grunting of the earl and rhythmic squeaking of the bed combined with Ilene's muffled cries of pain—the noises penetrating the closed door. Each sound announced the earl had gotten his way in a most vile manner. Unable to refrain, Huw slipped from the curtained dressing room and peered through the keyhole of the outer bath chamber door.

Shockingly, he saw Ilene's husband taking her from behind. Bending her over the footboard of the bed and holding his wife firmly by her hair, he forced her face into the thick bedding with each thrust. Ilene's dress lay on the floor, and her shift had been pushed up over her back and shoulders. Blood streaked Ilene's legs. The earl seemed to take pleasure in hurting and degrading his wife as much as he did sodomizing her, and he clearly enjoyed that immensely.

The sight sickened Huw to the core, though he'd heard such things did happen. Now he was torn between being an unwilling witness to a brutal rape and confronting the earl, making the situation even worse.

The earl was reputed to be an accomplished swordsman, known to have no sense of fair play. Dwyn's sword belt hung on the bedpost near his hand; it was never far from him. Rann Dwyn was infamous as a man whose duels always ended in the death of his opponent and was well-known to enjoy toying with his victims.

Huw knew without a doubt he was outclassed as a swordsman. Now he sharply regretted never taking his sword lessons seriously. And even if he were to take Dwyn by surprise, there was the problem of his men.

Tearing his eyes away from the disgusting scene, and rocking back and forth with his hands over his mouth to keep himself from shouting at the earl to stop, Huw felt the panic rising. He was scarcely able to control it, but the voice of reason overruled his insanity. Taking on Rann Dwyn in his own home would be madness, as his men would surely execute him and Ilene both, even if Huw somehow managed to kill him.

Then there was the law that said whatever a man wished of his wife was his by right. The law wouldn't be on Ilene's side, no matter how brutal her husband was. Were Huw to intervene and kill him, a magistrate would find him guilty of interfering in lawful intercourse between a man and his wife. He would hang for murder.

Nevertheless, with each strangled cry, Huw forced himself to remain hidden, biting his hand in an effort to keep silent. He knelt before the door. As much as he tried not to listen, Huw was privy to every distasteful thing that occurred.

Thankfully, and fairly quickly in Huw's estimation, the earl finished his business, grunting loudly and pulling Ilene's head back at an impossible angle with his pleasure in the final throes. Huw watched in horror. *He's a sick man who enjoys inflicting pain; he needs to hurt her in order to get his own release. I've heard of people like that, but oh, God! Poor Ilene!* After leaning heavily against her and resting a moment, Dwyn abruptly slapped her thigh, as if in appreciation. Then he pulled himself out of his weeping wife's body, buttoning his breeches.

Speaking as if nothing out of the ordinary had just happened, Rann Dwyn began talking conversationally, telling Ilene he'd be away for several days on business for the Grefyn. "I'll be going north now. I don't know when I'll return, but I'm hunting a wily quarry and I'll not be back until the valley is scoured clean of them. Oh, do stop your weeping, woman! I suggest you try to pretend some affection for me," the earl told her. "One day, you'll be the Grand Duchess—the mother of my heirs! Try to be grateful."

There was a faint jingling as Dwyn shrugged back into his coat-of-mail. "I'm off to do a most important task for your uncle now. I've news of traitors hiding in Moireton, posing as casual entertainers." Ilene said something Huw couldn't hear, and Dwyn replied, "It's no matter that Moireton answers to Weyllyn. Dayved Weyllyn has vanished! The Old Weyllyn is now without a male heir, and he puts up his missing heir's sister, Madewyn, in his place. No man with any sense of pride will follow a duchess. No man follows a woman unless he is weak. Now is the time for Clan Grefyn to seize the Long Valley of Eyn! We began the task with the extermination of rats in Ludwellyn. Your uncle says he'll cleanse the entire Long Valley of the bards' infection. Anvel Grefyn speaks, and I obey. By my prompt actions, he'll know *I* am fit to inherit the ducal coronet!"

Through the keyhole Huw saw him strapping his sword belt on.

"Surely he'll reward me, for it was I who silenced their guild master's tongue, putting the rope about his neck myself! I set the torch to the rat-infested tenement that was their hall. For the last four weeks I've been hunting traitors, and I won't quit until they're all accounted for. Some must have escaped, and I'm going to finish the task of eradicating them! That so-called guild was naught but a tool of the barbarian King of Wald. Spies they were, pretending to be entertainers but, in fact, feeding lies to Wald."

Dwyn's voice was scathing as he continued, "The bards all sang glorious songs of Waldeyn, as if two such disparate countries as Wald and Eyn could really be one. Look what propaganda gained the bards. I tell you now, there are none left here in the South, and soon we'll have the entire valley free of them. Every house that looks to Grefyn has rallied their armsmen. The valley belongs to Grefyn now, or it soon will, and it will be me who gives it to your uncle. He promised to reward the one who gives him the Crown of Eyn, and *I* will reap the reward!"

Dwyn laughed, a braying sort of snigger. "Those who thought themselves safely barricaded in their hall are well and truly roasted now. The fire burned for a week! Nonetheless, if there are bards anywhere, in any town or village, I'll find them. Weyllyn's hands are tied now, so let them just try to stop me ferreting out their tame bards!" Again he laughed.

Bile and hatred rose in Huw's heart, threatening to send him out to murder Dwyn with his bare hands. Red rage blinded him, and he reached for the door, yet his hand was stayed by some miracle. Biting his fist to silence himself, Huw heard the earl calling for his manservant as he swaggered out of the room. "Royal Eyn will rise again, and our fortunes with it. Pull yourself together and behave like a duchess, for the love of God, Ilene! You're a woman now, so act like one. No other woman balks so at doing her wifely duty!" With that, Dwyn told his manservant to assemble his men in the courtyard and be ready to depart immediately.

The door shut behind the earl, leaving his shattered wife once again trying to pick up the pieces of her wretched life.

Chapter 5 An Epic Tale For The Lady

Huw heard Ilene weeping piteously. He stood there, uncertain whether he should remind her of his presence or give her time to compose herself. His hands shook; he was a mass of seething emotions and still didn't trust that he could remain calm and silent. After a time, Huw heard the jingling of mail and the whickering of horses outside. Crossing to the high window, he watched as the earl rode away, followed by a band of armed men wearing Dwyn's colors.

The sound of Ilene's sobbing finally stopped and he opened the door. She sat, bruised and disheveled in her shift, trying to fix her hair with shaking hands. Tears streamed down her swollen face.

Huw's heart broke to see her so destroyed. He'd never, until that afternoon, understood the harsh realities of a noblewoman's life. Now he realized it wasn't the sinecure everyone pretended it was. Ilene had been wed at the age of fifteen in a carefully arranged marriage, as all women of her class were. It was an unforgiving life unless a woman was fortunate enough to be given to a man she could love. A noblewoman was a valuable possession, one that increased either her family's wealth or standing. She was an ornament, a prized possession, nothing more and nothing less.

Huw turned back and began running a hot bath. While the tub was filling, he crossed the room, saying, "Ilene, let me help you." The look of hopelessness and misery in her eyes stopped his words. Gently, he took the hair brush and pulled it through her locks, piling it in a knot on her head as he'd often done for Sinean. Naturally, she shied away from him. "Will you let me help you? I won't molest you, I swear! I just want to repay your kindness. A bath will ease your pains, I promise."

Then he took her hand and led her to the bath, pulling the bloody shift over her head. Ilene's legs gave out, and he lifted her into the tub, promising the water would ease her suffering.

Huw was shocked beyond words on seeing her battered body. Bruises from the foot-board of the bed stood stark across her belly and hips. Discolorations in the shape of handprints marred her thighs, shoulders and neck. Her many scars and contusions were both old and new, and numerous bite marks stood out sharply on her back. Gently he bathed her, telling her repeatedly it would be alright, although he had no idea how it possibly could be.

Through it all, she said nothing, though she trembled constantly. At last she broke her silence only to say, "It'll never be alright. Not until I'm as dead as his other wives, God rest their lucky, lucky souls." Her voice was thick, and she refused to meet his eyes. Eventually she stopped shaking. The heat of the bath helped her immensely, soothing her injuries. Rummaging around the shelves in her dressing room, Huw found a jar of healing balm, a clean shift and a robe. She'd begun to feel better, pretending she was fine and telling him she could take care of herself now.

"No, my lady," Huw replied. "You will allow me to care for you as your husband should have done." Helping her out of the bath, he gently dried her and applied the healing balm. Then he assisted her into the clean shift and robe.

Leading Ilene back to her bedroom, he helped her to a chair, unsure what to do next.

"Thank you, Huw. I'm so sorry you had to...to...." she stopped. When she started again, her voice was low, but more like her old self. "I think I'll heal much more quickly than usual this time."

A knock at the door made Huw jump. Startled, Ilene looked at him, and he quietly returned to the bath chamber. He pushed the door nearly closed, leaving just a slit to see through. It was a servant with Ilene's dinner tray. She thanked the old woman and set it on a table. After locking her bedroom door, she stood numbly looking at her meal, and Huw came out of the bath chamber.

"Get into bed, my lady," he said, taking her hand and leading her to it. "You rest and I'll feed you." Pushing her gently, he waited until she was sitting up, leaning against the pillows, and then he covered her with the quilt. Next he brought the tray over and set it on the bed, climbing up to sit beside her.

"You don't have to feed me. It's not as if I'm an invalid," she said, with a bleak attempt at a smile. "It's nothing I haven't endured at least twice a week and sometimes daily since our wedding." Her lips quivered, eyes downcast. "I'm sorry you had to witness my humiliation. I know you must have been embarrassed to be a spectator to such marital bliss."

"I couldn't have left discreetly without making your situation worse, my lady." Huw smiled, trying to comfort her, and began slicing the fruit into small bites. "I'm sure your husband would have been quite unhappy to find a man in your dressing room, even though we aren't lovers." Spearing a slice of melon with the fork, he held it to her lips. "Just a bite or two. Please?"

"Why are you being so kind to me?" she burst out. Tears rolled down her cheeks.

Huw was silent for a moment and when he spoke, it was with the full force of his self-loathing. "I behaved like a coward. I was safely concealed in the bath chamber while you were being ill-used. I wasn't man enough to stop him raping you. I'm hiding in his house, and I'm miserably aware I'm no match for him with a sword," Huw admitted, his guilt starkly written on his face. "No man should treat his wife in such a fashion."

"But he's my husband, and it's his right under the law," she said. Her characteristic bitterness had returned. Then she asked, "How is it you bards all sing of true and romantic love, making what happens between a man and a woman sound so beautiful and wonderful, when the reality is so disgusting?"

"The reality is you're married to an animal, my lady. Truly, a real gentleman would never behave like a rutting hog." He searched for the words to explain to her what he knew was true. "A real man pleasures his partner before seeking his own gratification. Love between a man and a woman should be a thing of beauty and romance, not an act of violence."

"What pleasure can there possibly be in such a revolting, humiliating act? There is none!" she burst out. "I don't understand how a woman can possibly want to do such, not even to beget a child!"

"Beget a child? In the way he used you today?" Huw was stunned. "Were you never told how babies are made?"

"Yes, of course," she nodded and said, "The morning of my wedding, my Aunt Grete told me my husband would force his body upon mine, and though it would be painful, I should endure my wedding night with a good heart because I would surely beget a child from it. She was wrong. I've never yet begotten a child though it's been nearly a year."

That's how Huw found himself explaining to Countess Dwyn how babies were actually conceived. When he'd finished, she sat there, stunned and trying to comprehend what Huw had told her. Finally she said, "If what you say is true, then I shall never conceive a child, for my husband regularly plants his seed in the wrong field!" Her lips quivered, but she didn't give in to tears. "On my wedding night, he took me the way you describe and has never done so since then. He got as little pleasure from it as I did."

Feeling ill, Huw held the bite of melon to her lips again. "Please eat. Please?"

After a long pause, Ilene said, "I'll eat one bite if you'll eat one. When was your last meal?"

"I was very well fed last night," Huw replied, feeling a mix of guilt and gratitude as he thought of the beating Glyn had endured, just for being in the service of Clan Weyllyn. "A good man risked his own life to feed me." He saw her holding a piece up for him. "Alright, if it's your wish, my lady. One for me and then you'll eat another."

In this fashion Huw was able to induce the countess to eat her meal. After they'd finished, Ilene quietly placed the tray outside the door. Then she locked it and left the key in the door so no one could see through the keyhole that she was entertaining a guest in her husband's absence.

"The servants will expect to find the tray there. I keep my rooms tidy myself because we have no chambermaids. None will work for us. I wonder why." Her voice dripped with scorn. "Stable boys leave as fast as we hire them. Nattie changes my bed when I ask her. She has no time to do more." Ilene found herself jabbering nervously as she drew the curtains about her bed. "No fire tonight. I wouldn't have the strength for one normally after his visit, and I won't change my routine. I don't want to give anyone a reason to check on me."

"They really do put a lot of food on your tray," Huw said, trying to ease her nerves. "They must care for you a bit, despite your precarious position here."

"I flush most of the food down the toilet, or the servants worry I'm not eating and pester me. I haven't eaten so much in days!" She climbed back into the bed. "I feel quite full."

Once she was settled, Huw stood up to depart, knowing he had to be on his way.

"Don't leave me just yet," Ilene begged him, placing her hand on his arm. "I feel so alone. Your friendship means so much to me. No one's ever treated me with such consideration. I mean it, Huw. You've asked nothing of me—you've only shown me kindness."

Reluctantly giving in despite his better judgment, he agreed. "I'll have to leave tomorrow though. Every day I linger here brings me closer to the gallows or if I'm truly unlucky, the gibbet-cage." He lay down on top of the bed next to her. "I really don't want to end my days in the gibbet, Ilene. I knew a good man who did, and it broke my heart."

"I know. I'll sneak you out of here tomorrow." She sighed. "I know you're endangering yourself to keep me company and I appreciate it more than I have words for." Smiling unsteadily, she said, "In the meantime, tell me a story, Huw, like you did for my fourteenth birthday, when my mother was still alive and we had music in our house. I know you can't sing it the way it should be done, but you can whisper me a story of romantic love and happy endings." She looked like a child, begging him for a story.

"You remember!" Huw said, with a sense of wonder. It always surprised him when people remembered his tales with fondness. "It was my first performance as a master." Fully clothed, he slipped under the blankets and put his arms around her. Clearing his mind, he began telling her the story of Merewyn and Aelfrid, a tale she'd never heard because it had long been banned in all Grefyn demesnes. His low voice was a whisper, barely loud enough for her to hear.

It was a tale of forbidden love and the struggle that culminated in the marriage which united the immense northern kingdom of Wald with the Long Valley of Eyn. Aelfrid and Merewyn's marriage had freed the Eynier people from the yoke of slavery under the pirate kings of Lanqueshire and brought peace for two hundred years.

"It's a beautiful tale," she told him when he came to the end. "If only life were really so, with adventure, love and good triumphing over evil!" Huw told her several more love stories, speaking softly in the dark, stroking her hair and holding her close. Toward midnight, Ilene drifted off to sleep with a smile on her face. Huw wondered if she'd ever been so relaxed in a man's company.

He lay there with his thoughts spinning wildly. He hated Earl Dwyn with every fiber of his being. His mind saw nothing but Balen's corpse dangling from the gallows and the burning guild hall. Huw's errant body very much wanted to make love to Ilene as it should be, and desperately wished not to feel such yearnings when she'd been abused so harshly. Still, snuggling Ilene as she slept eased his heart in an obscure way. The woman needed his consolation, and he needed the comfort of holding her.

Wide awake, the dark hours passed slowly while he sorted through his confused thoughts. *With his own hand, Rann Dwyn murdered my father and most probably Loris too. He put the torch to the hall and slaughtered the others as they tried to escape the flames.* His heart nearly stopped each time he thought about it. *I can't live knowing he exists. Some sort of punishment is in order, and I'm the only one left who can seek retribution. How pathetic. I barely even know how to hunt a rabbit.*

Eventually he made the only decision he could be at peace with. *So now I'm going to be a hero,* Huw mocked himself as dawn approached. *I'll have to forget crossing the river and heading east to Imrysdock, which just shows what a fool I am. I've never before killed anyone and yet I'm going to hunt an earl down and kill him.* He sighed heavily. *I'm going to Moireton after all. What makes me think I'm an assassin?*

Dwyn was bound to have guards attending him. But having seen what he did to Ilene, Huw realized the man had something to hide. *He has secrets with a certain stigma attached. A man with skeletons in the cupboard is vulnerable. He'll be unattended while he indulges in his sport unless he's even more perverted than I know him to be.* The privacy of his rooms would be where Huw had the best chance to get to Dwyn, as he'd be unattended, unarmed and unconcerned for his own safety.

Having made his decision to hunt down and murder Earl Rann Dwyn, Huw finally relaxed. He'd just about drifted off to sleep when he heard Ilene's small voice ask, "Would you show me what love between a man and woman should be like? I know only the bad. I wish to know the good too."

Despite the fact he desired her far more than was wise under the circumstances, Huw's conscience forced him to be honest. "I must be truthful about something, Ilene." There was bitterness in his voice as he confessed his deepest shame. "I'm less than a gigolo now. I've sold my body for nothing more than a meal many times since I left Ludwellyn, and not only to women. Do you understand? I didn't wish to, but I did and I'll do it again if I have to. I have no future. My life as I knew it is over. I'm no longer a man at the top of my craft. I've become a common whore. I'm not good enough for a woman like you."

Ilene was silent as she considered what he was telling her. "Anyone would choose to fill their belly," she said. "I think many people make such a terrible choice every day. It doesn't make them bad! And you've kept yourself under great restraint," she pressed her hand against the hard shaft of his manhood. "I feel your passion—you're trembling with it." She seemed surprised at what her hand found and continued touching him, feeling the length and hardness of him through his clothes. Her hand pressed harder, as if she were curious as to the shape of him.

Huw knew Ilene was unaware of what her questing hand did to him. Barely able to contain his need, Huw's low voice was raw. "Believe me—I'd enjoy nothing more than making proper love to you. But Ilene, you're not in love with me. It won't be as wonderful for you as if you were with a man who also holds your heart. There may be pain because of what you suffered yesterday afternoon, though I'd try not to hurt you."

She put her finger over his lips. "I know. But I'm afire with curiosity and some other wild emotion I don't understand. You love me a little. Your kindness tells me this. I'm married to a beast. If I don't seize this moment, then when will I have the chance to be with a kind man? I'm completely compromised anyway, lying here like this with you. Please, just let me have this to remember. Let me have a small piece of happiness to hold on to in the sea of misery that is House Dwyn."

Lying next to her as he had for so long, refusing to act upon his baser impulses, Huw had no defenses against such an open, honest request. Turning to face him, Ilene pressed her body against his and their lips met.

In that moment Huw's will to resist crumbled. Passionate need filled him, pushing aside his hesitation. Huw returned her kiss, burning with desire such as he'd not felt for any woman but Sinean. "This is how lovers kiss," he whispered, and lowered his lips again, his tongue caressing hers, taunting, giving her a mere glimpse of what she never knew she wanted. The pulse in her throat quickened and she responded to his kisses. He felt her delighting in the waves of sensuous pleasure that washed over her.

His own breath caught as her hands slid under his shirt, feeling the satin smoothness of her fingers against his skin as she touched the hardened peaks of his nipples, sensing her astonishment. In response, his hands found her breasts; teasing her, he moved to kiss them, suckling through the thin material of her shift, enjoying the way she gasped as his thumbs stroked her nipples. He kissed her again.

Standing up, he eased out of his clothes, and she watched him, seeing he had indeed missed many meals. Yet the hard contours of his slender body with its fine musculature were pleasing and her eyes widened. Diffidently, she reached out and touched his belly, feeling the softness of his skin. "Seeing you like this—I find myself in awe of how extraordinary this has become," she said, wonder coloring her voice. "I've never seen a man completely unclothed."

"Do you like what you see?" he asked as he sat cross-legged before her. His wicked smile and dancing eyes completely charmed her.

"I think so," she said with an answering smile, and hesitantly touched his manhood, as if she were unsure that she should. She found herself stroking it, cupping him, feeling the weight, and then caressing the length again.

"I'm glad," he said, his heart racing as her hand became surer in its explorations. "Ohhh, that feels good." He gasped as she stroked the velvet tip. "Too good. We need to slow down a bit or...."

Hoping to distract her hands, he helped Ilene out of her shift, and kneeling before her, continued awakening her senses with tender kisses on her lips, shoulders, throat, and breasts. Huw kissed every injury Dwyn had inflicted, always returning to her breasts and belly. As the tension within her mounted, he explored further, parting her legs and stroking her most sensitive place with gentle fingers, making her gasp in wonder repeatedly.

Gradually, his lips wandered down to the secret place he knew was the focus of pleasure for her. He took his time, gently kissing and caressing the soft mound that now became the center of her awareness.

Every stroke of his tongue brought her closer to some amazing thing that seemed just beyond her grasp; now it was she who trembled with need. Sensing the intensity of her arousal, he continued until Ilene hung trembling on the edge of something larger than lightning and more profound than thunder. Then at last, Ilene's world splintered into a kaleidoscope of exquisite sensations. With kisses and soft caresses of his tongue, he brought her to her first orgasm, thoroughly savoring and enjoying the moment she first experienced that instant of timeless rapture, drawing it out as long as he could, her stifled moans of pleasure gratifying him.

Ilene basked in the golden afterglow of the shattering orgasm, with a smile of absolute bliss gracing her disheveled beauty. Huw held her, congratulating himself for having placed that smile there. Stroking her hair, he told her that until that moment she'd been a virgin, no matter how she'd been abused. "Now you're truly a woman, my Ilene," he whispered. "Now you know what it's all about. Are you sure you're ready for me to show you the rest? I don't want to hurt you."

In answer she wrapped her legs around him, grasping his fully aroused shaft, drawing him inside her. She sighed softly as he entered her, caressing her in places that were secret no longer. Aching with the effort of not allowing himself to make wild love to her battered body, Huw pleasured her as gently as he could. Determined to make it the best experience possible for her, he brought her to ecstasy again. Though he tried to rein back, her hands clutching his back as she climaxed and her soft moans so near to his ear tipped him over the edge. Groaning long and low, he was swept away; caught up in the moment, he thrust deep into her, taking his pleasure in a thundering climax that left him utterly spent.

Exhausted and sweaty, he lay in her arms and their tears mingled. "Have I hurt you, my dear girl?" he asked, mentally cursing his lack of self-control and terrified he'd ruined it for her. "Oh, God, Ilene. It was too much after what that beast did to you. I never meant to hurt you." His arms tightened around her. "I shouldn't have taken advantage of you. Please forgive me!"

"No, Huw, no! I'm not hurt," she kissed his tears away. "I think I'm healed now in some wild way— maybe not my body, but my soul." Tears of joy and sadness streamed down her cheeks; joy for what Huw had just shown her, and sorrow that she'd never know such an experience with the loving husband the women in the tales had. "It was better than the stories can possibly tell. It was so much better."

<u>Chapter 6 Murder in the Dark</u>

Waking to the sound of a knock, Huw found himself cowering deep in the shadows of the curtained bed. Ilene met the servant at the door and took her breakfast tray, setting it on the table. "Thank you Nattie. I'm a bit unwell today, so please don't disturb me unless my lord requires me," she told the woman. "If my husband returns, please notify me immediately. I wish to be prepared to greet him properly as he'd expect me to. Yesterday he was less than pleased, and we want to avoid that in the future."

"Yes, my lady. We all wish that. Jessup was on his way to tell you, but the earl overtook him and sent him on an errand. We were worried for you. He's our master and there's naught we can do," replied the old woman. "Shall I start your fire?"

"No, thank you, Nattie. You three have enough to do. I think I'll rest today," said Ilene, "but thank you for your offer. I'll feed my own fire, and if Jessup leaves the coal in the bin by my door, I'll get it as I need it. That way he won't be overburdened. He has the stables to see to, and if Rogers can water the kitchen garden today, I'll be well enough to tend it myself tomorrow or the next day."

Apparently, it was a common occurrence for her to remain in her room after a visit from her husband. The old woman just nodded and said if Ilene needed anything, she had only to ring.

Ilene closed the door, turning the key and leaving it in the lock. "They'll expect me to stay here in the dark for two or three days, depending on how long his visit was." Her face held a mixture of emotions as she added, "They know he's violent, but they're bound to serve Dwyn, generation to generation, and don't know how to help me. Our servants have sent their children to work in other houses for their safety, and they've buried three young countesses before me. They expect to bury me soon, but they're kind, letting me pretend to be feeling a ladylike malaise and giving me the time I need to recover."

Huw was silent, overcome by an unpleasant mix of rage and hatred for the society that turned a blind eye to the harsh realities of the lives of women who were treated as property. Gritting his teeth, he managed to bury it, so when he turned to face her he had his usual wicked glint in his eye, and she laughed, calling him incorrigible.

Ilene convinced him to tie his hair back in a braid, emulating the nobility. "This changes your appearance greatly. Bards wear their hair long and loose because the women like it, but you're trying to avoid being mistaken for one. Young tinker lads who wish to be scholars all follow the styles of the nobility, whether they mean to or not. They wear their hair in a tail as do the nobles." She caressed his scratchy cheek and giggled. "You must shave this or I'll be rubbed raw!"

Later, as they shared her lunch, Huw confessed he'd decided to put off crossing the river until he'd managed to murder her husband. "If I'd not witnessed what I did yesterday, I'd be a much happier man. But I saw what he did, and heard…. Now I can't live knowing *he* lives. I have no forgiveness for him."

Ever practical, Ilene agreed she'd very much like to be a widow. "I hope you'll be able to kill him, but I won't believe it's happened until I'm standing over his grave wearing a black veil and tossing a rose in with the dirt." She grinned and added, "If you're successful, then I'll be widely known as the Notorious Countess Dwyn, the merriest widow in the Long Valley!"

Huw laughed and kissed her.

"I'll miss you, more than you know. But I'll never make a good wife now. I'm not cut out to be property. Once my year of mourning is up, I'll have many lovers and enjoy every minute of my life. I'll be known for my parties and my dashing friends from the artist's quarter…." She stopped, a look of sadness crossing her face. "I'm so sorry, love. Surely some playwrights and poets have survived. Surely the tinkers will have escaped. They are a clever people. Some of the traveling pipers and street singers must have, too."

Willing his tears to disappear and holding her close, Huw said he understood. "Some will have survived. After all, I'm here. The tinkers and other travelers will be laying low for a while, as they must know there's trouble for entertainers in the Grefyn lands. The tinkers know all the songs and tales. They wrote them, you know, long before we were bards.

Everyone makes music." He kissed her forehead. "You're too young and full of spirit to be kept down by convention. You'll have the best salons and parties, where all the brilliant artists will gather and share their talents. I'll always wish I could be a part of it, but you'll do what you can to keep the art and music of Eyn alive."

"And you must try to rebuild what we've lost, so the old tales and histories like the story of Aelfrid and Merewyn are never forgotten. My uncle Grefyn wants to rewrite history, and he murdered a craft to do it," she said, tears in her eyes for the other bards whose music and tales she'd had the pleasure of hearing as a child. "But heed these words, my dear. You must *never* let your guard down. Noble houses all over the valley on both sides of the river and in both clans are secretly relieved you're all dead. You'll never know which house will support you and who would kill you until it's too late." She kissed his cheek and tried to console him as best she could. "I love you, Huw Owyn, just a little. And you love me too, so stay alive! I'll write to you."

Indeed, he did love her and felt loath to leave. "I fear I'll miss your company far more than is good for me, my beautiful girl." Ilene had given him back the spirit of the man he used to be, something he thought lost forever when he was at his lowest.

"If you're in need, send me a note and sign it 'Jak the Tinker,'" she told him, smiling widely. "I'll know it's you."

"And you can send a note to me at the Green Man in Clythe, for I must stop there and finish my personal business before I leave this valley forever. Later, you can send letters to me there, and my friend will forward them on," replied Huw. "I'll have to let him know where I'm going. I owe him that much." He sighed. "Truthfully, I'm going to need his help if I'm to make it to the North alive. He'll help me to get hired on with a mercenary crew since he knows them all."

Huw stayed with Ilene for two more days, delaying the inevitable and enjoying her company. She made sure he was properly kitted out with a new kit-bag, a woolen blanket, soap and even a small pot of healing balm. "This kit-bag is much larger, and your lute takes up far less room. Even with the book, it doesn't show at all from the outside. Now you've plenty of space for odds and ends you may need along the way. I've not given you much, love. This is the only blanket I have that'll shed rain and isn't too big to strap to the top of your kit. You'll be able to get a waterproof along the way and maybe a pot or two. Now you look like the tinker-lad on his way to the University in Vyennes that you really are!"

"It's such an improvement over what I've had for the last month, you can't imagine," Huw replied, gratitude in his eyes and embrace. "I won't be shivering under hedges anymore."

Ilene insisted he accept a money belt with enough to buy him meals in towns as he came to them, all the way to Clythe. "A scholar won't have enough coin for lodging, but he'll have sufficient for food and other essentials. It'll be expected of you to sleep in barns and stables and to eat in tap rooms. I've no need for money, and this was mine when I came here. There's a lot more where this came from. My brother will be required to send it to me as my father's will stipulated! He's held it back because my husband isn't to be trusted with money." With a low, sardonic laugh, she added, "If you're successful, I'll cut myself off from my family. They loved me so much they sold me to Dwyn for the position this house once had, knowing full well he's a rutting animal." Her dark eyes hardened. "I vow I'll *never* be chattel again and I'll make public my reasoning."

"You're a woman who'll change the world, love. I just have to make it possible before I leave this valley, and it'll be a task I'll enjoy. He condemned himself with his own words." Huw's voice was low, but it conveyed the depth of his emotion. "Upon my life, I swear he's a dead man." He grinned wryly and added, "I just have to figure out how to do it and draw the least amount of attention."

Toward midnight, Ilene led Huw down to the road where they said farewell in the rain, both loath to lose each other. Embracing tenderly under the shelter of a tree, they whispered their good byes. Reluctantly, they parted.

"Good-bye love. I'm off to kill a beast," Huw said, with that wicked grin Ilene loved so much.

Laughing, she replied, "If you aren't successful, I'll find a way to kill him myself. Once I'm a widow, House Dwyn will look to Weyllyn, especially now the

Duchess Madewyn of Imrysdock leads them. She shall certainly have my support!"

At daybreak the rain lifted just long enough for the eastern sky to lighten with a red, angry dawn as a storm lingered on the horizon. A heavy mist set in, and Huw walked along the road hoping to hear news of his quarry. He smiled, thinking of how Ilene had blossomed over the days since her husband's brutal attack. *Ilene will be a real force for change,* thought Huw. *She's exactly what the valley needs more of.* His smile faded. *I just need to find a way to make her a merry young widow, and then she can live happily ever after, as the ladies in my tales all do.*

Huw walked quickly, heading north to Moireton. The heavy, grey, woolen cloak, standard attire for the men of the local area, blended with the fog making him as ethereal as a ghost. Huw's contemplations were as black as the lowering sky. Each time Huw thought about Earl Dwyn, his hatred threatened to overcome his caution.

Anger and desire for justice drove him, his feet moving in an angry counterpoint to his dark deliberations. Huw forced himself to think clearly, to plan his course of action once he found where the earl was staying.

Once Huw entered Moireton, he discovered Rann Dwyn had been there and since moved on. He went to the inn and stood in the tap room drinking ale, listening to the conversations around him. Bit by bit, he pieced together the story of a band of Crows that had ridden into town without fear of consequences, taking over the inn. They'd immediately begun interrogating the populace, demanding to know if there were any bards about. After two days, they were pressing the local men harshly, demanding to know where the entertainers were. When it finally came out one of the local boys could play the pipes and sing a good ballad, he was dragged out of his home, and the Crows hung him from the tree in his own garden. When his mother tried to save him, protesting he was just a boy and was never a bard, one of the earl's men struck her with his mail-clad fist. She collapsed at his feet, blood flowing from her ear and nose. She died not long after.

An atmosphere of sullen anger permeated Moireton, souring the air. In the tavern, the men were brooding and angry that Weyllyn could allow such a thing to happen in their town. Huw's thoughts were as grim as the local people's comments. He strode down the near-empty street heading for the gate, muttering to himself. "Weyllyn will lose the valley if this keeps up, and Lanqueshire will have us as a province. The old Grand Duke is losing his grip. He must be near death because he wouldn't tolerate these atrocities in his lands. Madewyn must take control and soon or she won't have a duchy to inherit!"

He decided to get supplies at the general store instead of spending the money on a meal, thinking he could feed himself for several days on what supper at the inn would cost.

The shopkeeper was cold and abrupt with him. "I'll take your coin, tinker, but be gone quickly. We've had enough of strangers in this town." Huw purchased a set of utensils for cooking his food. They consisted of items that nested in each other and took up little space in his kit. Then he bought a tin of waybread, a round cheese, some dried fruit and a packet of tea. A thin, tightly woven wool blanket and a waterproof ground cloth completed his purchases and didn't make his kit that much heavier. *Now I won't have to go hungry when the fishing is poor, and with the ground cloth to wrap around me and the extra blanket, I'll sleep as warm as the Grefyn,* he thought as he left the store. Because of the shopkeeper's general unpleasantness, Huw bargained harder than normal and spent only four coppers of the money Ilene gave him. He had no idea how long it would have to last and didn't want to waste it.

He continued on to Emmerton, where he felt sure his quarry would be looking for more victims. *No bards were this far north. They were all in the guild hall for the ceremonies.* He snorted to himself, thinking, *The only "bards" the bloody Crows will be murdering will be tinkers and casual entertainers.* Huw's thoughts were as forbidding as ever, as he trudged through the foggy fields.

Toward dusk he came to an inn called the Dead Man's Coins, built on the outside of the town walls. Entering the dark, smoky room, he saw men in the livery of Dwyn making merry in one corner. He stood quietly at the bar, listening to their conversation, and overheard his quarry was lodged upstairs, resting. "I wonder which of the town's lovelies his lordship is 'resting' with tonight," said one of Dwyn's men in low tones, winking broadly at his mates. His comrades all laughed and nudged each other. "In Moireton he near on kilt Gryn for spyin' on him when alls Gryn were doing was beddin' down in the hallway for a bit of warmth, so don't none of ye even think of it. We're kippin' in the barn again like always. 'S a lot warmer'n sleepin' in the bush, right?" Everyone agreed and continued drinking.

Quickly making up his mind, Huw decided to chance a meal, hoping to overhear something to help him with his task.

The townsmen were unable to defend either the town or their daughters, who'd been compelled to serve the earl's men. Emmerton was poised on the edge of violence, and only the steel the Crows wore so openly kept the peace. The local men couldn't stand against them, and they were miserably aware of it.

When the innkeeper brought Huw his stew and ale, he said there were no rooms available in the entire town and for his health, he should just keep walking. Huw agreed and thanked him for the advice. After he finished his meal, he continued north until he was out of sight of the town's gates. There he left the road. Stashing his kit in a hazelnut grove, he waited until dark and circled back, walking in the shadow of the town walls until he once again approached the Dead Man's Coins, this time from the rear. Many fruit trees grew there, and a sweet-maple stood beside the woodshed, which leaned against the kitchen. Slipping through the gloom, Huw hid behind the trunks, moving from shadow to shadow until he reached the sweet-maple.

The door opened and a man staggered out to the privy. Pressed against the tree, Huw waited patiently for the man to finish and go back inside before moving on.

The Dead Man's Coins had originally been built well over a hundred years earlier and extended many times. The various different angles of the roof offered Huw plenty of ideas as to how he could accomplish his task. The sweet-maple blocked the view of the kitchen roof from the stable yard and was connected to a broad covered porch. This ran along under the windows of the second floor.

Silently, Huw climbed the maple and stepped onto the kitchen roof, careful not to dislodge any tiles. Then he crept along under the windows, staying in the shadows. A large cherry tree stood by the porch, shielding the windows over the tap room from view. However, ahead of him Huw saw a long stretch between the two trees where someone could see him clearly if they looked up. In the dark, the shingles that covered the second story walls were weathered to a dark gray. Desperately, he prayed he wouldn't stand out too much if someone were to look up when he had to cross the exposed area.

He'd just reached the middle of the open expanse, when the noise of the raucous tap room surged and the door to the kitchen opened, shining a square of light onto the packed dirt of the back garden. Completely covered by his cloak, Huw pressed himself against the wall, holding his breath and willing himself to blend in. A thin, tired-looking girl carefully emptied a dishpan full of water onto the plants that grew in the neat rows of the kitchen garden. Taking a rag that hung on a nail by the door, she wiped the pan and went back inside. The sounds of the party subsided as the door closed.

Creeping as silently as he could, Huw once again began peering into windows. The door opened for a second time and two men wearing chain-mail came out. They wandered to the stable, talking in low tones. In the dark shadow of a chimney, Huw waited until they'd mounted their horses and ridden out of the yard. Then he moved slowly along, looking briefly into windows until he found the one he wanted. Fortunately, this one was shielded from view by the large cherry tree. It was no coincidence Rann Dwyn had taken this particular room; the tree hid his activities from all eyes.

The man sat with his back to the window, drinking from a large mug. He looked to be fairly deep into his wine, as a bottle stood empty near his hand and another lay on its side, rolled against the candelabra. Three of the four candles had guttered, and the fourth was nearly out, flickering wildly. The bed stood across from the window, but Huw couldn't see past the earl well enough to view it clearly, so he had to hope Dwyn was alone.

I'll have to wait until he's asleep to deal with him. It's the only way I'll be able to kill the beast. In the shadow of the cherry tree, Huw settled down to wait, planning exactly how to murder the earl and get away before his men discovered him dead.

The door of the tap room opened, and two men stepped into the yard. They closed the door, and stood speaking in low voices. From his hiding place, Huw could see they were Crows. He strained to hear their words.

"Dwyn must've found himself a bit o' pleasure. He was off to bed early," said one, a man with a crooked nose. "He don't share his wimmen, so what he does with 'em when he's done, I don't know." His slight Lanque accent proclaimed his origin. "The Grefyn wants him watched. There's been some ugly rumors come to the attention o' his highness, and he don't want no sort o' tarnish on his family name. Dwyn might've overstepped it, see? Folks don't like their daughters snatched in the dark."

"Well, I don't care fer what he done with that boy. Sure, he sent the boy up to his folk's room to collect his things afore he kilt the parents, so the boy din't atcherly see it, but it were a mistake. The lad's disappeared! He shoulda kilt him too since Dwyn were all fer killin' his folks. Now the boy'll come out against Grefyn, and we'll look bad agin." The man, who was missing an ear, wiped his nose on his sleeve. "I think these folks wuz bards about as much as you are, Borik, and you cain't sing a note. It's murder fer the fun o' it. I jus' think we oughta call it what it is."

Borik replied something in tones too low for Huw to hear, but his companion responded, saying, "Never had no problem with killin' when it's needed, you know that. But I don't kill fer sport. I'm just sayin' this is gonna come back to haunt us, is all. An' where's the boy now? He's probbly already gone to the next town, tellin' what was done to his folks." They turned and went back into the tap room.

Huw turned to look in the window at his quarry. The earl, at last, staggered to his bed and fell into a drunken sleep. Now Dwyn no longer blocked his view,

Huw could see a visibly shocked and battered young boy, lying awake beside him. With a feeling that bordered on nausea, he realized the boy had been raped. *If this were to come out, there'd be no place safe for Dwyn. The Grefyn himself would kill him. There's no stigma worse for a nobleman than that of being an abuser of little boys!*

Taking a chance the boy wouldn't give him away, Huw quietly slid the window open. With a finger to his lips, he silenced the numb-looking lad, who simply watched, obviously unsure of what would happen next.

Huw had taken his knife training quite seriously, and no one was better than he. With barely a gesture, a blade appeared in his hand. Silently, he motioned for the boy to gather his clothes and get dressed. The drunken earl didn't so much as stir when the trembling boy climbed out of the bed.

The thought of his father, hung in the street like a criminal, blinded him. Leaning over the earl, he whispered, "This is for Balen, my father, whom you murdered in cold blood." Slashing down hard, he slit the sleeping earl's throat, cutting so deeply he severed the man's windpipe. Blood spurted across Huw's chest, splashing hotly on his face and spraying the front of his cloak, before it soaked the pillow and the sheets.

The man's eyes opened in shock, and he made a strange, horrible, gurgling sound. The stricken earl convulsed for a moment clutching at his throat, but Huw's blade fell again, stabbing him through the heart and this time he twisted the knife. Finally Dwyn's body became motionless.

Looking down at his bloodstained shirt and sleeves, Huw stared at the streaks and spatters that so loudly proclaimed him a murderer. Naively, he'd no idea it would prove to be such a messy job, and unexpectedly, he found himself enraged by the sight of all the blood that betrayed his guilt so blatantly. Suddenly the image of his father's body twisting at the end of a rope while his dearest friends burned alive rose in his mind and overcome by a brief madness, he stabbed the earl's corpse again and again, hating him, his blood and everything he represented, repeatedly knifing him with all his strength until a shocked gasp snapped him out of it.

He turned to see the boy staring at him in horror. *Oh God. First he's raped and then he witnesses me botching a murder.* Realizing he had to calm the boy, he wracked his mind, trying to think of something, anything to ease the child's distress. "Don't worry. I'm here to rescue you," Huw whispered. "He'll never hurt you again." The boy just nodded and stared at the mangled corpse with an unfathomable look in his eyes.

Huw stood looking at the gory body, wondering how he was supposed to feel now. Murdering the loathsome earl hadn't made his heart any lighter. He hadn't gotten the sort of pleasure he'd anticipated, and as he carefully cleaned his knife on the blankets, he wondered why. With only a slight flick of his wrist, it vanished, hidden once again in his sleeve.

Then Huw did the only thing he could think of to delay the inevitable discovery of the dead man. He adjusted the blankets as neatly as a mother tucking in her child, hiding the mutilated corpse perfectly.

The blood that now stained Huw's cloak, face, hands and shirt affronted him, shouting to the world he'd assassinated a man in his sleep. His hands shook, but he tried to remain calm as he washed his hands and face in the basin on the dresser, feeling as if they'd never be unsoiled again.

He opened the window and tossed the basin of bloody water out. Using the last of the water in the jug, Huw rinsed his shirt clean and then hung it on a peg to dry. He took the neatly folded shirt that had been left out for the earl to wear the next day and put it on, feeling immensely better once he was no longer covered in blood.

Suddenly inspired, he exchanged his stained cloak for the earl's clean one. It was identical in every way to the one he'd been wearing except for the black epaulets on the shoulders and braid on the left breast in the shape of a *G,* all of which he tore off. In the absence of a wastebasket, he tossed the trimmings onto the floor and gave them no more thought.

Let them figure out what happened if they can, he thought. *Let them try to guess how his cloak got so bloody.* Carefully, he picked the telltale black threads out of the material of the new cloak. All the while the boy stared, first at Huw and then at the corpse.

"I know how he hurt you." At Huw's words the child closed his eyes and shook his head slowly, as if denying it would make it go away, but he finally nodded. Huw said, "I've been hurt in that way myself. I've medicine to help you heal. Are you able to travel?" His whisper was low, only for the boy's ears. "If you'll follow me and stay close, I'll get you away from here."

Mutely, he looked at the floor and nodded.

Motioning for the child to follow him, they left the way Huw had come, closing the window. They went slowly, pausing in the shadows several times as patrons stepped out to use the privy and returned to the tap room. The lad was in pain and moved stiffly; Huw had to help him climb down the sweet-maple. Eventually they made it through the orchard away from the inn.

Huw led the traumatized boy back to the grove where he'd stashed his kit. During the whole episode, the boy said nothing.

Once inside the grove, Huw sat, trying to think of what to do with the child. He was sure the lad was newly an orphan and suspected he was the one the two Crows had been talking about. At last he had a plan. "What's your name, boy?" Huw's voice was gruff from the tension, but not unkind.

"It *was* Ned Wells," he answered, with reluctance. "But now I have no name. You know why. No one will want me, with the stigma of what he done to me. They'll kill me for it." Ned's face was full of dread and misery. His lips quivered, but he didn't cry. "He wouldn't stop! I begged him, but he wouldn't quit."

"No one knows what he did to you but me, Ned, and I'll never tell. I know your secret, and you know two of mine—and mine are worse. We're even. But now, Ned, you must let me bathe you," Huw said. Dark eyes filled with shame and fear stared back at him. "If we don't get your wounds clean, you most likely won't heal right. I promise I won't hurt you. I'll only wash you and apply the medicine."

Silently, Ned nodded. As gently as he could, Huw set about bathing the boy, though he only had the water in his canteen. Passively, Ned endured yet another humiliating experience with as much reaction as a ragdoll, numbly doing as Huw asked. The canteen held enough water to clean the lad, and he made sure the child knew how to apply the medicine himself.

"You must bathe daily even if it's in a creek and use the medicine for three days until the pain is gone," Huw told him, kindly. "It was no fault of yours, what he did to you. You weren't the first he'd used so badly, and you wouldn't have been the last. Your family must be worried for you."

Ned confirmed Huw's fears. "I have no family, not now," muttered the boy, his face full of despair. "We're tinkers, but my da fell out with my granda and swore he'd not be a tinsmith as granda was. Da didn't have the gift of memory, so Balen didn't want him to be a bard, but we were making our way as traveling entertainers. We were saving up for a bit of land to call our own. I thought folks liked my parents. Now their bodies hang from the oak near the town pump, and our wagon was burned with everything we owned. Bepito, our ox, was slaughtered and the meat given away to the townspeople. No one cares what happens to tinkers, right? No prayers will be said for my parents, no one will sing at their wake." Tears rolled down his face. "Dwyn said he wasn't done with me, so he let me live for one more night. I've nothing left, he took everything." Ned's voice broke as he said, "He hurt me, but he pleasured me." A sob wracked the boy. "You should've let him kill me."

Feeling nothing but pity for the child, Huw said, "Listen to me, Ned. He pleasured you, but it's nothing for you to be ashamed of. You didn't ask him to. He raped you, and you weren't the first." Finally Huw asked him, "Do you trust me?" The boy nodded his head.

"It isn't wrong to find pleasure with someone if you love and desire them and they return your affection. It's wrong to *force* someone." Huw looked at him to see if he understood. "Dwyn raped you—no matter he tried to pleasure you in the process. You didn't want it, and he forced it on you. He chose you because you're only a child. He knew you could never fight him off. The rape of a child is a crime, Ned. The penalty is death." Ned nodded, but Huw couldn't tell if he understood or not. "He's paid for his crime."

"I guess," mumbled Ned, refusing to meet Huw's eyes. "Things will never be the same. No one wants an orphan—especially a tinker's orphan."

"I understand how you feel. My da was born a tinker and life is hard for our sort. Dwyn killed my father, my friends, and he hurt someone I love," Huw said, suddenly realizing how he could solve two problems. "But I know someone who'll help you and give you a place in her home. She's in need of a page to assist her with things, and you'll be safe with her until you're old enough to choose what you want to do with your life. The man I killed, Earl Dwyn...I need you to take a message to his wife."

Shaking his head, the boy backed away. Huw grabbed his arm and said, "Believe me, Ned. Since she was given to him against her will, she's suffered daily what you've just endured, but he never gave her any pleasure, only pain! Please carry my message to her." The boy faintly nodded, looking at him with disbelieving eyes. "Ilene will know who it's from when you tell her 'Jak the Tinker' sent you." Huw quickly wrote a note, holding the paper up to the moonlight to read what he'd written and then added a few more words. "Don't lie to her. Tell her, and *only* her, exactly what happened here tonight, everything. She deserves to know, and she'll never tell your secret because she shares it. She'll find a place for you. Will you faithfully serve her?"

Ned nodded with his eyes cast down, obviously thinking about Huw's words. After a long moment, he made up his mind and looked up, saying, "If she's been done so badly by him, she'll want to know he suffered. At least I would. I'll take the message and serve her if she'll have me."

"She'll have you. If you know any stories and songs, tell them to her and sing for her. She loves music. Now, do you know where House Dwyn is?" Huw waited expectantly.

"Aye," the boy nodded. "But we never entered their lands, for they're Clan Grefyn. Grefyn has a tin ear, my mum always said."

"Not after tonight," replied Huw, smiling grimly and looking south to where he thought House Dwyn might be. "Now they are Weyllyn. Now go quickly and stay out of sight of the road." He gave the boy half of the cheese and bread he'd bought in Moireton, wrapped in the earl's clean kerchief. "Here's some food for your journey. God be with you, Ned."

"And with you too, Jak. Thank you for trying to heal me, and for killing him. He needed to die, no one more so." Saying a final goodbye, Ned turned and began the journey to House Dwyn, walking briskly through the dark.

Chapter 7 Dunmora

As Ned disappeared into the night, Huw began to head east, traveling across the fields and meadows. By dawn, he was camped on the banks of the River Limpwater, where it flowed slow and shallow and was easily forded in many places during certain times of the year. The River Limpwater began a thousand leagues to the north in the high country of old Wald; Huw didn't know exactly where. It carved its way south, dividing the length of Waldeyn east and west. Just north of Clythe, the river plummeted from the high country to the lowlands of the valley in a spectacular series of falls.

In the lowlands, many bridges crossed the river as it looped and wound its way through the valley. From the town of Emmerton, the trade road followed it closely. It was used mostly by the merchant caravans that traveled north from Ludwellyn to Clythe and from there to the high country and the land of old Wald. The local people avoided the trade road, staying to the back roads for the most part, because thieves and highwaymen lay in wait for the unwary. There was safety in numbers, and the heavily guarded caravans travelling the trade road to and from the port city were often exceedingly long. They had right-of-way where the road was narrow, such as on the bridges or in the passes, so a farmer could wait for an hour just to get his hay wain across.

Huw sat on his bedroll by the campfire, unable to sleep. His thoughts had grown darker and more forbidding with every step he'd taken toward the river, and now his mind was a morass of dreadful, shadowy things. He wrapped his arms around his stomach, rocking back and forth, fearing he would throw up. Every time he closed his eyes, he saw the knife in his hand slitting Dwyn's throat, and smelled the peculiar iron scent of blood spurting everywhere. In the breeze that had sprung up, he heard the strange gurgle of the man's windpipe being cut.

Huw knew his life had taken an irrevocable turn. *I killed a man, knowing full well what I was doing. I did it, and I'll do it again if I find the others who helped him. I'll kill every Crow who had anything to do with my father's death, if I'm able.* Unable to stop thinking about what he'd done, he shivered. *Oh God! He needed to die, as Ned said. But why don't I feel better about it? I thought it'd ease my pain to kill him.* Huw's sight was clouded with a red miasma.

His voice broke as he spoke aloud, "I avenged you, Balen! I avenged you, my father…but I'll never be the same. Oh, God, I'll never be the same." Once again, Huw found himself sobbing his grief out, and this time he also cried for young Ned, Ilene and, strangely, for the man he'd murdered. "I'd do it again, Balen. I'd do it because it has to be done."

With the daylight, Huw came to terms with his guilt, at last finding peace and reconciliation in the knowledge he'd most certainly kept Ned from being raped again and probably even murdered. He also accepted his own need to avenge his father and friends. Aware he could never change what he'd done, he put it behind him.

Huw broke camp and began looking for a good place to ford the river. He crossed the chilly stream, holding his pack on his head to keep it dry. The river was running deep, and at one point, he feared he'd have to swim for it, but he made it across. Soon he was huddled in his blanket, shivering and warming himself by a small fire while his clothes lay drying in the sun. By noon he'd crossed the meadows and was on the road once more. At sundown, he entered the village of Dunmora.

In a twist of fate, the heir-apparent to the Grefyn fortunes, Duke Amstyce Lyndys, was staying in the hamlet on business. He and his men were harassing the casual entertainers in the name of the Grefyn. An impromptu gallows bore testament to his diligence in carrying out his uncle's wishes. Huw didn't recognize the bodies that dangled there; it was as he feared, the victims had not been bards. *There are no bards anywhere now. Only fifty of us had the necessary gifts of memory and pitch to begin with, and now they're all dead. I'm the last.*

Huw was curious about Lyndys. He was Ilene's older half-brother, having been born of their father's first wife, but Ilene had little affection for him. Amstyce apparently saw his sister only as chattel to be exchanged for property or position. Huw wondered if news of the murder of Dwyn had traveled to the far-flung members of House Grefyn. He decided to risk the tap room in an attempt to hear some news.

Duke Lyndys's approach was somewhat different than the method employed by the late Rann Dwyn. Lyndys's men weren't allowed to molest the daughters of the townsmen, nor did Lyndys himself appear to have the unsavory habits his deceased brother-in-law had enjoyed. He was occupied at a table in a corner of the tap room near the fire, jotting things down in a well-worn ledger.

Huw sat at a table with his back to Lyndys's men, as a man who was unfamiliar with fighting might do, but where he could see the duke from the corner of his eye. The window to his right provided good light for him to read by, and taking a book from his kit, he laid it on the table and began to read while he ate, occasionally making notes in the margins as he'd seen scholars doing. From his table, Huw observed Lyndys while searching in vain for some resemblance to Ilene and feeling somewhat disappointed when he found none.

Amstyce Lyndys was a man with no sense of humor and who was possessed of a surprisingly unfortunate countenance. He had no chin to speak of, and small, watery eyes to complement a somewhat querulous manner of speech. Still, while the good duke might have a boorish demeanor, he was apparently diligent in his work. He was quite intent on the tasks that lay before him. As Huw considered leaving, a messenger approached the duke. Lyndys had the man read him the message twice and then told the courier to gather his captains.

When they were all together, he said, "Come with me." Lyndys rose, and stepped outside, his men following. Huw resigned himself to not hearing the rest of Lyndys's instructions. Quiet voices drifted in through the window, and Huw smiled. Standing just under it, Lyndys said, "I've just received a message that changes everything. We must leave immediately." As each squad leader approached him, Lyndys carefully explained how he wanted their task carried out.

Then he spoke to them as a group. "My brother-in-law, Rann Dwyn, never understood how the common people have the ability to bring us down. He overstepped his authority and nearly cost Grefyn the entire valley with his precipitous spree of murder and arson. *We* were to deal with the bards, but it was to be done quietly and in such a way they would never realize they were being exterminated one by one.

"Now Weyllyn has dealt roughly with him! He was murdered in his sleep last night. His throat was cut and he was stabbed through the heart many times in what can only be ritual assassination. Knives were used, the sort that only an assassin would have. While Dwyn's death is no great loss to us, the very violence of it is a slap at Grefyn! We know the killer was bought by Weyllyn because the Grefyn badges were torn from his cloak and cast to the floor. No one else would *need* to send such a pointed message.

"Duchess Madewyn is now their regent, and with this murder has announced she'll rule their demesne with a woman's hand. She indicates it was worth the expense of an assassin to rid her towns of Dwyn's ill-conceived depredations. The murder is a message, a warning that we're being watched while we're in their towns. Or perhaps it was a favor, but either way it's a message. Therefore, your men are not to drink to excess." Lyndys glared at his captains. "Keep a rein on them, or I'll have them whipped!"

One of his men said something, and irritated at his comment, Lyndys snapped his response.

"Dwyn was a marked man for the way he let the fire get out of control in Ludwellyn. My uncle made it clear to me two days ago that Dwyn's days were numbered. My sister would have been a widow soon enough and this has saved us the cost of an assassin. So we'll pretend Weyllyn has done us a favor. My uncle has already selected a new husband for my sister to wed when her year of mourning is up. The carelessness in Ludwellyn was avoidable and cost us dearly. Two weeks passed before commerce resumed, and we all suffered terrible financial losses because of it, both Grefyn and Weyllyn."

Lowering his voice to where Huw really had to concentrate to hear him, Lyndys said, "We're not to confront Weyllyn openly at this time. Retribution for this slight will have to wait until the Grefyn has all the Port Lanque mercenaries necessary to take the valley. It'll take another month or two. Avoid openly antagonizing them!" Lyndys smiled unpleasantly. "We'll deal harshly with Weyllyn when we're ready, but until then we walk widely of them. Madewyn is only an untutored girl, playing at ruling a duchy. We'll let her believe she's frightened us off, and then we'll have our day in the sun and reclaim her lands. Henri of Wald will no longer be welcome here."

Despite his dismal demeanor, it was clear Amstyce Lyndys did keep a rein on his men, which Huw appreciated. "We're here to rid the town of traitors, not turn the populace against Clan Grefyn! If we anger the peasantry, it won't matter how weak Weyllyn is, the people will turn against us, which will ruin my uncle's plans. We return to Ludwellyn tomorrow. Once there, we are to oversee the rebuilding of the artists' quarter, minus one guild house, of course. This charity will elevate us in the people's opinion and negate some of Dwyn's bad odor."

Lyndys and his men reentered the tap room and resumed their original tasks.

Huw waited a while, reading and making notes in his book, still posing as a scholar. Having finished his meal, he left the tap room while the duke was busy with his own work, feeling he understood why Ilene would wish to turn her back on her only living close family member. *How can I get word to King Henri about the Grefyn's plans to bring in a Lanque army? I can't let anyone know a bard survives, or it'll get back to Ludwellyn. They might wonder who's been harboring me. Certainly, if they learn I still live, they'll hunt me to the gates of Hell.*

His mind conjured the image of Yannes, the close-mouthed innkeeper, whose tavern stood at the crossroads halfway between Dunmora and Imrysdock. He was known to be a man of the Weyllyns and had been useful on occasion in the past. *Perfect! Yannes will pass a message to Duchess Madewyn. If I stay low and don't do anything stupid, I can pass myself off as a messenger from Ilene, implying she's afraid to be openly associated with Weyllyn due to family connections. Then Madewyn can alert Henri. She might already be aware of what the Grefyn plans, but I can leave nothing to chance.*

Huw slept in a barn on the outskirts of Dunmora. The next morning found him on the rutted and winding East Road, still hoping to get to Clythe before midsummer. *Two more months should see me all the way to Bekenberg. I could get there while the weather is still decent.* Travel in the Bekenberg Pass was notorious for being fraught with dangers during the better weather and was doubly so during the winter.

Huw had traveled only seventy leagues toward his goal as the crow flies in the weeks he'd been on the road. He'd actually walked five times the distance because he'd been forced to avoid the trade road most of the time, taking the winding back lanes and tramping along the edges of fields.

Now he was finally on the Weyllyn side of the river, he'd be able to travel on the main road and go much faster. Still, even by the eastern trade road, it was nearly a hundred leagues from Dunmora to Clythe, and once he made it there, it'd be forty leagues to the Bekenberg Pass and safety. Those forty leagues would be the roughest and most dangerous part of the journey unless he could arrange to travel with a caravan or trader.

The mists that clung to the lowlands east of the river closed in, and again despondency became his companion as he sorted through the things he'd done and learned during his time on the road. Huw now knew with certainty he truly *was* the last living bard in Waldeyn. He would never have believed he would come to be a whore and a murderer, yet he was exactly those things. Trudging along, he tried to understand what sort of man he'd become. He was no longer the same green boy who'd escaped Ludwellyn in an ale keg. Was he even still a bard? He feared music had been seared out of him by his experiences. The events of the last weeks had changed him, and he no longer knew who or what he was.

He was only halfway to what he hoped might be a safe haven for him, but he was certain no sanctuary could exist in the entire valley. The people of Clan Weyllyn wouldn't concern themselves with anything but their own survival. If he were to seek their aid, he'd become a pawn—a bargaining chip to be exchanged for favors.

Just stay low, he counseled himself. *Let no one know your secret until you're so far north the Eynier Valley is only a rumor.* He hoped the worst part of the journey was behind him, but had his doubts. *Nothing is ever easy for you, Huw,* he thought as he continued his flight north, this time creeping through the alleys of a village he'd never been to before. His bout of self-pity was embarrassing, but he couldn't shake it. He immersed himself in his misery, in an effort to be done with it once and for all.

Chapter 8 Maldon

It was long after dark, and Huw's feet were killing him. A worn signpost indicated he was approaching Maldon, a small village in the far east of the valley, hard against the high mountains of the Eastern Wall and not too far from Imrysdock. Maldon had a bad reputation, but for the life of him Huw couldn't remember why. It wasn't brigands or Crows; those he would have remembered. Nevertheless, he couldn't linger in Imrysdock since he was sure to be recognized there despite his disguise. He'd spent many a happy hour playing his harp for the Grand Duke Weyllyn's parties and fetes, and if Ilene had recognized him from his voice, others surely would too.

He didn't stop long in Imrysdock. Instead he stood at the backdoor to the inn and handed a note to Yannes, keeping his hood pulled far forward, hiding his features. Using the thick local accent, he raised the pitch of his voice for the few sentences he spoke. Once Yannes accepted the note, he vanished in the darkness.

The Crows were watching Imrysdock closely, though they weren't bold enough to actually set foot in the town. He saw them riding the roads, ostentatiously heading back to the Grefyn side of the river. Huw was no military man, but it appeared they were too visible in their departure for it to be genuine.

His gut feeling told him they'd left spies embedded in the local population. *The Crows planned their taking of the valley well, until Dwyn threw a hammer into the works. Too well, as the Grefyn is not known for being at all subtle and this whole scheme has been very restrained. It's like there's a hand guiding him, but whose I can't imagine.* After thinking on it long and hard, he had a notion who would benefit the most and who must actually be pulling the strings.

The pirate-king? It must be him. He's said to be a crafty, resourceful man. This situation is perfect for opening the way for him. There're far too many Lanques immigrating to Grefyn houses for it to be a coincidence and the Grefyn is bringing in an army from Lanqueshire. I wonder if King Henri knows what's really going on here.

In an effort to avoid the departing Crows, he'd taken an overgrown, rutted back road out of Imrysdock. The old road met the Maldon River and followed it north in a winding path. *I need to go this direction anyway. Maury and my mum's cottage are on the Maab, and it flows into the Maldon. I need to see my mother before I leave the valley. She should be told what really happened and that I'm alive.* The road had seen very little use recently, which concerned him, but still he trudged onward.

Huw entered the village of Maldon through an untended gate. This surprised him. *What's the point of going to the trouble of building a wall and having gates if you don't use them?* No welcoming lights appeared in any window. He couldn't see which of the dark buildings might be the inn. As he plodded down the vacant cobbled street, he was struck by how dark and silent the town felt.

The grass was high and tufts grew between the cobbles, causing him to stumble in the dark. No smoke rose from the chimneys, no one walked the empty street, and no dogs barked to give warning about the vagrant who now trudged warily along. The town was apparently long deserted.

An owl hooted and the hair on Huw's body stood up at the sound. *Owls are bad luck,* he thought. He was tempted to turn back to Imrysdock, but definitely couldn't return there. All he could do was to try to walk through the eerie village as quickly as possible.

Huw came to what had once been the center of the abandoned town. As he approached, he could hear a squeaking sound, like a sign moving in the wind. Once in the town square, the creaking noise grew louder.

He came upon a tall oak tree from which dangled an odd sort of gibbet-cage. It was like a birdcage in shape and about five feet high by three feet across. The side was fitted with a door just large enough for a man to fit through, and a padlock was firmly latched on the outside.

As the cage swung in the breeze, the light of the moon showed brief glimpses inside. A young knight in chainmail, who appeared about eighteen, was imprisoned there. He was either sleeping or unconscious, although in the dark he looked, at first, to be dead. Dark marks like bruises decorated his handsome face, and dried blood matted his blond hair. He was seated with his legs folded in a position that must have been terribly uncomfortable, and it was impossible to tell how long he'd been there.

Looking around, Huw could see no one who might observe him. Still, he stayed close to the deep shadows of the tree's canopy. As he circled the trunk, he saw a large sword lying in an intricately worked scabbard beneath the knight's prison. *What's this? Why did they leave his sword here? Is it to torment him?*

Huw came to a decision. Carefully he climbed the tree and inched out onto the branch toward the suspended cage. The stench rising from the man was overwhelming, a fetid combination of urine, feces and misery. *Gah! He's been forced to live in his own filth since they put him here, poor sod.* The door was at the limit of Huw's reach, but by using his sword he was able to break the padlock.

At the sound of the lock falling away, the young knight started and woke. Still using his sword, Huw swung the door to the cage open. "Wait until I get down below you," he whispered to the battered man. "I'll catch you when you leave. Your legs won't work well, for a few minutes at least. I've had a similar experience, being forced to stay in a cramped place."

Nodding, the knight did as he asked. Once Huw was beneath him, the man tried to leave gracefully, but ended up falling out as he couldn't feel his legs or move them. Huw caught him and tried to hold him upright. The man's battered face betrayed his misery as he endured the pain of the blood rushing back to his feet. Unable to hold the large knight upright, Huw lowered him to the ground while the man clenched his teeth and groaned with the agony in his limbs. At last he sat up, and through parched lips he tried to thank his rescuer.

"Who are you and how did you end up in a cage in an abandoned village?" Huw asked, helping the man to his feet once he felt able to stand.

"I'm called Lackland," he said simply. "This place wasn't abandoned when I came here. I spoke to the innkeeper. The next thing I knew I woke up in the cage. I've been in there for two days, so far as I know. They come in the light of day and torment me." He swayed and clutched at Huw's arm. "Is there a well nearby? I'm perishing with thirst."

"I believe so, yes," Huw spotted what looked like the well, and looping the man's arm over his shoulders, helped the knight walk over to it, stopping and steadying him when he appeared about to fall. The bucket was none too stout, but it did hold water. Sitting on the grass, Lackland drank his fill and poured some over his head in an effort to revive himself.

While Lackland slaked his thirst, Huw reclaimed the man's sword and helped him strap it on.

"Now we must rescue my horse," the knight said, standing up with a grimace of pain. "If aught has happened to Farroll, there will be bloodshed!"

"You don't look too well," replied Huw. "I'd be happy to help, but you're still a bit wobbly."

"I know. My legs are feeling somewhat delicate," said Lackland. "I'm sure I'll be fine in a moment."

The two men sat on the grass by the well, and Lackland eased his aching limbs. Huw cleaned the injuries on the wounded knight's head and face, finding them mostly healed. When he was finished, the knight thanked him. "May I ask you a question? Are you by any chance, Dayved, heir of Weyllyn?" Lackland looked at Huw quizzically. "You have black hair and blue eyes and are quite comely to look at, as I'm told he is. Are you he?"

"Hah! No such luck! I'm Hu...Jak, the tinker's son," answered Huw, caught by surprise. "All who are born in this valley are dark of hair and blue of eye. There are so many of us you'll be asking every young man you meet," he laughed. "But I've heard Dayved has disappeared. It's presented a problem here in the valley, thus I must make my way north."

"Do you know of the man? I need to find him if it's possible," replied Lackland. "My cousin is concerned about his wellbeing."

Huw tried to recollect what the young man in question looked like but couldn't remember him, which seemed odd when he thought about it. "He'd be about my age now. It was two years ago. There were a lot of young people at Imrysdock for Madewyn's coming-out party, and he should have been one of them, being her brother, but he must have been absent.... I remember now. He was in Vyennes on business for the Weyllyn, being trained as the heir. Of course, Madewyn caught my eye. She was a gorgeous girl." During his breaks Huw had monopolized her, and she'd encouraged him, even allowing him to kiss her hand.

"Ah, I see. You're somewhat unwelcome in these parts, yet you're friends with the duchess," said Lackland, grinning at him. "Why are you running, if I may ask? You don't seem like a highwayman or a brigand."

Huw didn't know what to say. He had no idea what the knight knew or didn't know, or even whose side he was on. Most likely the man was a mercenary, set on the hunt by the Grefyn; he'd said his cousin was concerned about the heir. "No. Not friends. Nobles don't have friends like me. We were hired help, employed just for the party. My father was a tinker with ambitions, and I'm a scholar on my way to the college in Vyennes. I ran afoul of an earl when I was caught, um, instructing his young wife." Huw fabricated his story well, saying nothing that wasn't strictly true. In truth, his father *had* been born a tinker, and no one ever had more ambition than Balen Owyn. "I'm bound to House Weyllyn, so I walk wide of the Crows and let them get on with their business." Apparently he'd struck the right note because the knight nodded his understanding.

"So, you're no friend of Anvel Grefyn then," Lackland looked off into the darkness.

"No!" Huw's reply came out a little sharper than he intended. "No, I'm most definitely *not* his friend."

"Good." The knight's response took Huw by surprise. "I'm afraid I'm going to have to remove him, and it would grieve me to slay a friend of yours. You see, to kill a snake you must cut off its head. It's the only way I can see to put a stop to Grefyn consorting with Lanqueshire," replied Lackland, as pleasantly as if he were discussing the weather. "Jak, if you know anything that will aid me, please tell me."

Huw looked at him in shock. "You're going to kill the Grefyn? You have my sincerest blessings, but I heartily doubt you'll be able to achieve such a wondrous thing. He's completely paranoid and better protected than most men safeguard their gold. His guards are typically thugs of the Lanque persuasion, as he doesn't trust his own heirs to guard him too closely."

"This is good to know. Nonetheless, I've been given a charge, and I'll see it done. The king wishes for peace in the Long Valley, and wants the influence of the Lanques to be diminished. He told me to do what I feel is best to resolve the situation." There was a grim set to the knight's face. "I'll have to use stealth. What do you know of Anvel Grefyn and his demesnes?"

"I know he stays in Ludwellyn in his fine palace on the bluff in the High-town. It's said he rarely goes to House Grefyn or his birth-house, Lyndys, in the country. His attention is ever on his ships and trade," replied Huw. "I *do* know if you go about dressed like you are and riding a horse, you'll be killed outright. It'll happen long before you even get there. It's a miracle you made it this far before you ended up in a cage!"

"What should I do? How should I travel?" Lackland looked surprised. "I've never been this far into the Eynier Valley before, so it's all new to me. The farthest south I've ever been is Clythe. I'm sorry to say the people down here are most unfriendly."

"Clythe is the northern gateway and not like the rest of the valley at all. It's where northerners are encouraged to leave their gold, then turn around promptly and go home, for their own safety. Many powerful people despise the North with great passion and would murder you just for the color of your hair. They won't accept we're one country and stronger for it."

"I know, but it's been two hundred years! Surely by now they see the difference, the changes for the common man," said Lackland, with a quizzical expression.

"They do, actually. They see it as the root of the problem." The knight stared at him, obviously not understanding. "It's true the joining of Eyn with Wald freed the peasants from the yoke of Lanqueshire. No one disputes this. But the union also released them from serfdom to the clans—do you see what this means? Now the peasantry expects to be paid a decent wage, and demands opportunities such as education, the right to own property, and to pass property to their children upon death. On top of this terrible affront to their nobility, Clan Grefyn lost half of their demesnes when the houses in the northern half of the valley went over to Clan Weyllyn. Clan Grefyn only knows they're poorer, have less stature and must allow the peasantry some dignity, though they remain hard masters. They believe the golden days were those during which they were allied with Lanqueshire." Huw shrugged.

"But this is ridiculous," replied Lackland, with some heat. "I've seen the ledgers detailing the amount of goods traded on their ships. I tallied them when I was attached to the exchequer as a boy. They're the wealthiest clan on the continent!"

"I've long suspected such. They appear to have unlimited wealth to go along with their limited minds. But in regard to the lack of welcome you've received here, I assure you, there are reasons for that unfriendliness. First of all, you're on horseback and wearing chainmail." At Lackland's raised eyebrow, Huw continued. "Common people fear those who go dressed in armor and ride warhorses, because when the great houses are battling, as they so frequently do, the peasants suffer. They fight on our lands and in our towns. They take our sons from the fields and force them to work at sea or worse. They put them on the frontlines of their inter-clan wars. Then they get drunk in our public houses and violate our daughters. 'Trouble rides a horse while the commoner must walk,' as we often say in this valley," explained Huw.

"I understand now. I'll have to find a way to get around this prejudice." The knight stretched and cracked his back. "Well, now I can walk, I must see to rescuing Farroll," said Lackland, as he stood up. "Where are all the people? They must have him somewhere, and I need to get him back." He leaned on the stone side of the well and then slid down to sit, as his legs were still quite weak. "They were tormenting me just this afternoon."

"This afternoon...really?" Huw was puzzled. "You say you saw people, but looking around this godforsaken town, I'd say no one has been here for years. What does this remind me of...oh no, it can't be...I'm wrong! I must be!" Resting his head in his hands, Huw tried to find a way to avoid saying what he'd just realized. "I've some bad news for you in regard to the people of Maldon. What sort of an idiot am I that I'd forget such a thing?" Huw smacked his own forehead with the heel of his hand. "God help me.

If I'd remembered the tale of Maldon, I'd never have come here." The whites of his eyes showed his sudden terror.

"What is it, Jak? You look ill," said Lackland, surprising Huw with his genuine concern. "If you hadn't come here, I'd surely have died since none of the villagers were going to release me. Cheer up, lad! We'll soon be on the road once I find my equine companion."

"Lackland, I've remembered what I forgot about this place—it's known to be haunted! How could I have forgotten this?" groaned Huw. "I'm an idiot!"

"Haunted....Well, it does seem a bit bleak and rundown, but really...," Lackland's face showed his incredulity. "Haunted? Like spirits and ghosts? Haints?"

Unconsciously, Huw settled into his bardic voice, telling it to Lackland as he had told rooms full of avid listeners several times. "Maldon is the village Old Grim claimed. Long ago, Maldon was a town full of evil men who preyed on travelers, visiting all kinds of the most gruesome tortures on them if they couldn't ransom themselves. The women were in league with their men, luring the unwary to lewd orgies resulting in an early death, reveling in the suffering of innocents, participating in the most lustful and degenerate of merriments over each victim's corpse. Old Grim was so pleased with their work on his behalf, he appeared one night in this very square. He told their head man he wanted their sort working for him, promising them great rewards. The two of them struck a bargain then and there. At the moment the contract was sealed, Old Grim spirited them all away to his domain in hell because they were evil enough to be his favored people. There *are* no villagers here because they're in hell for all eternity. They've been gone for nigh on fifty years." Huw fell silent. His sudden raw fear made him want to flee as fast as he could.

"Well, fifty years is a long time, so you can be forgiven for not remembering. But it can't possibly be this village," said Lackland, plainly surprised. "You must be thinking of a different haunted village. I spoke to these people not two days ago, and the innkeeper took my money in exchange for a room. Of course, then he knocked me out and put me in a cage, but he was real. They've been poking and prodding me daily since!"

"Aye, Lackland, he was real, and your tormenters are real too," agreed Huw. "It was a sunny day, am I right?"

"Yes! In fact, it was raining cats and dogs until the moment I stepped into the village," Lackland agreed. "I thought it was peculiar, but many things are strange in this valley."

"It's the pact, Lackland," said Huw, clenching his teeth together to keep them from chattering. "The covenant they made with Old Grim in exchange for eternal life. In the light of day they're allowed to claim any innocents who walk into their trap for Old Grim. We have to get out of here, or we'll be done for!"

"I'm *not* leaving without Farroll," replied Lackland firmly. "He trusts me, and I must honor that commitment." His sharp eyes searched the buildings for some sign of life and found none.

Huw nodded, feeling a sense of urgency. "If we can find him on our way out of here, fine, but we must be gone *before* the sun rises! We can't be here in daylight," he declared. "Old Grim allows the villagers of Maldon to live in the sunshine whenever a traveler has fallen into their trap. It never rains in Maldon, though it pours everywhere else in this dismal valley. Where was your horse when you saw him last?"

"Well, I handed him to the ostler just outside the stable and asked him to see that Farroll had a good feed of grain. We'd been on the road for a long time, you see. A fortnight I've been traveling since Clythe," Lackland's gaze now roamed around the deserted square, as if he might find his horse hidden in the shadows. "Waldeyn is a large country. I had no idea how long this valley is, the maps don't do it justice. I'd hoped to be on my way home by now."

"You're a week away from your quarry if we find your horse. It'll be four weeks or more if you must walk."

"You might be correct, Jak," Lackland smiled brilliantly at Huw. "Let's find Farroll and leave this dismal place."

Huw replied with an answering grin, "The stable is where we should look first for your four-legged companion. It seems logical to me, since it's where you last saw him." The two men made their way to the overgrown and weedy yard behind the abandoned inn. Huw steadied Lackland as he rose. "But you'll never arrive there if you continue on dressed as you are while on horseback. The Crows are molesting everyone, and won't allow a lone rider, especially one so obviously from the North to pass into the southernmost end of the valley that they've claimed for Grefyn unless we can find an excuse for a lone northerner to be down here."

As they searched for the stable, Huw thought, trying to come up with a plan. Then he had an idea. "I think I know what you must do. But first we'll find your horse and take our leave of this godforsaken place. I don't know how near to dawn we are, but we absolutely *must* be gone before the sun rises. If we've not departed by then, we'll both find ourselves dangling in cages in yonder tree, and it's unlikely a third fool will stumble into this place to rescue us."

The stable loomed dark against the sky. Its doors hung off the hinges and the yawning blackness looked like the entrance to the underworld. "I promise it didn't look like this when I came here in the light of day, else I would have kept on traveling."

A lantern hung by the door with the stub of a candle in it. From a pocket under his mail, the knight pulled a silver box the size of a small snuff-box. At Huw's querying look, Lackland said, "Firesticks from Vyennes, very dangerous if you don't keep them in a metal case. They're majiked and catch fire easily, so you must always keep them safe." He removed a stick with a red end and looking at it, said the word that was the key to making the majik work. "Alight." Sure enough, the tip now sported a little flame. Lackland soon had the candle lit and blew the firestick out.

"Well, that was a mistake," said Huw as he looked at the gaping maw of the stable doors. "It looked better in the dark."

"It's best to be able to see your enemies," replied the knight, although he didn't appear too happy with the view. Drawing his sword, Lackland entered the silent building first, and Huw followed with his knives at the ready.

It was a place of indescribable horror. Every stall held the white bones of many horses, all of whom had perished of hunger and thirst in their stalls, surrounded by the skeletons of those who had died before them.

The barn floor was littered with pile upon pile of rotting tack and saddlebags and heaps of mysterious things that couldn't readily be identified. They'd disintegrated into nothing but moldy black lumps. As Lackland and Huw walked past the stalls, mummified corpses stared at them with sightless eyes, horses whose riders had no doubt perished in the cage that had held Lackland.

Toward the rear, in a dark, fetid stall, they found Lackland's poor starving horse. A scant bit of water lay in the watering trough and the last remnants of hay were in the very bottom of the manger, lodged in the corners Farroll was unable to reach. The ostler had apparently done as Lackland asked before disappearing into the netherworld. Lackland's saddle and saddlebags rested just outside the door to Farroll's prison, as did the last remaining possessions of countless unwary victims.

Huw picked up Lackland's saddle and began heading for the door, struggling to take the heavy tack outside where they could get it onto the horse.

"I know, Farroll, I know," Lackland soothed the great beast. "It wasn't my idea to leave you in such a dreadful place, I promise! I was locked in a cage, and this man rescued me."

Huw returned to get the rest of Lackland's tack, while the knight led the horse out of the crumbling barn. The poor creature was nearly mad with thirst, and they quickly led him back to the well.

"I'll have to saddle him for you, I think. You'll have to tell me what to do—I've never done this before." With Lackland helping as well as he could, Huw saddled Farroll while he drank; all the while Lackland warned the horse to be sure not to drink too much. Once watered, the unhappy horse desperately munched on grass while Huw began getting him laden with numerous heavy saddle bags and weaponry. "I know entire families who don't travel with this much baggage," muttered Huw, as he made a third trip with yet more of Lackland's luggage. "No wonder you require a horse of this size!"

"Now, now, Jak! You sound like Chicken Mickey, clucking away at me like that," replied Lackland cheerfully. "It's all necessary, I promise!"

"Chicken Mickey?" Huw was at a loss. "I don't believe I know this person."

"Of course you don't. The man is our provisioner, and he's an absolute genius at it," replied Lackland, lobbing the last saddlebag atop the horse. "You just reminded me of him. He's always accusing me of overburdening Farroll with my luggage."

"I see his point," Huw said, struggling to hold the horse still while Lackland finished tightening the last straps. "I have no idea what a provisioner is, but he sounds interesting."

"Interesting? Mick is definitely that!" His face lost its mirth as he considered the task of mounting his horse. His legs could barely hold him up, and he had to lean on Farroll just to stand. "I've no strength in my legs, and I doubt you could lift me to the saddle. I'll have to walk as best I can."

Nodding, Huw jumped nervously as pre-dawn sounds of birds alerted him to the danger they were in. He began to panic. "Lackland, we must get your horse moving! We must be away from here *now*!" He picked up his kit and looped his arm around the knight, half carrying him with Farroll supporting his other side. Then, at Huw's urging, Lackland walked as swiftly as he was able. Farroll was not happy about having to walk when he wanted to eat. Huw grabbed the startled horse's bridle and tugged, saying "Come, Farroll! They'll have you back in the hellhole we just left if you don't help me get your master out of here!" The occasional call of the birds spurred Huw as nothing else could have. The eastern horizon began to glow a fiery red, heralding the imminent advent of the dawn. "There's the gate! Hurry!"

Almost running, Huw dragged Lackland and Farroll down the street and out of town as fast as he could. They stumbled to the opening just as the sun's first ray pierced the sky, and with the light, the gates shuddered and began to close, creaking and groaning. Struggling desperately, Huw pulled the knight and his horse through. With a loud thunk, the gate swung closed behind them, catching the horse's tail.

Farroll kicked at the gate, but although his tail was stuck fast, his hooves passed through the wood as if through fog. Skeletal hands began pulling the great beast backwards by the tail. He whinnied and his eyes were wild; Lackland struggled to keep him standing still. Quickly Huw raced back and, dodging Farroll's stamping hooves, with a flick of his knife cut the tail free. He slapped Farroll's rump and the horse shot forward, knocking Lackland down.

"Gah! They nearly had us!" Overcome with terror, Huw pulled Lackland to his feet. Grabbing Farroll's harness, he dragged the two down the rutted overgrown road as fast as he could. He kept urging them on until they could no longer see the village.

"Slow down, Jak! I must slow down. My feet can't keep this up. They're killing me." Lackland's face clearly showed the knight's suffering. "I'll have to get my boots off soon, I fear. Now there's blood going to them, my feet have swollen. Mickey made sure I had a medicinal balm for just such an emergency. That will help once I can get my boots off."

Feeling contrite, knowing the man was in terrible pain, Huw slowed his pace. "Is it a balm such as the healing sisters work their majik on?" Lackland nodded, struggling to walk as best he could. Huw was familiar with the potions and salves prepared by the Sisters of Anan, women with the gift of healing-majik. "That's a rare and valuable gift!" Still half carrying Lackland, he set a pace the knight could more easily manage. "I'll hold you up for yet awhile, until you're sure you can continue on your own. We'll find a place to camp near the river," said Huw, relieved beyond words to leave the haunted town behind. "There looks to be a place up there a ways."

As the knight grew steadier on his feet, Huw released Lackland and let the horse eat grass again.

"Poor Farroll! He'd have come to a dreadful end, left to starve or die of thirst, whichever came first." Lackland stroked the horse's matted mane. "Don't worry, old boy, I'll take care of you straight away. You look dreadful."

The horse shook his head in disgust and looked meaningfully into Lackland's eyes. He snorted.

Lackland's jaw dropped. "Well, I can't help it," he replied, in affronted tones. He turned to look incredulously at Huw. "This muscle-bound pack-pony says I stink like a privy!" He glared at Farroll, saying, "I'll have you know they had me imprisoned in a cage that made the one you were locked in look like a palace!"

Farroll snorted again and tossed his head, and Huw could have sworn the horse was sulking. "As soon as we find a place to camp, you can take care of him," said Huw, grinning at the exchange. "We need to find somewhere we can stay comfortably for several days so you can rest and recover more fully from your ordeal."

Once again the horse nodded his head enthusiastically, as if answering.

"I confess my limbs are still quite swollen and painful from being cramped for so long," agreed the knight. "I never sit for very long in one place, and there was no way to get comfortable in that cage."

On hearing that, Farroll's eyes held a sad expression, and he touched his nose to the knight's cheek. Huw was stunned by the gesture. *If I didn't know better, I'd say the horse just kissed him by way of an apology!*

Apparently Lackland thought it was an apology too and patted the huge horse's neck affectionately. "I know, Farroll. You're forgiven…you had no way of knowing. It's just I could get no rest or ease in the thing."

"Well, it *was* a gibbet, and they're notoriously lacking in comfort," replied Huw, with his wicked grin. "They're quite popular among the nobler members of Clan Grefyn when they wish to make a point. Once you've watched your loved one die a slow death dangling in a cage on the walls of the Grefyn Palace, you're never the same." His jocularity faded as he thought of Sinean's father, and he had to look away as a peculiar lump rose in his throat.

"I see you've had some experience of this," said Lackland, his blue eyes serious. "Tell me what happened, if you will. I find I'm woefully ignorant about this valley, though I thought I understood the customs well enough. I certainly studied them long and hard as a lad!"

"You speak our language well enough, but your accent definitely has the sound of a northern nobleman," replied Huw. "I'll work with you on it, and you can help me with the speech of the North, which

I'll need a better knowledge of once I'm safely out of this valley."

"I *am* a northern nobleman, so I suspect it's why I sound like one," laughed Lackland. They walked down the narrow, untraveled road as quickly as they could, letting Farroll have the occasional nosh. Huw told Lackland about Sinean's father and how his death had fired a desire in her to crush the entire Grefyn clan. "My lady loved her revolution more than me," Huw concluded, feeling the old familiar wave of self-pity he thought he'd gotten over. He stuck with his fiction of being a tinker's son and a scholar who was driven out of Ludwellyn and named no names. He did admit she let him go north alone, abandoning him for her cause. "It was a bitter time for me when I first left."

"Perhaps she loved you more than you know. A woman like that is bound to have enemies. I would say her friends could be as dangerous as any enemy," said the knight, looking at him with a sharpness which belied his usual genial vagueness. "She may have felt your life would be safe once you were away from her. Have you ever thought she is tied to an extremely dangerous crowd? That *you* might be a weakness she wouldn't want known? If her enemies were to discover this vulnerability, can you imagine how they might exploit it? Your life was in danger from the moment you first shared her pillow."

Huw was startled and at a loss. For a long time he thought about Lackland's words, and finally had to acknowledge the truth of what he'd said. "You're very likely right." His face was bleak as he added, "But it feels like a betrayal nonetheless."

Lackland clasped Huw's shoulder sympathetically, and they walked on in companionable silence.

Chapter 9 Lackland

Half a league north of Maldon, Huw and Lackland came to a meadow on the eastern banks of the River Limpwater. Groves of alders and hazelnut bushes grew there, along with plenty of grass and fodder for Farroll. The meadow gradually sloped down to the river that flowed in a shallow, lazy manner belying the floods of only two months before.

Much of the luggage the warhorse carried consisted of camping gear. They laid out a ground cloth in the shelter of an alder grove. Over that they set up a lean-to made from canvas. The knight laughed when Huw appeared shocked at the amount of gear he was unpacking. "I don't care to be uncomfortable." Lackland courteously offered to share his lean-to with Huw, as it was wide enough for two bedrolls to fit comfortably.

While Lackland set up camp, Huw built a fire ring and found plenty of dry branches and sticks for several days' worth. Soon he had a merry little blaze going, and the place looked rather homey.

"I'll see if I can catch our breakfast while you take care of your horse," said Huw. "I've become quite good at keeping myself fed, thanks to a friend who taught me how to fish." The fire burned cheerfully, which only served to accentuate their hunger. He'd already found his fishing line and hook, and was preparing to go down the bank to the river's edge. "I'll be quick, God willing. I'm famished!"

When Huw returned with his catch, the knight was brushing his horse's mane, once again talking to him. Bemused, Huw listened while he began cooking their breakfast.

"And if you'll just play nice for a week or two more, we'll be able to go back home. I miss our beautiful Mags too. Hopefully, she hasn't taken up with someone else in our absence. You know how she hates to sleep alone."

Farroll snorted derisively.

"Well, it could happen! I'm not the only one who gets lonely on the road. Even so, no one will ever take her place, you know that." Lackland carefully brushed a knot out of the horse's mane, while Farroll made a whickering that almost sounded like scolding. "I know…. It was my fault you ended up in gaol. You really didn't deserve such horrible treatment."

The horse shook his great head. Farroll looked at Lackland, and Huw swore the horse was speaking to the man who replied, "I'll do a better job on you once I'm bathed and my feet are a bit better."

Farroll made a chuffing noise, blowing his nose in disgust. Then the horse shook himself all over.

Lackland nodded and replied, "You're right, Farroll. This is a fool's errand, but there you are—I'm a fool. Now, I'm going to get myself cleaned up so I can eat. I stink so bad it puts me off my own appetite!"

Lackland divested himself of his reeking garments and eased out of his boots, telling Huw he could hardly stand the delay of searching for his personal kit. Wading out to a shallow sunny spot, he sat on a sand bar, bathing himself and washing his clothes and armor. Finally clean, he rejoined Huw by the fire, hanging his damp clothes out on shrubs to dry and laying his armor on the grass.

"I've never smelled so bad or been so uncomfortable in my life," he told Huw. "Hanging in that cage with only my own filth for company was nearly unendurable."

"I did notice they didn't give you the key to the privy," Huw commiserated with him. "I suspect the lack of cleanliness they forced upon you was part of the fun. Why don't you go rest for bit and keep Farroll company? This won't be too much longer, I promise."

Huw finished broiling the fish and called to Lackland who, now clad only in his spare underdrawers, was seated on the grass near his horse, nattering away. The knight immediately dug about in his saddlebags and produced a bottle of wine, a tin plate and cup, and a silver fork. "I confess I'm hungry enough to eat grass, which Farroll thinks I'm silly to pass up. He was wondering why I didn't try some of the sweet grasses we passed on our way to this fine resting place. I told him it makes me shit green, and I don't really enjoy that."

Huw laughed, both at the knight's comment and the realization Lackland really did believe he was conversing with his mount.

"I can't believe you have wine in those saddlebags," said Huw, rolling his eyes. "I wondered what you could possibly have in them besides your weaponry. That bow of yours is astounding. I've never seen one so large!"

"I learned the craft of archery as a boy," replied Lackland. "My tutor, while I was still at home, was a member of the Brotherhood of St. Aelfrid, Friar Benjamin. He taught me all the basic skills I have. Though it turned out I have no ability with majik, as one must have to be a member of that select group, he saw to it I was well trained in all the arts of weaponry."

"I've always wondered about the Brotherhood," replied Huw. "They're rarely seen here in the South, other than to test our lads for the ability and whisk the talented ones away. Having the talent is a terrible stigma here, so once a lad shows the aptitude, the family can't wait to send him away with the friars. He'll be abused and perhaps even murdered if they don't get him to safety as soon as they can." At Lackland's raised eyebrow, Huw elaborated. "Folks fear what they can't comprehend, and no one understands majik here. Lads with the ability to cast a lightning bolt or a ball of fire are considered too dangerous to have around. So in their wisdom, instead of waiting for the friars to show up and claim them, their neighbors or even their family will kill them with less thought than they would a cockroach."

"To have the gift is an honor where I come from," replied Lackland, visibly surprised. "This is another difference between the North and South —one that astounds me. We are much less concerned about things that would be called stigmas here. I hate to say it, but I think we're happier for it."

"I think you may be right," replied Huw, thinking of Davey, the man who'd helped him so much when he'd been so desperate. "This is a hard land for anyone with any sort of a stigma to survive in. Sadly, our leaders encourage ignorance, hoping to keep the commoner both illiterate and uninformed. My father often told me education encourages independent thinking and threatens the rule of those who would be our masters. Some of the nobility still deem it a crime to teach a laborer to read."

"I see why you find yourself on the run, Jak." Lackland's sharp blue eyes seemed to miss nothing. "You espouse dangerous beliefs that would be better suited in the North. There you'll find many who think the way you do."

Worried he'd given too much away, Huw nodded and tried to steer the conversation into safer territory by asking about his life as a mercenary. The knight was quite happy to talk about the Rowdies, a group of mercenaries who lived and worked out of a half-built northern wayside inn that was, as yet, unnamed. They sounded like a colorful group with equally colorful names, and Huw found himself quite intrigued by Lackland's descriptions of them.

"So, Billy Ninefingers is your captain," said Huw. "It sounds very rural, though. How does a place so far removed from everywhere find any business?"

"Rural? It's that and more. You southerners have no idea what rural really is—even your countryside is well-populated and the people are all well-to-do. But a town will grow around Billy's inn, I guarantee it," replied Lackland. "Billy attracts good people, and his place is at the ideal spot for a town, on both the trade road and the river. It's a day's ride to either Castleton or Somber Flats, so it's the perfect place to stop. Henri has given Billy a patent to build a town. Travelers stop over with him all the time even though Billy isn't really set up for it yet. They're happy enough to sleep on the floor in his old cabin or in whatever bunk is available. But his inn will be something else, very high-class. He's built a fine bathhouse with indoor plumbing and everything!"

"Now that's something I'd love to see," replied Huw, thinking of Ilene's bath chamber. "I've seen only one manor with plumbing here in the South, and it was a marvel. I'd consider it a luxury to be able to regularly avail myself of such!"

After they'd eaten, Huw bathed and washed his clothes in the river. Later, Lackland lay on the bedroll, stretching his limbs and massaging his feet. Even shivering in his underwear, the man was the epitome of the heroic knight, firing Huw's imagination. His golden hair, blue eyes and chiseled profile were the template from which all the engraved pictures in romance novels were created. He was sure no woman could help but look at the knight with desirous eyes.

Suddenly, Huw was struck with the conviction there must be a hundred stories surrounding Lackland. As he covertly observed the strange northern knight, he knew without a shadow of a doubt his future lay wherever Lackland was. In a moment of clarity, he realized he'd never lack ideas for the most amazing ballads and tales of heroism. Not only would he have an endless supply of inspiration at hand, he'd be safe in the North. As he watched Lackland, Huw's mind spun; he'd already begun to craft the tale of *How Jak, the Tinker's son, rescued the Hero*.

All he needed to do was find out where Lackland actually lived and get there. After that, he only needed to figure out a way to stay near the man. His moment of revelation was interrupted by Lackland's shivering speech.

"The river is much warmer here in the South, I've noticed. Bathing is not such a shock as it is back home!" The knight's lips were blue and his teeth chattered from the cold of the late spring morning, but he looked much better. "Of course, where I'm from, the Limpwater is just emerging out of the high mountains, so it's fast and cold. It sweeps you away before you've had a chance to get your breath. Only dead men swim in this river up north."

Laughing, Huw replied, "Most of the time here in the Eynier Valley, the river is lazy. One can frequently wade across it as you travel further south. I did several days ago. But when the snow in the mountains begins to melt and the March rains fall unceasingly, the low lands become dangerous and in some areas, a death trap. All the rivers from the mountains east and west flow into this languid stream, and when the thaw is on, it turns into an angry giant. Immense floods inundate the valley every spring, which is the reason our houses and barns are always on higher ground and frequently built on stilts. It's the yearly inundations that make this valley fertile, giving us the finest farmland on the continent." Huw warmed to his subject. "This is what the Lanques want, you know. They want the farmland they lack in their mountain country. They yearn to subjugate us again as they did before the time of Aelfrid and Merewyn, take our land from us and make us work it for them as little more than slaves." Huw paused, looked up and saw Lackland gazing at him with his sharp, knowing glance.

"You're quite knowledgeable for a tinker, Jak." Lackland's words took Huw by surprise, and he turned away, unable to meet his eyes. "But you did say you were a scholar. Perhaps when you get to the Bekenberg Pass, you'd continue north instead of turning east and making the crossing into Vyennes. Maybe you'd consider joining up with the Rowdies. Billy's always looking for able people. He'd definitely welcome you."

"I confess I'm not really sure what I'm going to do when I get to the Bekenberg Pass," Huw prevaricated a bit. "I'm thinking the life of a tutor is not really for me." He laughed a little at himself, trying to impress upon Lackland he really was only a student and a poor one at that. "I managed to get run out of my last job!"

They camped by the river for an extra day while Lackland regained his strength. During the time they spent together, Huw came up with a good plan for helping the knight achieve his goal. "You've told me you're King Henri's cousin. When you leave here, you should go to House Dwyn on the western side of the river." Huw saw Lackland's face and quickly said, "I know they're recognized as being of Clan Grefyn, but the Dowager Countess will welcome you. I'll give you a letter for her."

"What do you know of the old dame?" asked Lackland, his eyes wary. "I'm not too eager to walk into a trap again, as you may imagine."

"She's a very young dame. The Countess was unhappily married until recently," replied Huw. "She was good to me and helped me escape her late husband's Crows. She intends to turn House Dwyn to Clan Weyllyn. This move will definitely be a surprise to her brother, the heir to Grefyn!"

"You say she's a widow, yet this news hasn't been made public," Lackland looked at him with perceptive eyes. Huw flushed and looked away. "She is, perhaps, very fond of you? Why aren't you there?"

"The earl's death is very recent, only three nights ago in fact. She's fond of me, but doesn't love me enough to tie herself to me or I to her. Trust me, I can only go north now," replied Huw, trying to keep the loneliness at the thought from showing on his face. "I'd go back to Ludwellyn if I could safely remain in this valley. It's been my home since I was appren...since I was a lad of nine."

"That's sad, Jak. It's a ballad waiting to be sung," replied Lackland, seemingly oblivious to how close he was to the truth. "Speaking of ballads, I've always heard the bards in this valley were the finest in the world, but so far I've seen none who were any better than a minstrel from Castleton might be. Of course, they were fine, excellent really, but I was simply expecting more based on what I was told."

"Ah...I...never heard that. Naturally we moved from place to place all the time as tinkers do, so perhaps we never heard one. But music is the soul of Eyn, so, of course, they must be wonderful." Huw decided it was time to change the subject. "I've never seen a horse like yours. Where did you get such an amazing animal?"

"You're right, Farroll is a remarkable beast! He was a gift from my cousin and a princely gift he was too." Lackland warmed to one of his favorite subjects, and Huw's diversion was off and running. There followed a long discourse describing Farroll's lineage back to the founding of Wald. "I must say he's a bit of a pansy though," confessed the knight, turning and whispering so Farroll couldn't hear him. "He's a prissy old thing and hates the mud."

During the time they were camped by the river, Huw learned a great deal about the young knight he'd rescued. Yet, he didn't hear enough to completely quench his curiosity. Lackland revealed he'd ridden straight to Imrysdock on a mission for King Henri. After conferring with the young Duchess Madewyn, he'd left the great house unsure as to what he should do. He was originally sent south on a mission to find the heir to Weyllyn. If he had no desire to be found, Lackland was to discover the reason, if he could. But he was also charged to discover what the Grefyn was up to and stop it.

"I've been assured Dayved Weyllyn is missing because he's voluntarily abdicated his position. Madewyn loves her brother deeply and is devastated by his decision. She told me a situation arose that culminated in his quarreling violently with their grandfather. This ended with his abrupt departure, although Madewyn refused to tell me what the argument was about. Whatever it was, the old man suffered a breakdown as a result and is unfit to rule. Madewyn is now the regent and heir. No one else has both the capability to govern and the ability to control the old man." Lackland shrugged, saying, "Duchess Madewyn seems quite competent and is intent on rallying the houses that look to Weyllyn. She's proving to be a wily tactician!" Lackland's eyes twinkled as he spoke. "Some who answer to Grefyn will be surprised at how clever and strong a leader she'll prove to be. Despite the unreasonable disdain the men of this valley have for a woman's ability to lead, she's earned support from most of the Weyllyn nobles, who are relieved to have her good common sense in the leadership role. When her grandfather began his descent into senility, he apparently made some very strange decisions."

"Yes, he did. I don't know if she'll be able to recover from the damage his inaction has caused for House Weyllyn in their border towns," replied Huw. "The people are angry Grefyn has been allowed to hunt for so-called traitors in Weyllyn lands. Crows have been killing people at random and defiling the townsfolk's daughters. People are not only angry and frustrated, they're desperate to retaliate, but cannot match the Crows' steel."

"I know. But the duchess immediately made some strategic appointments that garnered her and King Henri much in the way of loyalty within her clan. This will come in handy, as she informed me the Grefyn and his Crows are now mounting a war against both her and the Weyllyn connection to the throne of Waldeyn." Lackland's face grew stern. "I really can't allow such a thing, you know." The knight spoke almost conversationally, but there was an undercurrent of steel in his commentary. "Lanqueshire looms large in this from what I can see. Tell me everything you know about the Grefyn and his palace in Ludwellyn. How are the rooms situated?" His penetrating gaze held Huw's.

Surprised, Huw complied. "Ah, I've only been there in a servant's capacity, so I don't know how the private quarters are laid out. I believe they're much like the other large palaces with private rooms on the second and third floors, and of course, the public rooms on the first floor."

"You know how these palaces are laid out then, so tell me. Does it follow the same general floor plan that House Weyllyn in Imrysdock does?" asked Lackland.

"Again, I only know the public rooms of House Weyllyn, but judging from the outside, yes. There must be some similarities because they were designed by the same architect, and both are considered to be national treasures," replied Huw. "However, I have an acquaintance that's spent many hours in the Grefyn Palace, as she's quite highly placed in the clan. I've mentioned her before, and I'll see you're introduced. She'll be able to help you with this."

"I see. Would this acquaintance be the Dowager Countess whose husband rather suddenly went to kneel at the Throne of Heaven?" Lackland chuckled at Huw's obvious discomfort. "A handsome, scholarly lad like you and the bored young bride of an old man.... It's a volatile combination in any strata of society!"

"I'm sure I don't know what you're referring to," Huw tried to keep his guilty dismay from showing on his face. "In any regard, I feel sure the lady in question will definitely assist you." He decided to make a jab of his own at the too-handsome knight's expense. "Your unusual blond hair, manly build and romantic demeanor might well appeal to her adventurous nature, quite nearly as well as they did to the duchess!"

"I'm sure I don't know what you mean," replied Lackland, grinning widely, "although Madewyn is a wonderfully warm and generous hostess."

"You're an amazing knight, Lackland," said Huw, still on the attack. "A man who claims to be a mere mercenary, welcomed into the home of the Duchess Madewyn Weyllyn. I find it quite interesting."

"And you're something more than you appear, Jak," said Lackland smiling widely. "You say you're a tutor and a tinker's son. You've an exceedingly sharp mind for either occupation. But I'll tell you about myself if you wish.

"I am the landless younger son of a minor baron. My mother is a first cousin of the king, and my father endlessly schemes to turn our kinship into an earldom. My older brother, Mortimer, would love such a thing also, but hell will freeze over and Old Grim will skate before Henri makes such a mistake." He laughed and said, "I spent my youth from the age of eleven at court, training in the knightly arts. Too late I learned I'd never be allowed to do what I was trained for, to lead men into battle and defend the country. Only as a youth, poised on the edge of manhood, did I understand my lack of land and standing would require me to forever bow to those noble men of lesser skill."

"Why? Why would they go to all the trouble of training you as a strategist and then not use you?" The minds of the upper nobility never ceased to amaze Huw with their singular lack of common sense.

"Oh, they used me all right," the knight said wryly. A flash of something dangerous and frightening passed briefly through Lackland's eyes as he spoke of his situation, startling Huw with both its suddenness and intensity. Fascinated, Huw realized that underneath the urbane surface the knight displayed was a seething mass of emotion, held in check only by extreme discipline. "They picked my brain and employed my ideas. They took credit for my work without so much as a 'thank you kindly, now bugger off.' But what really pissed me off was the way they would just slightly alter the plans so it would look original, which totally bollixed everything! Not being stupid, Henri saw what was happening. He was reduced to cornering me in my basement rooms and asking what I really thought. Once I explained it to him, he then had to *tell* them what they were going to do."

Huw must have looked as astonished by the revelation as he felt, because Lackland elaborated further about his situation. "The higher nobility are the ones who must lead, because it's their tenants who make up the armies." Huw nodded his comprehension, chagrinned by his own ignorance. "You know how it is—it's the same here. I have no land and, therefore, can bring no army to a skirmish. I only have my ability to plan and execute a battle, which I'm quite good at. My cousin knew how the wind blew though, and he arranged for me to leave court and join up with the Rowdies. This put me in a better position to serve him, and now I don't have to bow to the idiots who surround him."

Lackland was, much to Huw's amusement, unashamedly proud of having left many a hardened veteran a bloodied mess on the tourney field before the age of sixteen, the official age of adulthood. The knight admitted, somewhat sheepishly, to having felt an unprofessional sense of glee at trouncing those who'd snubbed him.

"How is it you're named Lackland?" Unconsciously falling into his old role as a bard collecting information, Huw took notes, unaware he looked like the scholar he was pretending to be. "I know of no noble house of such a name, north or south."

"You really *are* a scholar," Lackland said with some surprise. "I confess I doubted your tale, but a tinker would have no need to know the names of the noble families of Waldeyn. You're right. I was born Julian De Portiers, second and most useless son of Baron Hugo De Portiers, of House Portiers. A daughter was needed as a bartering chip to advance the family fortunes in the marriage game, not a second son. Our lands are near the northern village of Dervy." He went on to explain how the young nobles who felt threatened by his superior weapons abilities had dubbed him "Lackland" as a way of ensuring he understood his place.

"One day, when I was about fifteen, it occurred to me that being 'Lackland' really means I have naught to lose! Nothing is holding me back from accomplishing anything I choose." He grinned, and for a moment dropped his façade; Huw saw the true face of the man who lived behind the mask of eternal affability, a man who was both sharp and deadly. "It's amazing what having no encumbrances can do for you. It occurred to me these imbeciles were not only my intellectual inferiors, they were in desperate need of my knowledge and if they wanted it, they'd have to be quite conciliatory to get it, the arrogant buggers." He laughed, and it was a joyous sound. "Once I understood that, I *loved* the name Lackland! I embraced it and made it part of who I am!"

Huw laughed along with him, enjoying the whole notion. Having met the knight, Huw imagined Lackland's casual disregard of noble privilege had been unwelcome to his peers, like a flood, unrelenting and unstoppable. It occurred to him the Duchess Madewyn had, perhaps, adopted a similar stance. "You know, Lackland, I believe ineptitude in either sex should be discouraged in all our leaders, no matter how traditional it is!"

Once again the knight laughed, agreeing wholeheartedly with him. They passed the rest of their sojourn together laughing and discussing the ways of the world. Huw grew quite fond of Lackland during that time.

Several days passed companionably. The morning mists were rising on the river, as Lackland took his leave. The two men cleared all traces of their camp before they parted ways.

"By way of thanks for saving me and Farroll, I'd like to leave you with this," Lackland said, as he presented Huw with a full pot of majiked healing balm. "I still have plenty in this other pot, and you may need this before you get to where you're going."

Pleased with the expensive gift, Huw tucked it into his kit. "Now, remember, when you speak to anyone wearing black, you must tell them you are contracted to Dwyn, come to teach arms," Huw cautioned the knight. "Your hair is too fair and they'll know immediately you're from the North. Let them think you've come all the way from Lournes. Everyone knows the barbarian King of Lournes plots against Henri through his daughter, Henri's wife, Morganna. He frequently sends arms instructors to bolster Grefyn interests." Huw had traded cloaks with Lackland, so he'd look more like a lone Crow, now the man was passing into Grefyn lands.

Lackland's eyebrows rose. "I didn't know this."

Huw grinned at the knight's consternation. "You've the accent of our speech down well enough now to have had a long association with us, and you know most of the little odd things that make our tongue unique, but there's still a hint of the North in it. The Crows will allow you safe passage if you tell them

Prince Maldred has sent you. They consider Dwyn to be lacking in ability, so it'll ring true. They may know of his demise and they may not, so behave as if you don't know the man is dead. Show them the letter I've given you."

"I'm sure I'll be fine, Jak. You've coached me well," replied Lackland, his eternally sunny expression belying his serious task. "I'll take your instruction to heart. Who knew tinkers had need for such subtlety in politics? Henri could use a tinker in his court!" He grabbed Huw, hugging him exuberantly, before he mounted Farroll, who looked ready to get on the road. "I'm heartily glad I met you before I met Old Grim! You saved me and Farroll, and we couldn't be more grateful."

"Oh, I'm sure you'll be back doing the same for others as soon as you have the chance," replied Huw. He waved as the two rode away. "I'm going to miss him and his horse," said Huw as they disappeared, speaking to dispel the quiet of the woods and a sense of loss. "Stories are waiting to be told about those two, I just know it. We'll meet again if I have my way!"

Huw began to make his way to the main trade road, hoping he'd make it to Clythe with no more trouble. Humming as he walked along, he pictured himself telling the tale of how Lackland was rescued by a tinker. And he *would* tell it, once he was safely in the North and could travel as an entertainer.

Suddenly he stopped. A horrible thought occurred to him, and he spoke out loud. "What if the Grefyn has

154

spies in the North? Of course he has! Use your head, Huw! You know the crafty old man must have some way of knowing Henri's hands are tied in regard to Dayved Weyllyn's disappearance. I wonder.... Queen Morganna is known to be a sympathizer to the Lanque cause."

Huw's spirits slumped as he realized no place would be safe for him unless Lackland was successful. *If anyone can kill the Grefyn, it's sure to be Lackland. I've never met a man more likely to be a hero than he, but even if he's successful, there's always the chance someone will recognize Huw Owyn, son of Balen Owyn, the last guild master of the bards. The next Grefyn will never forgive me for either my father or my craft. And most nobles would prefer I remained dead; the lack of outcry from them tells me Dwyn did what they all secretly wanted to do. I'll be forever hunted.*

Shaking off his bleak thoughts, Huw continued walking toward the next town. *Once I make Clythe, I'll be only a week away from safety. From here, so close to Maldon, it's only a week's travel to Maury. If I can continue traveling on the King's Road from Maury, it's another week to Clythe. I haven't seen any Crows so far. Three weeks and Jak the Tinker will be safely on his way to Bekenberg. Once I make the pass, perhaps I'll try to find this person Lackland was talking about, Billy Ninefingers, and see if he's finished building his inn. He might need an entertainer, and Lackland will be there. He won't be the only hero loitering there, I feel sure of it.*

Chapter 10 Maury

Many days had passed since Huw parted company with Lackland. As he worked his way north, his mood gradually began to improve. Sometimes he found himself humming as he walked alone on a long stretch of the remote back roads. The old trade road had left the river, and for four days Huw hadn't been able to fish for his supper. Although he'd purchased bread and cheese at a farm, he was again in danger of going hungry. He passed inns and had coins, but his family was well-known in these parts. He'd spent much of his time as a journeyman playing in the tap rooms. He had to stay low and only travel after dark or risk being recognized. This was the most dangerous stretch of his journey; Huw Owyn was going home to say goodbye to his mother.

At last, Huw approached the village of Maury, the place of his birth. His plan was to visit his mother and tell her the truth—that her husband had been murdered, but her son still lived. It was likely his mother, Karolyn, would know she'd been widowed, because news traveled in the Long Valley, and rumors of the fire were on the lips of people in some of the most remote places. She probably knew the moment Balen died since she was "witchy" and possessed second sight. Despite the fact they were separated far more than they were ever together, Balen had loved Karolyn dearly and she him.

In the back of his mind, Huw feared something had happened to his mother, but he pushed his anxiety aside, hoping against hope she'd remained well. *Perhaps my origins aren't well-known. I was apprenticed to Balen when I was only nine; maybe the Crows have forgotten my father had a wife.* His stomach knotted up. *Bards are thought to have no attachments, and Balen was as free with his affections as any other. A bard's best chance to get information is sharing a pillow with a highly-placed, terribly bored spouse. Possibly Mum is safe after all.*

His mind began to imagine all sorts of scenarios, wondering if his mother had paid the price for loving Balen Owyn. Maury was a weavers' town. It was once a source of pride for one of their own to be a bard of great fame and influence.

Oddly, as a young child, Huw had not really thought of Balen as his father. Balen's frequent long absences during his childhood made him seem more like a favorite guest when he was home.

The day Balen had taken Huw back to Ludwellyn with him, he'd felt in some ways as if he were leaving with a stranger, but being apprenticed to his father was the best experience of his life. If Huw knew his mother as well as he thought, she'd missed her son only briefly, because he was at the age he'd have been apprenticed somewhere anyway. He was blessed with his father's gift for both music and mischief, and had the perfect pitch and eidetic memory, so where better than the Bards' Guild?

Karolyn Owyn had been the perfect bard's wife, as she was quite happy to be on her own and was secure in the knowledge of her place in Balen's heart. Balen was not a faithful spouse; no bard could be. Nevertheless, despite his many "close friendships," he never loved anyone the way he loved his Karo. Balen returned home for a month or so two or three times a year, which was sufficient for her. She was always overjoyed to see him, but was glad when he left.

Karolyn was an artist and needed solitude to imagine and craft the wondrous creations with needle and thread highly coveted by the nobility. Every design was different from the previous one. Each was drawn from her mind's eye view of the world around her and made in five pieces. A completed set would have two cuffs, two yokes (front and back), and a collar. Each collection would be pinned together and sold as one. The women of the aristocracy were eager for clothing made with pieces of Karolyn's handiwork set into it, and she made a comfortable living from her art.

Her embroidered tapestries of wildlife set in pastoral landscapes graced the walls of some of the highest noble houses throughout the country of Waldeyn, even in the North. She produced four a year, and each one was as detailed as the finest painting.

When she'd piled up enough sets, she would take them into Maury and sell them to the cloth-factor, who would in turn peddle them to the dressmakers and tailors for use in their designs. The cloth-factor in Maury catered to her, doing anything he could to keep her happy and busy creating things for him to sell to the traveling wool and cloth merchants.

Huw waited at the edge of the hamlet on the southern side of the River Maab, hoping to be able to cross over in the dark. Unfortunately, this high in the foothills of the mountains surrounding the valley, the river was running swift and deep, and his chances of dying in the wild waters were unlimited. The footbridge had no rail and was dangerous to cross even in daylight. It consisted of a single, fairly wide split log. The split side faced up, forming a flat enough path, but the perpetual mist from the tumbling river encouraged the growth of algae, making a deadly, slick path.

Huw hadn't crossed the log bridge since he was a boy of twelve; no one in his right mind did. When he crossed it with his father, Huw had been terribly afraid he'd fall in and be swept away. He'd felt the terror even though he was securely tied to the rope Balen had pulled across the bridge and then tied to a tree. Huw had never used that bridge again, because on subsequent trips home, they'd come from the North on the forest trail that led directly to Karolyn's cabin.

They never journeyed openly on the trade road, though they could have used the King's Bridge to cross the river. It had wide stone railings to prevent carts, horses and people from accidentally falling into the torrent and was wide enough for a horse-drawn carriage. Balen had always taken the less-traveled paths through the woods to and from home, which only he and a few others really knew about. *"We don't want folks to know our business, boy. We won't need anything from town, and they don't need to know we were here, right?"* Balen didn't want anyone to remember his connection to Maury, and now Huw knew why. *How could I have never understood what he tried so hard to tell me?*

The King's Bridge was the safest to cross, but Huw didn't dare use it even in the dark with most folks asleep, because it was on the main thoroughfare through the village. The fact he still lived would be all over town before he stepped off the bridge. He didn't trust the gossips to keep such news quiet. His best course was to continue staying out of sight.

Toward midnight, he took a chance and crossed the narrow log bridge by the light of the moon. Praying to God he wouldn't lose his footing and slip into the maelstrom, Huw carefully made his way across.

He'd just reached the center of the span when his foot slipped. He found himself falling hard, seriously scraping his legs up to his inner thighs and just barely managing to stay on. He nearly lost his kit, but by some miracle saved it. Somehow he avoided injuring his private parts, but groaned with both the pain of his legs and the realization he still had half the bridge to cross. Resolutely he crawled on his hands and knees, carefully feeling his way and pausing between each inch forward.

Finally, he reached the hard-packed soil of the bank on the other side. Leaning against the old oak that stood there, he recovered his nerves. His knees were weak and his bowels were loose from the terror of making the crossing, but he managed to keep from soiling himself. Now he had to work his way through the village to the hidden path that led to his mother's cottage. He pulled his cloak around him, making himself into a shadow, and slowly slipped past the dark structures that housed the great looms powered by huge waterwheels.

No lights shone in any buildings except for the Weaver's Rest, the inn that also served as the tap room for Maury. The lantern over the porch was flickering, as if reaching the end of its supply of oil. This encouraged him, because if they weren't tending the lamp, it meant no guests from out of town were staying there. The stable behind the Weaver's Rest was dark. Looking into the tiny window, he saw no horses stabled. *It appears the Crows have overlooked Maury,* he thought, feeling a surge of hope. *It's been over two months since the trouble.* Still, he didn't let his guard down.

Huw slipped down the alley behind the cottages of Weavers' Lane, hiding in the shadows of the privies and ash heaps dotting the landscape. Finally he reached the far side of town.

The seldom-traveled path to his mother's house began in a copse of hemlock trees growing along the cliff above the river behind the wool-barn. The entrance to the path was well concealed, but even in the dark Huw found it easily. After a half hour's walk through the gloomy woods, he arrived at the clearing behind his childhood home.

Karolyn had fallen for Balen Owyn as a young girl and married him at fifteen. She had borne Huw at the age of seventeen, and he was the only child she'd conceived. Karolyn was a good mother, and Huw was very close to her. *Mum is only thirty-five, but she'll never remarry. She loved Balen that much.* In his mind he pictured her curling black hair with only a little silver as he'd last seen her at Yule. Her deep blue eyes were sharp and her conversation as witty as ever. Huw thought her the most beautiful woman in the world.

Even in the dark, he knew something was wrong, as the bushes by the privy seemed overgrown. Karolyn was always careful to keep the shrubbery trimmed. She'd kept the cabin neat, and the gardens were never allowed to get out of hand.

With a sinking feeling, he came to the back door, noticing no smoke coming from the chimney. The growing sense of dread threatened to overwhelm him when he found her door ajar. It looked as if it had been left open for weeks. Leaves had blown into the pump-room and from there into the kitchen. *No...she would never allow such a mess.... No...God, please, no....*

Huw's mind knew the bitter truth, long before he found her on the floor in the tidy sitting room, her long-dead body unrecognizable except for the clothing. The breeze that blew the leaves through the cottage would have carried away the stench, but she'd been there long enough there was no longer a smell.

His mother had been dead at least several weeks. It looked as if she was murdered within days of Balen's death. Her body was left where they killed her, an obvious message meant for either him or Balen to find should they have escaped the massacre. There was no blood, no way to tell how they'd killed her. It was impossible to tell if they'd violated her first, but he chose to think not.

Huw wasn't surprised no one had moved her to a grave. She was known to be a hermit and often went months without going into town. It was very likely no one in Maury even knew she was dead.

Burying his mother was the hardest thing Huw had ever done. When the rising sun finally burned off the mist, Huw was just finishing his task, setting a stone at the head of her grave. With a hammer and chisel he etched her name, his father's name and the date into the stone. It was all he could do for his father to see he wouldn't be forgotten. Huw reflected upon the wry justice that their bodies rested so many miles apart and yet their spirits were together, just as they'd always been in life.

He spent the rest of that day and all of the next cleaning her home just the way she would want it. He washed all of his clothes, putting on his father's garments and wishing he could wear them when he left. But the rich embroideries proclaimed them to be a bard's, so he would burn them along with his mother's things.

While his own clothes dried, he looked through all of his mother's possessions. Tears rolled down his face as he came across a letter she'd begun writing to him, perhaps the day she was murdered. It was full of the little day-to-day things that told of her life. He tucked it inside his shirt, next to his heart. The small pile of embroidered cloths near her chair told him she'd only recently taken her work to town to sell to the factor, and many months would pass before anyone missed her.

Her kitchen was untouched. Except for the light coating of dust and the leaves on the floor, it was as immaculate as she'd always kept it. The flour had not yet set weevils, so Huw made as large a batch of hard biscuits as he could carry, using the dark brown ale still sealed in its jugs in the pump-room to leaven the dough. He was only able to take one jar each of her carefully preserved jam and pickles along with the biscuits, knowing it would be a long time before he'd be able to find a meal he didn't catch for himself. Having to avoid the inns in the area would make his journey harder. Her chickens had turned wild as had her goat, and neither would come near him. Still, he was able to find a few eggs.

While his biscuits were rising, he burned all his mother's treasures he wouldn't be able to carry. He kept her locket with Balen's picture on one side of it and hers on the other, clasping the chain around his neck and slipping it under his shirt. From the mantel, he took the small picture Balen long ago had framed in silver, drawn of the three of them when Huw was a small child.

He found his mother's savings, safely hidden under a floorboard. Using her needles and thread, he fashioned another money-belt, securing his small inheritance around his waist. *We were never poor, but I had no idea we were so rich,* he thought as he counted up the golds and silvers that had lain beneath their humble cottage when the murderers had come.

Mum, you'll never know how much I'll miss you, he thought as he finished packing his kit and closed up the house. *I'm truly alone now. My parents are dead; Sinean has set me free. Everyone I ever loved is gone. At least I had you for a while, mum.*

With one backwards glance, Huw surveyed everything he was leaving behind, committing it to memory. Tears welled, and rolled down his cheeks as he resolutely closed the door and stopped by the grave. Brushing a stray leaf from the headstone, Huw said his final goodbye.

Walking north through the woods on the faint trail that would join up with the King's Road, Huw composed a tragic ballad to tell the story of his parents' love and their lives, fighting his tears as he did so. Balen's small harp that had hung on the wall for all of Huw's childhood was now slung over his shoulder, hidden in his mother's cloth-bag. It was the first harp his father had ever made, and was a very fine instrument for an apprentice piece. Huw wrapped it with the last tapestry his mother had finished and padded it with the pieces of her work he'd found by her chair. If he remained unmolested, at least he'd have a part of his parents with him.

All that remained of his life to this point, Huw now carried with him. His kit was full and heavy, but he was loath to lose any more of his possessions. Whether he'd still have any of it when he arrived at the town of Bekenberg was another matter entirely.

Chapter 11 Clythe

Eight days after burying his mother, Huw walked into the village of Clythe, which stood at the bottleneck of the Eynier entrance to the high Bekenberg Pass. Three countries had once met there, but with the marriage of Wald and Eyn, the only other country to touch it was Lanqueshire. The two countries met high in the mountains to the west, where Huw would not be going if he had any say.

Half a day's ride north of Clythe was a steep climb out of the long Eyn Valley into the high country of old Wald, one that would take at least seven full days to make though it was only forty leagues. Three distinct sets of gigantic waterfalls, culminating in the colossal, soaring Eyn Falls, were the real delineation between the old countries of Wald and the Eynier Valley. For the most part, the trail wound along the River Limpwater, but at the base of the falls, the road began the climb into the mountain passes and the high country beyond.

Once past the falls, he'd be safer from marauding Crows in what was definitely Henri's country, where the king was able to run things more to his liking. Huw had heard many tales and rumors of the uncivilized North and knew many strange beasts still roamed wild in the vast expanse of wilderness. Great distances lay between villages, and he was quite worried about his safety once he climbed out of the Long Valley.

Lackland had told him to invest in a horse, although Huw had only a vague idea of how to care for one and what it would take to feed such a large creature. "You need to be on a horse to be bigger than a beast can comfortably eat," he'd told Huw.

"What do you mean by 'eat'? It's just a folk tale, right?" Huw's incredulous face had made Lackland laugh.

"Jak, the wilds up there really *are* wild. All the beasts you ever read about live up there. Firedrakes, dragons, all those creatures and more live in the high country, and they sometimes come down to the trade road looking for easy meat. A man on foot is easy meat."

Huw passed through the familiar cobbled streets of Clythe, walking toward the northern gate, to the dark forest and the Green Man. Clythe was known as the gateway to the Eynier Valley, but the Green Man was really the place where Eyn and Wald joined. The rest of the valley considered Clythe to be the edge of the wild frontier and in many ways it was, but the average resident was as much an Eynier as any person in any village in the valley. When merchants came to the South, the Green Man, located several furlongs outside the northern walls of Clythe, was where they stopped, rarely continuing on into the town.

The villagers preferred they stay away, being suspicious of foreigners, meaning anyone who was not of Clythe. Merchants met and did business there, guarded by mail-clad northern mercenaries, but the locals didn't mingle with them, staying away when strange horses were stabled at the Green Man. While the locals would sometimes stop in for a mug of ale and join in a round of music the way country folk did, they didn't really approve of the northern mercenaries.

The Green Man was owned by the man known by all simply as "the Bear" Tavysh. He was Sinean's uncle and had been the Bear for so long that only he remembered his given name. What Huw's reception would be when he arrived there was uncertain at this point. When Sinean and her crew left Clythe, Huw had been in her company. The Bear wasn't worried about the proprieties of things, but he'd wanted Sinean to forget her romantic notions of leading a revolt against Grefyn. He feared she'd end the same way her father had, dying in a gibbet. The Bear couldn't stand the thought of that. His anger with Huw was not for his relationship with her, for she'd refused Huw's desperate pleas to marry him, turning him down in front of her uncle. The Bear's anger was for Huw's tacit encouragement of her mad schemes instead of talking sense to her.

The Bear had been captain on the "Sea Witch," a ship owned by one of the great Weyllyn families. When his brother died a slow death imprisoned in a gibbet-cage on the walls of Anvel Grefyn's Ludwellyn palace, the Bear had taken Sinean, raising her as his own. When his mother fell ill, he'd returned to the village of his childhood, taking over the old inn and raising Sinean there. His worst nightmares always had Sinean ending the way his brother had, dying a miserable death of thirst, starvation and despair in an iron cage. "No revolution is worth that," he'd told her many times, but she was set on vengeance, as if one angry girl could accomplish what Clan Weyllyn had never been able to do.

Huw wasn't looking forward to admitting Sinean hadn't returned with him. The Bear warned him she'd never marry him, no matter what she said during pillow-talk, but Huw wouldn't listen. He loved her and knew her peculiarities, accepting them as the price of living with her. Besides, he was convinced he could talk her around. After all, if a bard couldn't convince her to give up her vengeance, no one could.

Still, the Bear had tried. "You're the kind who marries forever, boy. She's not made that way. She loves you, but she won't be there when you need her." How he was going to face the man, Huw didn't know, but he had to do it. He needed help for the next part of his journey. The Bear would know who needed a guard on their next trip to Bekenberg, and how to outfit him for the journey.

When he passed through the village, it seemed to have a subdued quality. There were no fine horses in the stable, nothing to indicate the Crows were roosting in Clythe, but he could sense they'd been there.

Huw stood in front of the broad steps of the Green Man. Walking up the steps and through the door he made the decision to sit in a corner of the tap room, just as he had in the few inns he'd visited since leaving Maury. Opening a book, with his back to the door, he hoped he looked like a scholar to any Crows who might decide to stop over.

His eyes burned with unshed tears when a woman who closely resembled his mother approached him.

"Stew, thank you," he replied, trying to maintain his composure. *Mora...She's mum's cousin....Thank God she doesn't recognize me. I wonder what she's doing so far north....*

He was just finishing his meal when an immense shadow loomed. It seemed the Bear had decided to sit with him. "You remind me of someone I recently heard was dead," rumbled the Bear. "But he had a beard like a real man and a strapping girl, last I saw him."

"He *is* dead," replied Huw, looking up and meeting his eye, keeping his voice low. "He's gone forever. The girl was well when he last saw her. She was planning yet another revolution even as he was smuggled out of town in the dark. My name is Jak, and I'm on my way to Bekenberg. Do you know of a caravan who might need an extra sword?"

"I knew it was you. Sure, you're dressed like a common traveler, but you still carry yourself like you always did. Your face looks completely different without the beard, but your voice is unmistakable. I can see you've skipped a few meals and seen some hard times, though." He sighed. "Come up and sit in my rooms and tell me what's happening. Mora will keep things afloat down here."

Huw followed him up the stairs. The Bear led him down the hall to his private rooms, saying, "I got lonely after you two left for the South. Married me a good woman. Mora's a widow, never had any children, so we keep each other company."

"You'll be surprised to know we're family now," replied Huw, with a wry grin. "Mora is my mum's cousin. I haven't seen her for many years, but she's still the same, still looks like Mum...did." His voice caught and he stopped speaking.

Surprised at the relationship, the Bear just shook his head in commiseration, guessing what Huw had to say about his mum. "It's a small world sometimes. Here we are," he said, opening the door.

Once inside his sitting room, the Bear gestured to him to sit down on the old settee. Huw did so, feeling completely disoriented at being back in the rooms he'd visited so often when he was a journeyman and posted in Clythe. No sign remained of Sinean; her angry presence was long gone. In its place, a cheerful hominess had taken root. Mora's touch was everywhere, as was only right.

The Bear gazed at him, a long searching scrutiny. Huw had nothing to say, so let him look his fill. Finally the older man said, "Well, I told you it'd end in tears. But I didn't bargain on Balen being the one to pay the price." Huw's eyes burned again. The Bear continued, saying, "What really happened down there? We know there was murder done, but we've not heard why. We haven't seen a bard since you went back south with that scapegrace niece of mine. Of course, we didn't really expect to this far north of the great houses. But even the tinkers and traveling people have little to say."

"You'll never see a bard again. You've obviously heard my father is dead. Well, they hung Loris next to him, and then they burned the guild hall with everyone inside, so Waite told me. The spring conclave became the funeral pyre for the guild this year." The Bear shook his shaggy head in disbelief. "Sinean and I were late going to the hall. Disguised as a maid, she'd finally infiltrated the Grefyn's shipping office on the docks. She had to work until mid-afternoon, and I didn't want to go without her. I had no apprentice of my own to award a pin to anyway, so I'd agreed to wait tables at the dinner that evening as my reward to the new journeymen. We were just about to leave for the evening festivities and dancing when the riots broke out. The Crows came through, searching for traitors. We hid in our room and Sinean found a disguise that worked well enough that the Crows didn't recognize me. Afterward, Waite got me out of town, stuffed into a reeking ale barrel, and I've been on the run ever since."

"What happened? Why are the Crows molesting street entertainers? No one dares to hum a tune for fear he'll be hauled away. And why hasn't Weyllyn put a stop to it? Grefyn's Lanque Crows are swaggering around like they rule the valley." The Bear's expression said he wanted the full answer, so Huw told him the entire truth, which he'd never told anyone until that moment.

"It all goes back to the telling of a tale that skated too close to reality. Balen died for the truth, as did the rest of the craft. He told *The Tale of the Grefyn's Bones* to King Henri's new governor, Lord St. John, one evening during a Yuletide party at House Corlyn. Balen used the opportunity of the Corlyn Yule festivities to alert the governor to the way history is repeating itself with Clan Grefyn selling itself to Lanqueshire. He must have known there'd be reprisals of some sort, but he did it anyway. It tells of the sale of the Eynier Valley to Lanqueshire five hundred years ago, which began our occupation and slavery. It's one of the tales forbidden in Grefyn houses, and Duke Corlyn was horrified Balen had done such a thing in his home. His anger nearly cost Balen his life that night, but with all the witnesses, Balen escaped punishment. His public dressing-down was the first consequence from his telling the story in that particular house. The second bad result of the tale was to come later.

"The point was taken, and St. John put a stop to Anvel Grefyn's booming trade by insisting all commerce with Lanqueshire be registered through the Crown's port authority and taxes be paid on it. The governor delivered Henri's edict when normal court business resumed in January," replied Huw.

"Balen must have known Clan Grefyn was planning something. His informant told him there were to be attacks on individual bards, just as Grefyn is doing now to casual entertainers. Still, Balen had no idea a minor player like Dwyn was planning an assault on the guild hall, acting alone in an effort to have himself declared heir to Grefyn. Dwyn waited to spring his trap, knowing there would soon be a suitable moment to be rid of us all at one stroke. He had his opportunity at the end of March, when St. John returned to the North to attend Parliament.

"In a twist of fate, two more things happened that opened the way for Dwyn's master plan. The first was the disappearance of Dayved, the heir to Weyllyn. That paralyzed Clan Weyllyn. And then, not long after the governor left, the annual spring conclave of the Bards' Guild was held.

"St. John departed Ludwellyn, leaving his secretary, William De Neuve, one of the younger earls from the North, in charge. De Neuve is not a bright man, so when the disaster struck he'd no idea it was deliberate. He has no inkling there's trouble in the valley to this day! The bards were all there in the guild hall, honoring the hard work and dedication of our apprentices and journeymen, and Rann Dwyn seized the opportunity to put himself forward as a potential heir of Anvel Grefyn.

"Dwyn and his Crows set fire to the hall. He knew there'd be no retribution, because Clan Weyllyn was in turmoil over their internal matter. The Grefyn had plans in the works to be rid of us in a much less spectacular fashion, but took what he was handed. Dwyn hanged my father and Loris in the street like common criminals and burned the hall, knowing full well any building in that part of town to catch fire would likely burn out of control and take several more with it, which would make it appear accidental. Someone else took the opportunity to murder my mother as a warning to me, should I have escaped the fire.

"But Dwyn was clumsy. When the guild hall burned, the fire spread to all the buildings on the street and from there to the rest of the Artists' Quarter. Half the town burned, and in the chaos and terror, the fault of the fire was declared a terrible accident. In the wake of so much devastation and death, what were two murders down on the docks?

"Clan Grefyn was able to slaughter the guild and countless innocents simply because Dayved disappeared and Clan Weyllyn was in chaos." Huw fell silent. The Bear waited until he was able to go on. "The Weyllyn had a quarrel with his heir. I have it on good authority the man vanished on purpose, although I'm not privy to why it may be. The old man went into decline, but his granddaughter, Madewyn, has taken the reins, and she's now leading Weyllyn as regent. She's reputed to be quite capable, perhaps more so than her brother, but was unable to get the necessary support from the lesser nobles of Weyllyn until her grandfather had completely lost control. Only when they had no choice but to allow a female to lead did they grudgingly give her their fealty. Now she's taking her border towns back and forcing her clan to follow her."

"I see. How do you know all of this about Weyllyn's heir?" The Bear's dark eyes peered sharply at Huw. "What else have you been up to since you left Ludwellyn?

"I made a wrong turn and found one of King Henri's knights hanging about in Maldon, so to speak," replied Huw, grinning. "We traveled together for a day or so."

"Lackland," said the Bear, nodding his understanding. "It could only be Lackland you met in an ill-favored place like Maldon."

"The very knight! It figures you'd know him. But he, unknowing of the curse, had wandered in during daylight, which I was careful not to do," replied Huw, trying to put a positive spin on his own stumbling into the haunted town. "Once I released him from the cage and rescued his horse, we camped for a few days while they got healthy again. Then he went on to Ludwellyn. He had a new task in mind, since he'd been given a letter stating Dayved Weyllyn voluntarily abdicated his position as heir. So, tell me how you know Lackland? He's a babe in the woods, but I sent him to a friend, one who'll help him in his new task. He was planning, in his words, to 'cut the head off a snake' for Henri." Huw sat back, fully prepared to listen to any tale that involved the wandering knight. "I pray to God he succeeds."

"We all pray for that, though I doubt it'd change anything. There isn't one noble house in Clan Grefyn that wouldn't simply continue the habit of courting Lanqueshire in their effort to overthrow Waldeyn. The kings of Lanqueshire know Grefyn's weakness is gold, and while the Lanques lack everything else, they have gold aplenty. They're always willing and able to buy the allegiance of Clan Grefyn." Huw nodded his understanding, and the Bear continued. "But, as to how I know Lackland, he's a cousin to King Henri. As such, he's been sent to the Green Man several times on business to meet with members of Clan Weyllyn. This is the first time he's ever gone south from here. He wouldn't be diverted, despite my best efforts, and I *did* try to change his mind."

"No, I'm sure he wouldn't," agreed Huw. "Did you tell him he stuck out like a sore thumb? He was impossible for me to hide, with the sun glinting off all that shining armor of his."

"Hah! He wouldn't dream of going about unarmored. He told me so. Besides, he said he felt naked without it. I tried to explain only thugs and the masters-of-thugs wear armor south of here, but he wouldn't listen." The Bear shrugged.

"I gave him a letter of introduction to the Dowager Countess Dwyn, who's turned to Weyllyn since her husband's death."

The Bear raised an eyebrow. "You *have* been busy, lad," he murmured. "Fancy that. The very man who destroyed everything you ever loved dies suddenly in the prime of his life, and you just happen to be close friends with his wife."

Huw ignored the comment, sensing Bear's suspicions and not wanting to confirm them. Still talking about Lackland, Huw said, "I impressed on him if he *must* go about looking like a lone Crow, he should pose as an arms instructor being sent to Dwyn from Lournes." Huw wondered how the meeting had gone and if he'd ever find out. A twinge of jealousy, just a small one, assailed Huw at the thought of golden-haired Lackland, his fine horse and all his shining armor meeting with the passionate Countess Ilene, but he quickly buried it.

Grinning at Huw's rather visible moment of jealousy, the Bear said, "The man is completely mad! Not two weeks ago, he took on a band of Crows who were beating young Jemmy, the smith's son. The boy made the mistake of sitting out on his stoop in the evening playing a flute. On seeing such a travesty, Lackland-the-madman took all of them on singlehandedly. He kept warning them off, saying he didn't like to fight unskilled men, and each time he killed one, he apologized to the others and suggested politely they should flee. Rather quickly they were all dead, and he stood over them, cleaning his sword and praying for their souls!" The Bear rolled his eyes.

"Sadly, despite Lackland's intervention, the poor boy later died. They're naught but beasts, Clan Grefyn. They'll have to murder every man, woman and child in the Eynier Valley if they're going to kill anyone who hums a song or plays a pipe!"

"For some reason, the Crows are all tone deaf and can't tell the difference between a bard and a fishmonger shouting his wares in the street," Huw agreed. "A great many stories linger untold around Lackland, and I'd like to be the man to tell them," said Huw with a faint smile. "If I make it to the North alive, that is." His smile faded as he said, "Anyway, you were right about Sinean and I was wrong. I'll send you a message telling you where Jak the Tinker has found lodging once he arrives in the North. If she should wish to find me, she'll know where I am." His heart knew she'd never ask the Bear about him.

"You're young. You've seen hard times, and you've lost everything." The Bear patted his shoulder, feeling a clumsy desire to comfort him. "You think your life is over."

Overcome by a wave of self-pity, Huw nodded, unable to trust himself to speak.

"Well, I'm here to tell you it's not over until you're kneeling before God's throne! You'll get past this and though it'll leave its mark, you'll be stronger for it."

Again, Huw nodded, feeling obscurely better for having the Bear to lean on, if only temporarily.

"What're you going to do? Do you intend to just walk away from the craft your family began and nurtured, or are you going to resurrect it from the ashes? Nothing's stopping you from making your way as a bard once you get past Bekenberg. You're a master, Huw." The Bear's hands on his shoulders forced Huw to look him in the eye. "You earned the pin younger than most, but you earned it proper, and it says you've the right to take apprentices. Go north and rebuild the craft one apprentice at a time, but do it! You owe it to your father."

Huw sat there silently. Finally he said, "One thing *must* be done first before I can even consider it. I must get to the North, alive. I'm a danger to you while I'm here, even if Lackland succeeded in beheading the snake before he left the valley, because Grefyn will never let me live, should I be discovered."

Huw continued, "You say he was through here two weeks ago. If Lackland accomplished his task they must temporarily be in confusion, but it won't last long unless the king gets a stronger presence down here. Grefyn won't go down easily, especially if Duke Amstyce Lyndys is the new successor. He's as much a danger to me as anyone, even if his hand didn't hold the torch that sparked the fire in Ludwellyn. He and his men have been committing murder up and down the valley in the Grefyn's name, executing folks who had nothing to do with the Bards' Guild and likely never even heard of it. He does this in cold blood because of the troublesome matter of truth. Lyndys considers bards to be traitors to the Crown of Eyn, a crown that hasn't existed for two hundred years.

"This means he's my enemy," said Huw. "Somehow, someday, I'll tell the world what he was a part of, and I *will* name names. I owe it to my father."

"You do owe him that," agreed the Bear. "So…I have a letter here for a lad named 'Jak the Tinker' with the seal of House Dwyn on it. Oddly enough, it's sealed with the blue wax of Weyllyn. You wouldn't know anything about that, would you?"

"I am he," grinned Huw, suddenly eager to read his letter. "It's from the Dowager Countess. I did her a favor." He laughed at the knowing look on the Bear's face. "She was good to me and helped me when few others would."

The Bear rummaged around until he found the letter and then went down to see how Mora was doing in the tap room so Huw could read it in privacy.

Breaking the seal, Huw read the neat handwriting.

Dear Jak,

I hope this finds you well and making progress on your journey. Many things have happened since we last spoke. I've acquired a new page, a lad whose situation was terrible until he was rescued by a tinker. He has healed well, though he is, at times, melancholy for his parents. Nattie has taken him to her heart and he is thriving. I am seeing to it he learns his letters and numbers, as Jessup has decided to train him to take over as butler when he retires. Ned is an apt pupil.

There is news on the home front. It appears my husband left me with child on his last visit home, just days before his untimely death. This is wonderful news, because it ensures I'll not be required to marry whatever cretin my uncle has selected for me. Instead, I will manage all the holdings of House Dwyn for the babe, and when the child is grown, he or she will inherit. This lack of compliance on my part offends the males in my family. Because of my unladylike demeanor, my brother and uncle have washed their hands of me, which is no great loss.

I've turned House Dwyn to Weyllyn, as I told you I would. A dear friend sent a charming young knight, Sir Julian Lackland, who was able to help me with removing Crows nesting in my lands. He was of great assistance in finding among my own armsmen those loyal to me and the babe, men who are willing to stand with me and Clan Weyllyn against the pirates of Lanqueshire and the people who would court them.

I've had to take a firm stance in my financial dealings, but now everyone knows they must do my bidding in matters of commerce. I was raised in House Lyndys—I understand business better than most men! What was quite surprising to me, our people greeted my arrival in the shipping office with something akin to joy—my late husband had neglected our interests shockingly. We have begun to turn a profit and have no trouble meeting our obligation to the Crown exchequer. Next year I will look for a small but respectable villa of my own in Ludwellyn so I can continue to keep a firm hand on business. The heir of Dwyn will have something to inherit besides a crumbling manor and four sinking ships! I have hired new captains, and they are good men, Dragons of House Weyllyn every one of them.

I've become quite good friends with Madewyn, the Regent of Weyllyn. I am frequently invited to guest at the Weyllyn's villa in Ludwellyn; she insists I remain with her until the babe is born. It is easier to manage my shipping and other interests of House Dwyn there anyway. She and I often reminisce about a handsome young bard whom we both loved, but shall never see again, as he surely perished in the great fire.

Amstyce was required to release my inheritance to me, much to his disgust. I'm using this time of guesting with Madewyn to have House Dwyn redecorated and the gardens restored, removing all traces of my late husband's presence. When the child is born, it will be a house of light, love and laughter.

There was more and after he finished reading, Huw sat staring at the fire contemplating her letter. That Ilene carried his child was certain. That he could never be a part of the child's life was clear, and he understood it well. *Such a strange life I lead. If it weren't for all my losses, I'd have nothing—my grief is all I have left.* For a moment he was overcome with the pain of knowing he'd fathered a child he'd never be able to acknowledge. Then the irony of the situation set him laughing. *Oh God! The child of my body will inherit the lands and fortune of the man who murdered my father! Now that's justice if ever I heard it!*

Chapter 12 Jaky-lad

The Bear's new wife, Mora, took to Huw, adopting him and telling her husband "He's as good as a nephew, and besides, his mum was my cousin." With a laugh she turned to Huw and said, "I remember you as a wee lad in Maury. I left when you were about six years old. You were full of the dickens then, and I bet you're still a naughty boy." The resemblance to his mother in her merry smile brought tears to Huw's eyes.

He was overwhelmed to think he did still have family, albeit distant kin. Mora was horrified and devastated at the sad tale of his parents' deaths. "Who'd ever have thought our sweet Karolyn would come to such a terrible end." She hugged him through her tears and insisted he guest in their rooms.

Mora created a perfect disguise for him, one that had them all laughing. She thought of it when she recalled a disgusting trick he could do with his right eye as a child. "It made you look walleyed! It really used to make me laugh. It scared your grandmother though. She was terrified your eye would stick, and you'd have a stigma for it!"

"I don't know why I used to do such a silly thing," Huw replied, chuckling. "I used to stand in front of Mum's mirror and make horrible faces for hours on end!"

And so, with his hair trimmed roughly at his shoulders like a peasant's, a "wart" on the side of his nose and a little black on a few teeth, Huw became a guesting relative. "My first husband was an actor, but he didn't have the memory so wasn't accepted into the guild," Mora told him. "I know a few tricks of the trade, and everything we need can be found in the kitchen." They decided to see if Huw would be recognized by the locals, doing the menial tasks that a slightly less than intelligent young relative might be given.

"Jaky-lad, sweep the floor" and "Jaky, take out the slops" were the refrains of the day. Huw enjoyed the game, slouching and looking a bit slack-jawed, as if he was indeed the afflicted relation. Every time someone looked at him, he let his eye wander, giving him a completely daft appearance.

No one even looked at him twice, which eased his mind. He'd once been fairly well known in Clythe, but in those days he'd worn a bard's fine robes, a neatly trimmed beard, and hair that fell in long curls over his shoulders to his waist. By now, everyone knew the sad news that the handsome bard who'd once stayed in their town, Huw Owyn, was dead in the guild hall fire along with the rest of the bards. It never occurred to them he was hiding in their midst. If they thought poor, ill-favored Jaky Tavysh looked familiar, they laid it down to being the Bear's nephew, and that familiarity eased his acceptance into their closed society.

With Huw's disguise firmly established, the Bear took him to Felim the Chandler, a man who sold a little of everything, but mainly candles and food. Felim also had other things folks would trade for. Bits of armor, saddles and tack, all sorts of used items found their way to the chandlery in Clythe, where they changed hands several times, often returning somewhat bloodstained.

"We need to see some armor," said the Bear. "There might be a trip up north or out east for my nephew." The Bear had all of Huw's money, posing as a dutiful brother carrying out his sisters final wishes. Huw knew he would bargain hard.

"Takes a special man to make the trip to Vyennes guarding a caravan, Bear. You know that. You rode guard for Older Murfee same as me, afore you went to sea. They get halfway there an' decide the wild North just isn't fer them. They still have firedrakes an' all sorts of elemental beasts roaming wild up the Bekenberg trail. No one goes anywhere alone, unless they're that idiot knight who was through here riding like there was no tomorrow." The grizzled old man shook his head. "I told him to slow down. Life's too short to be running around like a chicken with yer head cut off!"

"You mean the knight what beat up those Crows?" The Bear knew exactly who the old man meant.

"The very one. And I have to say, I was glad to see it. The Crows we been seeing lately all come from Port Lanque, an' I should know! I came here as a young man, younger'n yer boy here, just to get away from their sort. They're naught but animals, an' they're the ones in charge there. Always have been, and always will be." Felim's old face was grim, and he changed the subject. "What kin I do fer you today, Bear?"

"Like I said, my nephew here needs some mail since he's decided to see the world," the Bear pushed Huw toward the chandler. "Stand up straight, Jaky-lad. You look a bit smarter when you do. I promised my sister I'd get him set up proper-like."

Huw straightened up, grinning vacantly at the chandler.

The chandler looked doubtful, seeing the lad was missing a few teeth, and his right eye sort of wandered off on its own. "Yer sister's boy? Didn't know you had a sister," he said. "Sort of a quiet lad."

"Cissy was my older sister from my dad's first marriage. She ran off with a tinker when I was just a boy and my dad cut her off for it. The boy's smarter than he looks, although he doesn't really talk much," confided the Bear. "He's quick with his sword, and it's all that matters for a guard. He's determined to see the world. He's lived all his life down Ludwellyn way, but he gets seasick so the sea isn't for him."

"Throw up all over everything, I do, out on the sea," Huw confided. "Ah'd like to see a oliphant, or mebbe a dragon. They got 'em up north." His voice was rather thick, as if he had a cold.

The chandler had to force himself not to stare, as the unfortunate lad's right eye kept wandering as if it had a life of its own. A large wart on the side of the poor boy's nose vied with the nomadic eye for attention.

"S'more likely you'll be seeing the arse of the horse in front of you," said Felim, desperately trying not to look at the wart or the eye. "Thass all I saw on my trip to Vyennes with Older Murfee. Course, he's dead now, got killed by highwaymen. His son's running the show. Younger Murfee might be looking fer an extra sword. He's planning a trip to Bekenberg in a few weeks. He's the only one, so far as I've heard. Yer lad could go east from there with one of the big caravans. Won't see no oliphants unless he goes over the Eastern Wall an' down into Vyennes. But yer lad don't look too…um…well, he don't look 'zactly like a fighter."

"I s'pose he don't, but I promised Cissy, so I'll see him properly set up. The boy's been scrapping all his life, since there's always someone as thinks it's funny to pick on him because of his crazy eye. It's a stigma, and you know how folks are about things like that. But he's a fighter, and a good lad. And he doesn't drink ale, so there's no chance of him going off his head and causing trouble on the road." The Bear clapped Huw on the shoulder in uncle-ish fashion. "We were thinking you might have some chainmail lying around that would fit him. He's a bit weedy now, but he's going to be big once he gets his growth."

Huw grinned his gap-toothed smile again.

"Aye, he's already as tall as you, so he should be growing a bit more in the shoulders. Lemme see what I kin find. I think I got sommat will fit him well enough fer now an' might last him a while." The chandler rummaged around on his dusty shelves. "He'll need one of these." Felim hauled out a heavily quilted shirt, somewhat blood-stained, but otherwise still quite good. "Take it from me, lad. Chainmail gets bloody cold once you get up in the mountains. Man could freeze to death." He rummaged a bit more. "What about a helm?

187

He sure don't want to be head-injured, seeing as how he's already a mite…er…here, this'll do good fer him. Put it on over yer knit cap, Jaky, an' it won't freeze yer ears."

Huw stood there with the helm on, wearing the padded shirt.

"Now this…." The chandler hauled out a heavy shirt of chainmail. "This might just do it. He won't outgrow it too soon, an' it's long enough to protect his legs." Felim looked up at the Bear, saying, "Folks always fergit their legs is vulnerable. Speshly when they're riding a horse. Does he ride?"

"Always wanted ter ride a horse," mumbled Huw, "Mucked out aplenty after 'em. Know how to care fer 'em."

Felim turned to the Bear. "If you sign him on with Younger Murfee, come back an' I'll see to it he has what he's going to need in the way of tack. You'll have to get him a horse, though. Murfee don't provide them." Felim dug around on his shelves and came up with some heavy leather trousers in black. "These, along with the mail shirt an' some leg-guards, will do the trick. It's going to cost you sommat."

"I know, but Cissy left him enough when she passed on. He has the coins," replied the Bear. "What about mail gloves? Something to ensure he comes home with all his fingers."

"Don't got no mail gloves, but I got some with steel reinforced backs," Felim rooted around in a drawer and pulled out a pair of black leather gloves.

"These'll be better than nothing, an' they'll keep him warm."

"Do you have a northern-style woolen cloak, something to keep the rain and snow off?" The Bear pulled a purse out of his own cloak. "We wouldn't want him to look bad with rusty mail."

"Most of this came by way of some Crows who suddenly decided to leave the trade, but I do happen to have a cloak like you're askin' about, barely even worn. Come from Vyennes, it did," replied Felim, standing on a stool and looking around on a high shelf. He unfolded a new-looking cloak, heavy and mottled gray, green and brown, with a deep hood large enough to cover a helm and still shade a face. "Sad, how I came by this, but what can I say? Everyone knows to boil the water, but some folks think it'll never happen to them."

An hour later, Huw and the Bear were back at the Green Man, and Mora was going over everything they'd bought, tut-tutting at the bloodstains. "What's wrong with folks that they bleed all over everything and don't clean it up?"

"The dead don't do laundry unless they've gone to hell, Mora," the Bear laughed at his wife. "They're too busy kneeling at God's throne and singing His praises!"

"Well, still, selling him a shirt with the bloodstains still on it," she groused. "It's not right that one of ours should go about in such a state." She looked at Huw, who grinned at her. "Oh, for the love of God, boy, go clean the black off your teeth! You look positively lack-witted!"

The Bear had heard Younger Murfee suffered some losses due to the turmoil in Ludwellyn, and knew the portly merchant wasn't quite ready to make his journey to Bekenberg. Despite his obvious misgivings, Murfee took Jaky on as a favor. "He'll be ready to go when you are," promised the Bear. "You'll be pleased with him, you'll see. Our Jaky's a good lad and he's quicker than he looks."

It was apparent Murfee didn't believe him, but nodded his head in agreement anyway. "Someone has to be bait for the biggies, Bear, and it's usually the newbies. Could be your nephew, so don't blame me if he doesn't come back. We can't be babying him, right? He's got to pull his own oar."

The Bear grinned and shrugged. "You'll see. Jaky's good with the sword. I'm working with him every day, and he's pressing me. I know he doesn't look it, but he's observant. He knows to listen to the woods for sounds that shouldn't be there."

Often when a caravan came south through the Bekenberg Pass, they had an extra horse due to accident or attack, so a few good ones were always available in Clythe. As soon as Murfee agreed to take his relative on, the Bear acquired a horse, and Huw learned to ride. He tried not to think about the fates of the former owners of either his gear or horse, but they found their way into a ballad he wrote down in his journal. He'd written a great many of them since he left Ilene's house posing as a scholar.

His horse, a young gelding named Blackberry, was well-behaved and fairly smart. Once the Bear showed him how to get Blackberry to respond to his commands, Huw enjoyed riding. "I never thought parading around on a beast would be so enjoyable," he commented, after his first day. "I see now why some folks are mad for them." Having met Lackland's horse, Farroll, Huw frequently found himself talking to Blackberry, who seemed rather surprised but pleased, flicking his ears and nudging Huw's shoulder in appreciation.

"You're going to be best friends for the rest of your life, if you're still intent on going north. Nobody walks up there or they're dead meat. The beasts will get you, them or the bloody Lanque highwaymen who make it up the treacherous Lanque Trail to the Bekenberg Pass. Some creatures will attack you on your horse, but at least you stand a chance. And you're going as a guard, so you won't be alone. Once you prove yourself, someone will have your back, as you'll have theirs."

Huw wanted to break his nether regions in to riding slowly, but was unable to spend more than an hour each day at it on a regular basis. The chandler had warned him a saddle-sore arse was a painful condition, and he had no doubts in that regard. "It ain't just yer arse as will be raw, if you get my meaning, boy." Huw understood what the man was saying, but he stood there grinning like a fool anyway. Despite his obvious doubts about Jaky's abilities, Felim had found him some good tack, and Blackberry was as well kitted out as possible.

While he waited for Murfee's shipment to be ready to go north to Bekenberg, Huw stayed busy. Every morning found Huw and Blackberry fully geared up in mail, trying to toughen up his body to get it used to the armor and saddle, traversing the paths of the thick forest behind the Green Man. Sometimes he rode all the way to the jumble of low hills that marked the base of the sheer cliffs where Wald and Eyn met. If there were no guests he could take Blackberry out some evenings too, but had to avoid being seen by the townsfolk. He was careful not to draw attention to himself; he couldn't afford to have anyone look at him too closely until he was safely out of the valley.

Frequently there were no overnight guests, so the Bear had him put on his armor and practice sword-work with him in the stable. "Your dad trained you well enough with the knives, but you can't rely on them. Those beasts they call 'biggies'—the only way you'd have any effect on them with a knife is if you managed by some miracle to nail one in the eye, and even then it's unlikely you'd kill it unless your knife was thrown hard enough to cut through to its brain. Dragons and firedrakes wouldn't even be hurt by a knife to the eye, they're that big and tough," he told Huw. "You must be able to use this sword as well as you possibly can. It'll save your life."

"My father always said the same thing, trying to get me to work harder at it," replied Huw, feeling the familiar sense of sadness that always accompanied thoughts of Balen. "But I didn't know I'd need to pretend to be a mercenary. I was that stupid."

"You aren't pretending, Jak." Bear and Mora always called him Jak even in private. "This is for real, boy. Balen and your old life are dead. You are a mercenary now, and you'd better think like one."

The townsfolk became fairly used to the Bear's unfortunate nephew and didn't press their company on him, knowing he was leaving town soon. He was an industrious worker and stayed out of everyone's way. Folks feared the Bear and knew he wouldn't bother them unless they harassed his nephew, so Jaky-lad was generally treated well, if ignored somewhat. This was good, as Murfee's men often drank in the tap room in the evenings. They became quite used to seeing him diligently helping his uncle and aunt, and knew he wouldn't be lazy when he joined up with their crew.

It wounded Huw deeply when the local men gathered and brought out their pipes and drums. He didn't dare join in, sitting in the shadows with his hair hiding his face. Still, he was gratified to hear them playing despite the Grefyn's depredations. "Music is the soul of Eyn," his father had always told him, and now Huw knew it was true. "They killed the bards, but they can't stop the people from making music," he told the Bear, suffused with pride. Nonetheless, the minute one of the gate guards saw a man on horseback, the simple instruments disappeared. When strangers passed through Clythe, they heard no music in the entire town. Huw suspected it was so throughout the Eynier Valley, all the way to Ludwellyn.

Various bands of Crows made brief sweeps through Clythe. The town was so far north, it was well outside of their normal jurisdiction, but they were making a statement, vying for bragging rights within Clan Grefyn. Some small amount of glory could be had for having "swept the Long Valley all the way to Clythe and back." The motley gangs of assorted thugs, mixed with the occasional down-at-the-heels noble, paid scant attention to the lad who swept the floor and stabled their horses.

The most recent group of ruffians had once been tied to Rann Dwyn. They were now at loose ends, having been suddenly absolved of all duties. The governor, Lord St. John, closed the port to all traffic with Lanqueshire. Unable to travel south to Ludwellyn, they found themselves in Clythe, trying to decide what their options were, not really wanting to take the harrowing and dangerous road north to the only land route into Lanqueshire, the Bekenberg Pass.

Increasingly there were more mutterings and grumblings among all of the Grefyn bully-boys when they passed through, and some of the swagger had gone out of their walk since Huw had seen them last.

At last, Huw heard the news he'd been waiting for. Someone had murdered the old Grefyn as he looked out his third-floor bedroom window one night. An arrow of unusually large proportions had lodged itself in his heart as he stood taking in the night air. How this had happened when he'd been so well protected was a mystery, especially to his guards, but the old Grefyn had definitely "woken up dead," laying on the floor with an arrow the size of a tree branch in his chest.

For some reason, this news didn't bring Huw the satisfaction he'd thought it would. Perhaps he would never feel his father was truly avenged; maybe the losses he'd suffered were so great that no amount of retribution could recompense him. Despite his great interest in the news, he felt detached from it, more like an observer.

Duke Amstyce Lyndys was residing in his townhouse in Ludwellyn at the time of his uncle's murder. Within an hour of hearing the news, he'd taken possession of the Grefyn Palace and seized control of all Clan Grefyn's assets. He claimed the coronet and personally dealt with the careless guards in his usual efficient way. Their corpses still decorated the walls of the palace. The mournful sound of gibbet-cages creaking in the wind was an audible warning to any who thought they'd eliminate him the way they had his uncle.

Many people were glad to hear Anvel Grefyn had gone to meet Old Grim. Everyone knew he could only have gone to hell, as a man as evil as he'd been would never be found kneeling at the throne of God.

A vicious dogfight arose among the possible successors, all of whom now fought to the death to reclaim the coronet from Amstyce Lyndys. An epidemic of murder spread among the high-ranking nobles of Clan Grefyn, and the streets of Ludwellyn once again ran with blood. Several inter-house wars were still being fought over the scraps, but it looked like Duke Amstyce and House Lyndys had the upper-hand. He'd moved his family into the palace quickly, taking possession of the ducal seat. But before he could have the coronation ceremony, he'd have to defeat House Doleyn. The Crows of Doleyn weren't going to give up easily, as the loser in this war would forfeit everything, including his life. It was a winner-take-all battle.

Huw busied himself with scrubbing tables and sweeping floors while the Crows had their supper. His ear was busy too, sifting through the heavy Lanque accents some of the men had.

Bent-nose sat with his back to the corner, glaring around the full tap room. "Seems ter me as like the Grefyn got hisself shot by one of his heirs," he mumbled to his mates. "Oi says it's Lyndys! Who else wuz ready ter take over so quickly? We knows fer a fact thet Lyndys done his brother-in-law, Dwyn. An' Dwyn hisself tol' us he were in line fer thet cor-o-net. Everyone knows Lyndys wanted his sister ter hold Dwyn."

One-Eye replied, "O' course Lyndys din't count on his sister goin' over to the Bitch Duchess, now, did he? Thet's why ye can't trust a woman. They always got sommat in mind what ain't in yer best interest."

"Ah bet Lyndys din't 'spect his own sister would open her doors to King Henri's men. Now she's got a garrison o' knights billetin' there, an' we's either goin' back to Port Lanque or bowin' to thet barbarian king from up north. I'm thinkin' o' headin' back to Port Lanque, meself." Pretty-boy leaned back and belched. He was handsome by virtue of the fact he wasn't as scarred as the others, and was missing fewer teeth. "I like a king what gets out an' does a bit o' plunderin' fer his country. King Karl is the man fer it."

"There's opportunity fer advancement," agreed Bent-nose. "Black Franck wuz all talk an' no fight. I don't 'member him mounting one raid. Still, he did cozy up with the Grefyn here on this side o' the mountains. Thet did help us all out."

"Thing is," said One-eye, "We cain't go south. Both sides o' the river are closed to us now, what with Grefyn pretendin' they don't know us, while they're scrappin' over thet cor-o-net. We has to go the Northern Trail, and thet's the hard road. We'll be in trouble once we enter the Lanque Gap, no matter what sort o' supplies we can find here."

"And we'll have ter pay fer 'em, so don't spend all yer gold on ale, Rafe," replied Pretty-Boy. "The locals here are diff'rent from the ones down south. These folks are mostly ex-mercs and they ain't afraid ter fight back." The others grunted their agreement.

Despite his interest in their words, Huw had to move away from their corner as he'd finished his task and couldn't hang about gawking, much as he'd have liked to. Still he managed to pick up a lot of information as he circulated in the tap room unobtrusively.

From what he gathered, Duchess Madewyn Weyllyn had taken charge and rallied her forces. As the duly accepted regent, Madewyn was free to act as she felt was best since her grandfather still lived and would wear the coronet until he died. She'd moved quickly to consolidate her position as regent for Clan Weyllyn. Her men had mounted severe retaliatory raids for the atrocities Grefyn had committed, which had endeared her to much of the populace. She'd regained control of her towns and the once bold Lanque Crows were now being harried all the way back to Lanqueshire. The great Grefyn ships were loaded with them, and their docks were empty of men in their mad effort to escape.

Most of the citizens of Ludwellyn still believed the fire and the total destruction of the bards was a tragic accident instead of a carefully planned massacre. Their own losses when the Artists' Quarter was consumed were enormous, and in the face of so many deaths, the Crows' murders had gone unnoticed. Amstyce Lyndys, now calling himself the Grefyn, had gained some support from the people of Ludwellyn from his generous efforts to rebuild the area.

Huw spied most diligently on the Crows who passed through Clythe, but as time went on, they were swiftly run out of town by Weyllyn's forces. Thus, when the Crows of Dwyn and another group began to make themselves at home, the Bear sent a message to the local Weyllyn nobleman. "Twenty Crows nesting here is an army," he told the mayor, who agreed with him. "We need to evict them now, or we'll have a town full come winter."

Earl Bry Dayle arrived promptly with his armsmen to rally the village and drive them off. The duchess had thrown her support behind him when he was raised to the Earldom and sent men and weapons to help secure his position. As a result, he was fiercely loyal to both her and Henri. The earl would give no quarter to enemies of the Crown.

The swift, bloody battle was fought in an oat field just south of the village, leaving several men dead. Though he disliked doing it, the young earl personally dispatched the wounded Lanques, quickly and efficiently slitting their throats. "No use taking prisoners, Jak," Bry said, upon seeing Huw's shocked face peering at the carnage. "They just weigh you down, and these sort come back to haunt you." He obviously took no pleasure in the task, but wouldn't ask his men to do such a disagreeable thing. "No, it's best to just be rid of them."

Shaking so badly he barely remembered to stay in character, Huw said, "I just never knew war could be so awful, my lord. It's a dreadful thing to have to do. But I can see we don't want them to come back since they'd not be grateful you spared their lives. They'd kill us for our kindness. But still, it's a terrible thing."

"Yes, Jak, it is. But it's necessary to keep the Lanques from taking everything we've worked for. We won't allow the Long Valley to slip back into their clutches!" The young earl put Huw and several others to work building a cairn for the dead Crows. Huw pondered a long while on the events of the afternoon.

Finally, Younger Murfee was ready to make his trip to Bekenberg. With a heavy heart Huw prepared to leave Clythe. Secretly, he was miserable at the thought of leaving the Bear and Mora. He'd come to feel like he really was their nephew, and knew they, in turn, felt as if they were sending off a son.

"I know you left home with my madcap niece, believing she was going to marry you, and she let you down. Sinean's not done with her cause yet, and maybe never will be. But you came back, which is more than she's ever done. I'll miss you, boy." The Bear hugged him roughly, and Mora shed a few tears.

"You and the Bear are all the family I have left, Mora. I'll write once I get to wherever I'm going. I think I'm leaving the Long Valley forever," Huw said, hugging her. He told the Bear, "I don't think I'll ever return, not even for Sinean. I'm finally over loving her. Coming back here helped me get things straight in my head. I know my future lies in the North."

The Bear just nodded, saying, "You're still our kin, never fear. We have to stick together, so be sure to write."

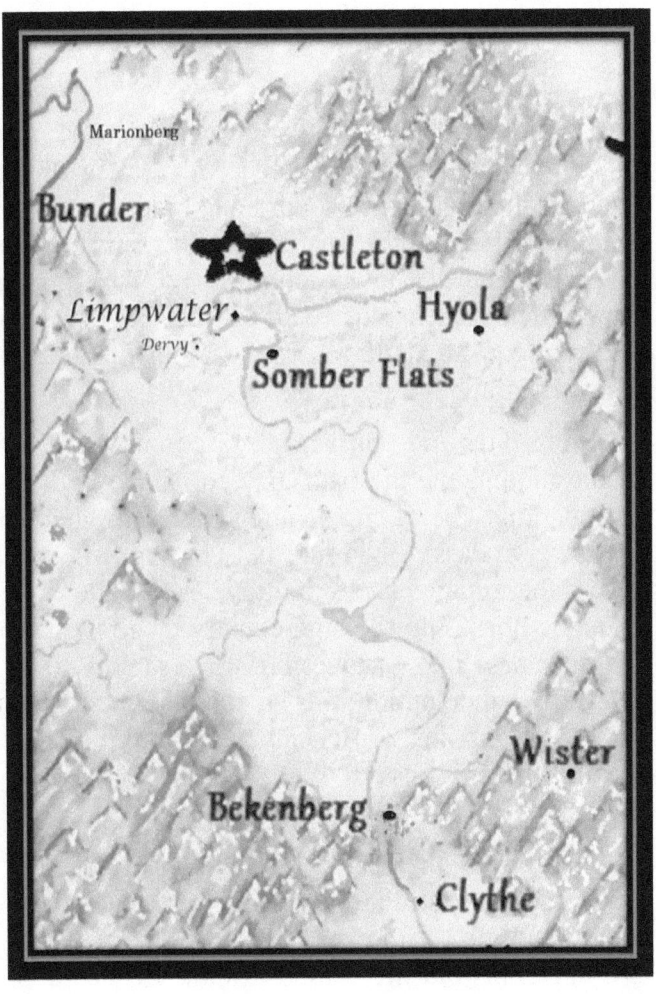

Chapter 13 The Bekenberg Trail

Huw was silent as he brought up the rear of Murfee's caravan, taking the heavily rutted dirt track that was the great north-south trade road. Once the trail left the lowlands, the changes in the landscape were obvious as they slowly climbed up the Limpwater Gorge. The treacherous road was barely wide enough for a wagon in some places, winding up the narrow canyon through the steep cut.

Four days' ride further north, at a crossroads deep in the mountains, the path divided. Three high passes surrounding the Long Valley met at the famed Bekenberg Pass, dividing the country of Waldeyn across the middle. There the traveler had the choice to continue north into the high country or go west though the only pass into Lanqueshire traversable year round. The only other option was to travel east through the remote trading post of Bekenberg, and from there, cross the treacherous Eastern Wall into the low country of Vyennes.

Sometime after eating a lunch of dried meat and waybread while still in the saddle, they began the steep, winding climb. With every step Blackberry took, Huw Owyn left his old life behind. Riding tail-guard behind the string of heavily laden wagons, Huw's mind dwelled on the changes that had occurred in him since spring. He'd not played his pipes or lute in nearly four months, nor had he sang in public, not even when the men of Clythe had played their unique and compelling music, although hidden in the shadows, he'd tapped his foot. He'd listened with a strange combination of yearning and fear, wishing he dared to join in as he had so often in the old days. His instruments had remained buried, safely tucked in the bottom of his saddlebags. He hadn't unwrapped his father's little harp since leaving Maury.

At times he wondered if he was even still a bard, despite the Bear's constant nagging to rebuild the guild. Everything that ever made him want to sing was gone. All he knew were sad songs now. Numb from the knowledge he really *was* leaving behind everything he'd ever known, he focused his attention on following the arse of the horse in front. Simply listening to the sounds of the woods around him became a solace of sorts.

His own insignificance was brought home to him as he rode into a forest that was taller, darker and more dangerous than any place he'd ever seen before. Naively, he'd always assumed the woods in the Long Valley were as tall and thick as any forest, but those woodlands were less than half as tall as the giants he now traveled through, knee-high to these lords of the forest in actuality. Gazing in wonder, Huw passed among trees with trunks as big as houses. As he rode along, he wondered what Murfee would think when Jaky lost the warts, his eye straightened up and he grew his teeth back. Smiling in anticipation, Huw began to cheer up. Maybe this would be fun after all.

It was late afternoon, and despite all his efforts at getting his arse in shape, Huw was now heartily wishing they would stop soon. They slowly followed the column as the oxen climbed the steep path. Gradually, Huw became aware the sounds of the horses, the creak of leather and the jingle of mail were the only sounds in the forest. He wasn't sure what the silence could mean. *There should be sounds, shouldn't there? Birds? Something.*

They rolled on, the great teams of oxen laboriously pulling the heavily laden wagons up the road, and with every step forward, Huw became more nervous. The hair on the back of his neck rose, and his stomach knotted up. Unable to stop himself, Huw began searching the woods around him, trying to see what could be causing the silence. *I don't know what to look for. Something's out there, I know it.*

Warily, he began to draw his sword, feeling like a frightened fool but stricken with a gut-feeling of anxiety. He'd just gotten his blade free when he was startled by a crashing noise in the brush near him.

One of the men yelled, "Mountain lion!"

The beast leapt right at Huw, and all he could see were talons on paws the size of dinner plates and fangs as long as his fingers. Terror made him clumsy, but instinctively, Huw stabbed, thrusting madly, trying to keep the cat out of his face. Miraculously, Huw's sword was at the perfect angle to impale the creature through the heart.

As it fell scratching to the dirt, the cat's claws made a large rent in Huw's cloak. Blackberry skittered a bit close to the cliff-side edge of the road, but somehow Huw got him under control before they tumbled off the mountain. He had to let go of his sword, or the weight of the beast would have pulled him out of the saddle.

Murfee's voice drifted back, saying, "Did you see that? Jaky got himself a biggie! You couldn't have done any better, Bil!"

Dismounting, Huw handed his reins to Derik, who rode just ahead, and attempted to retrieve his sword from the dead lion. At first, it seemed to be stuck, so he placed his foot on the cat's body and yanked until it came out. When it finally did come free, he stumbled backwards, staggering like a drunk. Fighting the urge to laugh hysterically, he steadied his nerves as he stood, nonchalantly cleaning the bloody blade with his rag, trying to remember what the Bear had told him about disposing of anything he killed. "Always clear the road once you've dispatched a beast or a highwayman. Act like you've done it all your life, no matter how badly you're shaking in your boots," he'd said.

The great cat's corpse partially blocked the trail, and Huw knew he couldn't just leave it there. He wasn't sure he had the strength to move such a large carcass alone, but had to at least try. Looking around, he couldn't see a ditch, so decided to move it to the cliff-side edge and try to shove it off there. Straining with all his might, he dragged the beast out of the road. It turned out to be a much more difficult task than he expected, as the creature seemed to weigh as much as a horse. Nevertheless, by rolling first the tail end and then the head, he finally had the cat perched at the edge of the cliff.

Making every effort *not* to look over the abyss, Huw pushed the dead lion toward the brink, trying to nudge it over without losing his balance. Unfortunately, the great body stuck on a low shrub and stubbornly refused to go any further. In desperation, Huw put as much force as he could into it and with a mighty heave he strained to get the huge cat rolling.

Suddenly the tail end of the immense carcass lurched over the edge, yanking the rest with it, sending it tumbling down the cliff.

Of course, this threw Huw off balance. The combination of his efforts and the lion's momentum as it plummeted into the gorge, nearly sent him over the edge. Desperately grabbing at shrubs and bracing against the rocks to hold himself back, he clung to the cliff, speechless with terror. Frozen, he watched the cat's body careening down the sheer mountainside, occasionally bouncing like a rock. Through it all, he had to fight a nearly overwhelming urge to scream madly. Indeed, he couldn't speak for fear of bursting into girlish hysteria.

Silently saying heartfelt prayers of thanks to God and all His angels, Huw remounted Blackberry, all the while keeping his jaws clenched to stop his teeth from chattering.

"Jaky made quick work of the cat. I reckon he'll do as well as his uncle said he would." Once again, Murfee's words to the guards who were riding point drifted back to the rear of the caravan. "Let's get moving! We have to get to the ridge tonight. We should be the only ones in the shelter, since there's no one else scheduled down the main trail today. Tomorrow we'll be meeting up with a train out of Vyennes."

Shaking his head with amazement, Bil said, "I ain't never seen no one sling a lion over a cliff like that, all by his lonesome."

"Wonder why he didn't ask for help? Most men would. I would have done, anyway," Fat Pat commented, as he hoisted his immense frame back up to the driver's perch. "I suppose our Jaky's not much used to asking though, things being what they are, and him with a stigma and all." Fat Pat shook the reins on his wagon, calling to his team, "Gee-up you lot! Let's go!"

The caravan started moving again, accompanied by the discordant song of creaking leather, faintly squeaking wheels and jingling harnesses and, now the lion was gone, the occasional call of a bird or chatter of a squirrel.

"It's always the tail-guard what the big cats go after," muttered Derik. "You handled it well, Jaky. Maybe your uncle was right about you."

Huw just grunted in agreement and kept riding, exhibiting a calmness he didn't feel. *Holy God in heaven! It was bigger than me! It nearly had me, and then I almost fell down the bloody mountain. God, have mercy on me—this is the worst job I've ever had.* The rest of the day Huw rode with a terrible sense of paranoia, sure he was going to be attacked with every step they took.

On the positive side, he'd forgotten how sore his arse was.

At mid-afternoon, they approached the wayside shelter that was the first stop on the high road north out of Clythe. King Henri's sire, good King Herrold, had built accommodations along the main trade roads throughout the high mountains all over Waldeyn to encourage commerce between the far-flung rural towns. They were simple, but immense. Each was comprised of thatched longhouses with shuttered windows, twelve bunks, two rough tables and four benches, cold stone floors and a fireplace for cooking and heating.

The building was divided in two by a wall. Half was a rough living area for the merchants and guards. Through a connecting door, one could enter the good-sized barn for the horses and oxen. A deep-dug well, surrounded by stone and covered, stood nearby for use when the snows had melted. A well-kept privy was situated downhill from the longhouse, a safe distance from the well. The merchants themselves kept them clean, since their guards had to muck the stalls before they could leave.

The caravans brought in their own bedrolls and any meat they wanted to eat, and left the place tidy. There were plenty of dried beans and a few other staples if they were snowed in for any length of time. King Henri had his men regularly replenish those necessities along with hay and fodder to keep the goodwill of the merchants and encourage trade. God forbid a blizzard should stretch for longer than a week, since cabin fever would drive them all mad long before they ran out of beans. Fortunately the longhouses were warm in the winter, and the merchants were pleased the monarchy had placed such a high value on them as to provide shelters as well appointed as these.

"You won't be treated this well in Fornost, should you ever work there," said Derik, as he claimed his bunk, grunting as he slid his gear underneath it.

Huw nodded and took the bunk nearest the door, as he'd been warned to do. "It's the drafty bunk. The door will be opening and closing all night long, what with folks going out to the privy at all hours," the Bear had said. "If you don't claim it first they'll move you there, so you may as well start out on the right foot with them."

As soon as he had his gear stowed under his bunk, Huw went back into the animal shelter to see to his horse's comfort. Blackberry was tired and grateful for Huw's ministrations, nosing his shoulder with a chuff of thanks. As he curried him, Huw talked in low tones, expecting no answer and receiving none.

When he finished taking care of Blackberry, Huw brought water and filled the mangers with hay and oat biscuits, giving every horse an apple and a carrot from the bins near the doors. Afterward, he bathed himself in the cold water of the well, pondering the events of his first day on the road north. Huw was tired and not really interested in working anymore, but he busied himself with bringing in more firewood. The others were glad for his help and felt more inclined to look on Jaky favorably since carried his own weight, and then some.

Once he was inside the bunk-room, he stayed in the dark corners, not speaking much. With his face cleaned, and the black off his teeth, he wondered how long it would be before they noticed Ugly Jak had grown somewhat prettier. The shadows and his hair shrouded his features, he nodded and agreed with anything said directly to him but stayed out of the center of things as much as possible, doing the washing up after supper as the new lad ought. The others ignored him, but not unkindly, much as they had at The Green Man. He listened to their conversations with a great deal of interest, as Murfee discussed the fire in Ludwellyn and the way it had affected his business.

When he finally fell into his bunk, it seemed like he'd only been asleep for an hour when the others started stirring, and it was time to prepare to get on the road again. Before they pulled out of the yard, Huw, Derik, Bil and Benet quickly mucked out the stable, leaving everything as clean as when they arrived. The task went quite quickly since it was done on a daily basis.

They were back on the road as soon as it was light. After a few hours, they stopped at a creek to water the horses and stretch their legs. It was slow going for the wagons, as the trail was steep and still climbing, and it grew progressively rougher and more rutted. At mid-morning they passed a crew smoothing out the worst places. The gang was a group of prisoners in black and white striped uniforms, chained and working under the watchful eye of hard-faced guards, all of whom wore the purple and grey colors of the Crown of Waldeyn.

Huw was surprised to see how cheerful the prisoners seemed to be despite their hard labor and grim guards. The men laughed, joked and worked with some enthusiasm, which seemed at odds with their circumstances. "Who'd think convicts would look so happy with their lot?" he commented to Derik.

"Mostly the road crews are made up of regular poor folk who come up from Lanqueshire to escape starvation. Many have been forced by circumstances into thievery. They were caught stealing bread or a chicken to feed their families," Derik told Huw. "They ain't done bad enough to be hung, but we can't encourage them to be thieves, so they work for half a year, and their families are sent to shelter with the nuns at Hyola. The women are treated well, and the children are taught to read, write, count and do figures. Everyone benefits," Derik shrugged. "We get the roads maintained and while they're on the road-crew, they get two good meals a day, a dry place to sleep and gaudy but warm clothes when the weather turns cold. When they've done their time, they can apply for a patent to farm out in the wilds on the coast towards Galwye, or they can go back to Lanqueshire." He shook his head sadly. "It's amazing how many choose to stay and farm the coastal wilds even though there's no protection from the beasts out there." After they passed the work crew, the road smoothed out and they were able to make better time.

Huw was silent, thinking about the prisoners for the rest of the afternoon. He had a sharp remembrance of what it was like to go hungry and have no hope of feeding yourself. *I'd take the offer of a farm too,* he thought to himself. *King Henri is clever. By treating them with respect even when they've done wrong, he gains the loyalty and service of generally good, hardworking people. Clan Grefyn buys the loyalty of the bullies and gains only the thugs and villains. The South fights new ideas and suffers, while the North embraces change and benefits from it.*

Huw knelt upstream from the horses, washing the trail dust off. It was late summer now, and even in the higher elevations, they were feeling the afternoon heat. Huw knew better than to drink the water from the creek.

"We'll be stopping at the Lower Falls shelter," muttered Derik. "There's supposed to be a caravan from up north stopping there today too. They always have women guarding them, mixed in with the men. You'd best mind your manners, or they'll put you in your place right quick. These northern women choose who they dally with, and don't you forget it!"

"My cousin's a merc down in Ludwellyn, and she chooses for herself. She'd have found me a place with her crew, but the sea wasn't for me. Besides, I always mind my manners, women or men," replied Huw, still using the thick southern accent he'd been adopting since arriving in Clythe. "Women don't pay me much mind, so I stay out of their way." He grinned behind his hair, congratulating himself on what a liar he'd become.

"Ah, yeah, I s'pose so," said Derik, obviously feeling bad for reminding poor Jaky about his being so ugly and all. "My ma always said there's someone for everyone though. You're a good worker, and don't chatter too much. Maybe on your travels you'll meet a woman as will look past your unfortunate lack of beauty."

"Could be. I don't really expect it though," said Huw. "My ma said the same thing, but so far it ain't happened." He decided it was time to change the subject. "Who gets the bunks when two groups meet up at the shelter?"

"It's easy," replied Derik. "The first ones there get them, and the others make do with the floor, it's why we're hurrying. Younger Murfee hates to sleep on the floor! Of course, the first ones there start supper, so it takes the sting out of things somewhat."

Murfee's caravan arrived at the shelter mid-afternoon, ensuring Murfee had a bunk. He was in a good mood as he made a huge pot of bean soup with plenty of bacon, opening a tin of waybread to dunk in the soup. Things were warm and welcoming by the time the other convoy arrived.

The caravan from the North arrived at dusk with heavily laden wagons pulled by oxen the same as Murfee's. There were three obviously northern guards, tall, with light hair and blue eyes; two men and a woman, all of them mercenaries, Ravens out of the town of Bekenberg. The woman seemed to be in charge, and she had her crew well organized. A rather muscular, blonde woman with a delicate, heart-shaped face, Sara Murtrey was easily as tall as the tallest man among them. She was quite capable, taking care of her horse and tack with practiced ease. She obviously knew Murfee and his men well, because she tolerated a great deal of innuendo and suggestions by all of the guards, most of which were bravado.

Sara kept her distance with a sense of humor that she had no need to reinforce with her sword. "Now Murfee, you know I don't mix business with pleasure," she said when the portly merchant offered to share his bunk with her. "I'm a woman with high expectations. It's bad for business when a prospective client can't keep up his end of the bargain! I'd hate for you to be too embarrassed to face me again! You're a wonderful source of employment for my Ravens!"

All the men roared, including Murfee, who replied "And that's the truth of it, lass! I'm not the man I was!"

As usual, Huw stayed in the shadows. Despite his wishes to the contrary, his eyes followed her; something about her attracted him. He was uncomfortable, feeling a stirring he thought he'd buried long ago. It was purely physical—he wanted her and that's all it was. *You're an idiot, Huw Owyn! She most likely has a man. At any rate, she'd not appreciate your offer of brief companionship. She's made that clear to Murfee's lads.* Despite his efforts to be circumspect, he was intensely aware of her no matter where she was in the cabin, a feeling that made him terribly uneasy. He wasn't used to having a continual tightness in his loins as if he were a green boy. *Besides, you're Ugly-Jak, and don't forget it, or you could end up in trouble!*

In desperation, after they'd eaten supper, Huw took the dishes out to the well. He needed to do the washing up in the peace and quiet of the dusk just to get away from the proximity of Sara. He felt the sexual tension in him fade as he left the stuffy cabin, and the cool of the evening refreshed him. Breathing a sigh of relief, he set to washing the dishes in the fading light.

It was full dark, and he was just finishing up the big kettle in the light of the rising moon when a strange, rotten-flesh smell assailed his senses. He turned, seeing a looming shadow that seemed wrong. A chill in the pit of his stomach told him something bad lurked there. Without hesitation, he drew his long-knife, throwing it at an eye that gleamed impossibly high, shining briefly in the moonlight. With a resounding thunk, it pierced the wood-wraith, sinking in to the hilt. Shrieking madly, the horrific creature stumbled about the moonlit yard and fell down, writhing on the ground. After a long moment of screeching and scrabbling in the dirt, the thing became still, and its other eye glazed over in death. Horrified, Huw stared at the dreadful-looking creature. Rough, bark-like skin covered it, making it appear much like a ten-foot tall dead tree with an immense, gaping maw lined with hundreds of knife-like teeth. He'd never even imagined such a thing could exist.

Another shadow loomed, and a second knife leapt to his hand. As soon as he saw it was Sara, the knife vanished. Her eyes met his, and he felt a jolt as if something electric had passed between them. She looked away first, staring at the dead wood-wraith. The door to the shelter banged open, and the men all poured out, swords drawn. When they saw the fallen creature, they sheathed their blades. Jonah, the merchant the Ravens were guarding, said, "Good work, Sara. I never heard of anyone taking a wood-wraith down with naught but a long-knife!"

"Would be you as could do that, Sara," said Mortyn, one of the mercenaries who rode with her. "At least this place is safe now. Those sorts of nasties always eat their competition!"

"It wasn't me who killed the beast," she replied. "It was the new lad as did it." Everyone turned to look at Jak, who stared down at his feet, hair hiding his features. "That little knife-trick of his is a thing of beauty—he's quick."

"Ah, that's our Jaky," said Murfee. "He got a mountain lion yesterday. Skewered it through the heart with his sword, then jumped off his horse and threw the carcass down the mountain, cool as ice!"

"Where'd you learn to throw a knife like that, Jaky?" asked Sara, with interest. "The only man I know of who could do such was a bard down in Ludwellyn. When I was a child, he would do tricks with his knives for me. He told me it was part of a bard's training...."

Before she could finish her sentence, Huw said in his thick accent, "My uncle was a sailor, ma'am. He taught me what I might need to know before I signed on with Murfee."

Murfee agreed, "It's true. His uncle is Bear Tavysh, who owns The Green Man in Clythe. He was captain on a Weyllyn ship until his mum passed on and left him the inn."

"I know the Bear," said Sara, peering closely at Huw. "We're old friends. He rode with my da for Older Murfee when they were young, before my da formed the Ravens. I heard his niece ran off with a bard. I didn't know he had a nephew."

Huw pulled his hood closer about his face. "My da was a tinker. You know how folks are about their sisters running off with tinkers, don't want to admit to it. He's dead now too."

"It's a good man who takes care of his nephews and nieces," said Murfee, as they all trooped back into the cabin. "No one does better by his family than the Bear." The door slammed behind the last of the men.

Huw looked at the ugly corpse of the wood-wraith and realized he was going to have to dispose of the giant thing or it could attract other, perhaps worse, beasts. Sighing, he gripped the twig-like appendages at the head-end and dragged the corpse to the edge of the road opposite the shelter and dropped it down the ravine. The wood-wraith was much lighter than he'd expected; it was like dragging dry branches. He had just finished when the cabin door opened again. He sensed her crossing the road to stand over him, watching as he cleaned his knife, forcing himself to not acknowledge her.

He could feel her eyes on him. The hairs on the back of his neck rose as did another part of his body. A peculiar current crackled in the air, connecting him and Sara, a combination of urgency and lust. Desperately, he tried to think of something, anything to take his mind off wondering what Sara would be like to make love to.

"You're a strange one, Jaky Tavysh. I admit I'm curious about you," she said, eyeing his backside appreciatively. "Murfee's men all seem to think you're good tempered, somewhat lacking in wits, and have an amazingly ill-favored face to boot. Yet, it's not what I saw when I looked at you earlier. You keep yourself hidden. Why is this, I wonder? For a man said to be short on intelligence, you managed to divert me quite nimbly when I mentioned a man whom you resemble most closely. It isn't the Bear, either, lovely man though he is."

Huw stood facing into the woods, trying to compose himself. When he turned to look at her, a combination of confusion and desire swept over him. "But you won't give me away, Sara Murtrey, free mercenary woman." His tone was light, and his roguish smile charmed her. "I just have to make it through the Bekenberg Pass. I have to reach the North and get away from Murfee's men and anyone who might be from the South. Keep my secret until then, please?"

"But why?" Her mind suddenly made the connection. "Balen Owyn—you must be his son. Your voice is his when you forget to use that silly low-country accent and so is your face, as his must have been as a young man. You're the right age, he told me he had a son near my age. Why are you on the run and posing as the lack-witted nephew of Bear Tavysh?" Sara was exactly the same height as him. Huw found himself enjoying that her face and his were at the same level, so close he could kiss her. He was perilously close to abandoning caution.

She possessed a certain strength. It reminded him of Sinean without the hard veneer of bravado Sinean had always affected, while trying to make her way in a man's world. Sara was a competent woman, completely sure of herself, with nothing to prove. Huw could tell she also felt the physical attraction that sparked between them, as the interest in her eyes betrayed.

"The Bear is actually married to my cousin Mora. He took me in and helped me, because Balen's dead and there's no guild for me to take over," Huw said, trying to keep the bitterness out of his voice and failing. "There're no bards left in the Long Valley at all now I'm gone, of this I'm quite sure. I'm dead too, so far as anyone knows. It has to be this way, do you understand?"

"No! I don't understand. This is terrible," she said, her voice conveying the truth of her words. "I'm sorry to hear Balen is dead, more than sorry. He was a dear friend to my father and me." Tears sprang to her eyes, and Huw was grateful for her compassion. "I don't understand, but I accept it's true."

"If you go to the Long Valley, you'll hear the sad tale. I really can't talk about it now. Someone might overhear." He felt compelled to turn the conversation to more cheerful things. "I confess I don't enjoy playing the lack-wit, but the circumstances require a good disguise," Huw said, and assumed his vacant grin and let his eye wander. "How's this?"

"Oh lord, Jaky! You *are* ugly when you do that even without the warts and missing teeth, which I've been assured decorate your unfortunate face!" She laughed, wiping her tears away with the back of her hand. "I know your name's not Jaky, but I don't remember what Balen told me his son's name was. I was just a girl then."

"Jaky will do until I make my way to Bekenberg," he replied, desire lighting his eyes and mischief in his grin. "The Ravens work out of Bekenberg town, so Murfee's men say. I hear you're their captain."

"Yes, I lead the Ravens," Sara said. She was breathless, and her pulse beat in her throat. "Are you looking to join up? We could use a lad like you."

"You travel to the Eynier Valley and Ludwellyn far too often," Huw said, with regret. "I can't go back there, ever. If *you* recognized me, someone else will, so I dare not chance it. Far too many people, both Grefyn and Weyllyn, would kill me if they find out my secret. They'd do it for the golden reward offered by Clan Grefyn for the merest rumor of a bard. The fact I'm a tinker's son wouldn't help either, nowadays."

"What are you planning to do?" She boldly took his hand. At her touch, the world stopped for a moment, and Huw had to force himself to breathe. Her invitation for more than conversation was clear and honest.

Huw had become used to his enforced celibacy by not thinking about it. Sara's arrival at the shelter had made him intensely aware of that scarcity in his life. Now, with lust nearly blinding him to everything else, Huw managed to answer, "I'm going to the far North, perhaps to find a friend of mine, a knight. He's a mercenary, so you may know him." He answered her unspoken question. "Lackland. There are many stories swirling around him, and I want to write them. The Bear tells me I'm still a bard, and if I am, then I must follow Lackland."

The physical attraction between the two was palpable, sizzling like lightning. "Oh, I do know him." Her breath caught as she remembered the last time she had seen the knight, despite her attraction to Huw. "Why am I not surprised to hear Jaky Tavysh knows the Great Knight? Lackland truly *is* the sort of hero bards tell epic tales about!"

Huw felt a flash of jealousy and chided himself. "Every woman must surely desire him. It's part of who he is, the knight in shining armor."

"He's that and more," she laughed at his brief flare of possessiveness. "We have on occasion been lovers, but Lackland's heart belongs to Lady Mags De Leon and always will. He worships her, but she's like me. She won't give up her sword and marry him, ever. Many stories surround Lackland and they all have a kernel of truth to them," Sara replied, her clear grey eyes meeting his dark blue ones. "I'll tell you where you'll find him. He lodges in the village of Limpwater, at an inn called Billy's Revenge."

"Thank you, Sara. When I last saw him, the place he said he lived was young and unnamed."

Unable to stop himself, Huw pulled her close to him, kissing her deeply, surprised by her eager response that set his blood on fire.

Her hands were firm but sensual on his back, sending chills up his spine. As her lips touched his, warm and demanding, desire swept away all sense of caution. The tightening in his loins made itself quite evident, pressing against her. She responded with an intensity that matched his, firing his ardor even more.

Glancing over his shoulder at the longhouse, he took Sara's hand and pulled her toward the woods, saying, "At least we know the wood-wraith is dead. God knows what else lurks out here."

Following him, she laughed, saying "Why don't you show me what else lurks out here, Jaky. Is it something I'm going to enjoy?" They stopped once they were out of sight of the shelter. She began unfastening his belt and unbuttoning his breeches. They came down and he stepped out of them. Her hands stroked the length of his manhood with appreciation.

"I think you might," he said breathlessly, as he unbuttoned her bodice, pushing her gown down over her shoulders and taking it off. "I think you might like it a lot." As her breasts came free, white and beautiful in the moonlight, he kissed first one and then the other. She closed her eyes, lips parted in pleasure. Huw's lips returned to hers, and his hands cupped Sara's buttocks, pulling her against his hard manhood.

Soon they lay on Huw's cloak. He caressed her smooth skin, enjoying the feel of her breasts in his hands. "I've been without a lover for a long while," he whispered in her ear. "It wasn't a problem until *you* walked into the shelter."

"You're a passionate man, Jaky, but don't be thinking I've fallen in love with you. I'm a big-hearted woman," she replied breathlessly, responding to his kisses. "Tomorrow I'll be on the road going south and this'll be but a happy memory until the next lad comes along." Her breath caught as he nuzzled her neck and gently nibbled her earlobe. "Ohhhh...a *very* happy memory, I'm sure." Her body rose to meet his kisses.

Huw laughed, low and wicked. "Forever isn't on my mind either. But we're here now, so why not enjoy tonight while we have it?" In response, Sara's lips and hands were warm, demanding and very sure. Huw's own breath caught as her hands once again found the shaft of his manhood, caressing him. He whispered, "Go slowly, love. Don't rush it. This is about you as much as me." Her throaty laugh stirred his blood, but her hands obediently moved to his waist and back.

Huw lay completely spent, utterly relaxed and feeling as if more than the sexual tension within him had been eased in their lovemaking. Lying in the moonlit woods, they held each other, talking quietly about what he'd have to do to get to the village of Limpwater. "It's a new village, just starting to grow up around Billy's Revenge and the Rowdies. King Henri insisted on granting Billy a patent to build a town there," she told him. "When you get to Bekenberg, go to the Raven's Nest. It's outside the gate on the East Road to Vyennes. I'll give you a letter to show Matteus, my partner and lieutenant. You may have to wait a week or more, but someone will have business in Castleton, and you'll be able to make the trip to Limpwater with them. They'll stop but one night with the Rowdies and leave the next day, but you'll stay and join up with Billy."

They lay there, talking until the mosquitoes found them. Laughing, they hurried into their clothes and began walking back to the shelter.

"Let's stop in the stable, Jaky. I'll give you a proper mercenary's haircut by the light of the lantern, one a bard would never wear. You don't need to hide your face anymore, and you look bloody awful," Sara said. "From now on, Jaky Tavysh is on the run from some sort of trouble involving a woman." At the sudden grin on his face, she laughed and said, "It's probably true! You do like the ladies, and I'd bet they all like you. I surely do." She caressed his bicep. "A proper trim will change your face completely. You must keep the low-country accent while you're with them, though."

The stable end of the shelter loomed in the dark, and her eyes gleamed as she nodded toward it. "Maybe we should sleep in there tonight, what do you think?" Her hand strayed down below his belt, and she laughed low and sexy, as his interest in her was once again apparent and standing firm. "This part of you is in agreement with me!"

"You might keep the others awake, with how much you enjoy my companionship," Huw replied with an impish grin, enjoying her boldness and unashamed sexuality. "You're not a shy lady, not at all!"

"No, Jaky, I'm not. I know who I am, and what I want. You'll find all the lady mercenaries are like me in this regard." She giggled, tugging at his ragged curls. "If I'm too long without a man, even ugly lads with bad haircuts begin to look good to me! My scissors are in my saddlebags. I'll trim you up first, and then we'll have more fun!"

Pulling her firmly against his lean, hard body, Huw kissed her, saying, "I confess I'll miss my peasant hair!

In some ways I've had more fun being poor unfortunate Jaky than you can imagine. You've no idea how much I've learned by being invisible!"

The next day Sara and her crew continued south, and Murfee's caravan climbed toward the high falls, where the River Limpwater fell from the high plateau to the head of the Long Valley far below. Huw could feel Derik's eyes on him intermittently all morning. Indeed, at some point, every man in Murfee's crew looked at Jaky speculatively. Finally Derik could stand it no longer.

"Jaky…last night…you and Sara…." Derik didn't know how to courteously ask his burning question. "Well, she does have a reputation for liking men who aren't real pretty, but, ah, you were out all night with her. She don't usually offer a man a whole night of her company."

"I was raised to be polite, Derik. I won't discuss her, it's not right." Huw maintained his thick accent as Sara had advised. He continued riding, letting his hood fall back. "It's going to be warm out again today, isn't it?" He fingered the thin braid just under his left ear, all that was left of his hair that Mora had cut to shoulder length. Sara had left it and braided it for him, saying, "This little tail marks you as a northern mercenary and from here on out, you'll never cut it. The length of it marks how long you've been in the trade."

Before Mora had hacked off his long curls, they had fallen nearly to his hips. He'd never cut it, because long flowing hair was part and parcel of the trade. Even the ones who were bald on top had worn what they had long and loose and kept it well cared for. "Hair as long as a bard's" was a saying that had worked its way into the general speech of the valley. Now, except for the thin braided tail, it was as short as a northern soldier's. He liked the freedom of it so much he decided he'd wear his hair in the mercenary style forever, no matter what course his life took. "I think it's going to be as warm this afternoon as it was yesterday."

Derik stared back at him in shock. "Warm...yes...." Derik began laughing, roaring so hard Murfee turned on his wagon seat to see what had him in stitches. "God, Jaky! Aren't you the dog! We haven't looked at you since we left Clythe, you sneaky bastard!" Derik's hoots echoed through the forest. "And she cut your hair in the northern style too." Howling with laughter, he demanded to know what he was on the run from, to go to such lengths to escape the valley. "It has to be trouble over a woman, after what went on last night!"

"I ran afoul of folks of the Crow variety," Huw replied, slightly red-faced. "Jak, the tinker's son, is no longer welcome in the Eynier Valley. My mum passed on and the Bear thinks enough of me to help me out, so here I am."

"The Bear *must* think highly of you, going to all the trouble he did," replied Derik once he quit laughing. "You played the part so well, none of us wanted to really look at you."

Huw let his eye wander, just enough to send Derik into a fit again.

Chapter 14 Death on Two Legs

Murfee's caravan arrived at the Upper Eyn Falls and the shelter that marked the high point of the lower trade road. This was where the trek through the Claith Mountains truly began. The river fell in a torrent, tumbling down the canyon in a series of waterfalls so high that Huw couldn't see the bottom. A constant mist rose from the several tiers between the top of the falls and the bottom, some 3,000 feet below, marking where the river continued to the Lower Falls. From this point on, Huw was well and truly out of the Eynier Valley, had reached the high country and would be traveling in a mountainous wilderness. Even the valleys and plains of Wald were much higher in altitude than the Long Valley of Eyn.

He stood clutching a tree, looking down the cataract, amazed by the incredible sight of all that water roaring and tumbling, dropping from a great height to land in the valley below. The thundering noise deafened him, but it also soothed him in some obscure way. He thought about the creatures he'd seen in the last three days. The bear that prowled behind the longhouse looking for scraps in the compost heap seemed friendly and safe in its commonplace normalcy. It was neither friendly nor safe, as Huw knew full well, but surely nothing could be worse than the wood-wraith.

"Jaky-lad! We need to talk." Murfee's bulk loomed, and Huw turned and walked over to his side. "Why didn't you fess up to me in Clythe? Don't you trust me?"

Huw had been expecting this. "Yes sir, with my life. But the Bear tells me to do something, and I do it. He knows what's best." As he'd hoped, Murfee nodded, accepting the truth of it. "You know he has to cater to the Crows as well as Weyllyn. Some who'd kill me come through town regularly when they're sweeping the valley, and he didn't want any trouble in his tap room. It was my own fault I had to run, and he didn't have to help me, but he did. I owe it to him to do as he wishes."

"How the bloody hell did you get involved with the Crows anyhow? You're not as stupid as you pretend to be, but *that's* stupid." Murfee's sharp eyes held him, demanding the full story.

Huw didn't want to be dishonest, so he didn't lie. "I can't tell you the whole truth, Murf. If it was only *my* life, I'd tell you it all, I swear, but several on the Grefyn side of the river helped me, people whose lives depend on my keeping what happened close. I was run out of the South over something I can't talk about, and if it comes out I'm alive and well this far north, questions will be asked about who helped me along the way. I can't have that, Murf. I've lost too many loved ones over this already.

"If you believe me to be a thief or traitor, I'll have to live with it, and I'll understand if you don't want my assistance anymore. The Bear is married to my mum's cousin, Mora. My mum's dead now, and they took me in. Mora came up with my disguise so the Crows wouldn't recognize me when they came through town, and here I am. I'm going north where I've a friend, and I'll start over there."

"I know you're not a traitor or a thief. I've a sixth sense about such. Anyway, the Bear wouldn't vouch for you if you were, relative or not. I sense the truth in what you're saying. A woman must be involved or you'd be more forthcoming," Murfee laughed at the look of shock on Huw's face. "But lad, you'd best keep your breeches buttoned if you want to avoid trouble in the future." He winked, saying, "Sara's known to be willful in that way. All the women mercs are."

Red-faced, Huw nodded, thankful that Murfee accepted him. Much to his relief, the men accepted Jaky's transformation and didn't recognize him as Huw Owyn. Perhaps it was because of the new haircut. He still behaved exactly the way he had since leaving Clythe, accepting his place as the new lad and doing the chores expected of him. He stayed quiet, hanging in the background and rarely offering an opinion. Over the last months, Huw had grown used to speaking with the slow, thick, low-country accent the others all had, and his speech pattern was still that of Jaky Tavysh. He rarely had to think about it anymore.

Huw was unaware of the true changes that had transformed him. He'd lost every trace of the youthful arrogance that marked him so clearly when he was posted in Clythe the year before. His humble demeanor was no act; he was a different man than he'd been only months before. Few people would connect him with the proud bard who'd once graced them with his presence.

"The Bear's wife must really have cared for your ma to go to that much trouble to see you safely out of the valley," an older guard, Lorne, said as Jaky brought in an armload of firewood.

"Everyone loved my mum," Huw replied with absolute truthfulness. "She was a good soul who never hurt anyone. She deserved better than…a fool for a son." He was silent for the rest of the evening, consumed with thoughts of his mother.

After a good night's sleep, he'd shaken off his melancholy, and as they began the final climb to the pass, he was feeling quite cheerful and had to forcibly restrain himself from humming. Huge drops of water occasionally fell from the branches overhead, meaning a torrent must have been falling for anything to filter down to the narrow dark road. By mid-morning the rain became a drizzle, then stopped, but the damp air was muggy. They removed their cloaks, vainly hoping to get some vagrant breeze to cool them inside their armor.

At midday they halted briefly at a wide clearing where many caravans had stopped before, to have a bit of lunch and cool their horses and the oxen. Huw was relieving himself just beyond a low shrub when the hairs on the back of his neck rose. For some unaccountable reason, he had the notion that something big and bad was watching him.

Tucking himself back into his breeches, he glanced around, seeing nothing. Nervously he looked up, and saw one huge, golden eye peering down at him as a robin might look at a worm. For a moment he was disoriented, wondering if he was imagining it.

Suddenly, he was knocked off his feet as Fat Pat's immense body slammed into him. Just as they hit the dirt, a blast of fire blew over their heads, setting the little shrub alight right where he'd been standing only a few moments before. Something huge raced over the top of them, narrowly missing stepping on them as together, the two of them rolled away from the gigantic three-toed feet. "What the hell *is* that?" The terror in Huw's voice made him shrill. "It nearly mashed us flat!"

"It's a bloody firedrake," groaned Pat as he rolled off of Huw. "God help us—it's a big one, too!"

"Firedrake! Firedrake!" The sounds of men scurrying to do battle were interspersed with Murfee screaming at his drivers to get the wagons to safety.

Pat leapt to his feet and frantically stomped out the flaming shrub. "Once we get the teams to safety, us drivers will put out any fires the damned thing starts while you guards are fighting it, Jaky—we sure as hell don't want to be caught in the middle of a forest fire!" He yanked Huw to his feet. "Stay nimble!"

"Thanks for having my back—I owe you!" Huw ran toward the clearing and the noise, drawing his sword as he came to the scene. Pat made it back to his wagon, wrestling his team around and forcing them to go further up the road, away from the battle.

The beast was both horrific and amazing. Standing more than twice their height and obviously male, he had an immense body covered in red scales that shone like copper when he wandered into the few shafts of sunlight that pierced the foliage. His legs were long and tremendously strong, clearly made for running. At each side of his massive chest was a short little arm, which seemed strange on such a gigantic creature. Both had wicked-looking three-fingered hands, which ended in deadly, sharp talons. Those tiny hands were doubtless quite good for grasping and holding on to his prey while eating it.

His long, sinuous neck and huge, triangular head whipped back and forth as he tried to decide which human he was going to fry. Occasional blasts of fire lit up the clearing.

At the rear of the beast was an incredibly long, whip-like tail that lashed faster than any Huw had ever seen. This was one more deadly weapon in the creature's arsenal.

Grison reached the opposite side of the clearing at the same time as Huw, and Bryce stopped at Grison's left side. The men began circling the firedrake, which seemed surprised they weren't running and watched them warily.

"This is the biggest firedrake I've ever heard of," muttered Bryce, shifting his sword from hand to hand. "But I've only seen one once, four years ago. I thought it was big," he laughed harshly. "It was only half the size of this thing. I fear we don't have enough men to do the job on this."

Bil shouted, "Spread out, lads, and stay nimble. Don't let it get you with its fire-breath!"

"Watch out for the tail! It'll knock you senseless," Lorne called to Huw. "Once you're down, he's likely to crush you, because he doesn't see too well unless you're moving. If he steps on you, you're dead."

"Jaky!" From across the clearing Derik shouted, "Your only chance is to keep him confused. Throw things past his head once in a while to keep him distracted." Derik threw a branch and the huge maw snapped at it, catching it mid-toss, and as it did so, Bil and Grison got in a few slashes with no effect on the creature. Huw began searching the ground and tossing things, alternating with Derik. Lorne and Bryce alternated with Bil and Grison. Periodically, the men were able to get in a few whacks, but all too often they were dodging fire, ducking the nasty, whipping tail or evading the firedrake's vicious snapping jaws.

The air reeked of sulfur and some other noxious fume that burned the inside of Huw's nose and lungs, clouding his eyes with tears. The cacophonous bellowing and thunderous stamping of the beast's feet deafened them. Huw knew without a doubt he was going to die this time. *There's no way we can kill this thing...Aaugh!* He ducked and dodged to the left, barely avoiding the fiery blast and flinging a medium-sized stick past the monster's head as he did so. The firedrake caught it. Splinters and wood chips sprayed out the sides of its massive jaws as it crushed the branch. *Holy God in heaven, he's quick!*

Confusion ensued as the men each dashed forward to slash at the enraged beast while it was occupied with lashing out at the others. Alternately they leapt back, ducking or tossing a branch to distract it. The men struggled relentlessly to stay moving and out of the maddened creature's line of sight, and still get in a few good hacks with their swords.

The mêlée seemed to stretch on forever, and as Huw became tired, he began to slow. Suddenly he was grazed by the fire-breath. His left arm caught the blast and he rolled away in agony. His glove and the parts of his sleeve not covered by armor were set ablaze. Quickly he smothered the flames, the sleeve of his chainmail red-hot and cooking him. That torture spurred him to nimbleness like nothing else. All he could think was, *I don't want to die this way! God in heaven, I don't want to go like a sausage that fell into the fire!*

Desperately Huw continued fighting despite the intense pain in his now useless left hand. Somewhere along the way, Huw noticed it was just he, Derik and Bil still fighting.

After what felt like hours, Bil got in a lucky swing and had the creature hamstrung. It lay thrashing on its side, but still the men could rarely get close enough to the beast to do any more damage. Huw stumbled across a sword, and without thinking he picked it up and threw it, hoping to hit an eye. He heaved it just as the creature opened its mouth to snap at Bil.

The sword entered the gaping maw and sank to the hilt, impaling the soft tissue in the creature's throat. The firedrake writhed in the dirt, gagging, struggling vainly to dislodge it with his little arms. The high-pitched keening shredded the hearing of everyone in its range. At last they were able to swarm the creature, the three of them hacking at it until they succeeded in finally cutting the great head off, ending the battle.

The silence was deafening, and Huw reeled. "I don't know about you lads, but someone else is going to have to bury this thing. I'm knackered." The pain of his injuries rushed in, causing him to drop his sword. Huw fell to his knees, puking his guts up. The last thing he saw was the clearing slowly spinning, as he fell forward into a soft pool of darkness.

Chapter 15 Tinker's Tales

Groaning and feeling as if his left hand was on fire, Huw woke, wondering where he was. Finally he realized he was lying in a moving wagon. "We're almost at the pass, Jaky. Don't worry, we're almost there." He knew he should recognize the voice, but it was too much effort, the pain overwhelming. He was in agony all the way up to his neck. "Majiked healing balm…friend gave me…my saddlebags…." Once again the merciful darkness claimed him.

When Huw woke again, his arm felt as if it were encased in ice, which was far better than fire, but still not really comfortable. As his senses returned, he saw they were in a roadside shelter. When he looked around, Murfee said, "Good. I dosed you with poppy, and the healing balm is starting to work. You've been out for a good while—it's close to supper time. We just buried Lorne, Grison, and Bryce." His eyes filled with tears as he said, "I've never lost any lads to a firedrake, and I don't know how I'll tell their wives. Bryce was my sister's son."

Huw nodded. "Bil and Derik—are they…?" His voice came out as a croak.

"Other than a few singes, scrapes and bruises, they're fine, lad, just tired," replied Murfee. "They're outside, still helping Fat Pat to sort out the teams and wagons."

"Pat saved my life when that thing first ambushed us," said Huw. "I need to thank him. Thank you for helping me, but I should get outside and help them now." He noticed he was only seeing out of one eye. "What happened to my eye?" He tried to sit up. His throat was raw from the acrid fumes of the firedrake's flames, and he ached everywhere.

Murfee pushed him back down. "A firedrake happened to it, lad! You fell on a rock when you fainted. You've a black eye. I put a compress on it, and it'll heal. You can't do anything until the balm has time to work its majik on your arm anyway, so just lay back. We'll be here for several more days while you finish healing, and everyone gets a chance to rest up. We can't really move you just yet, and the boys are all shook up," said Murfee, not looking at him fully. "You waking up enough to tell me about your majik balm was a stroke of luck. I had to root around a bit in your saddlebags, but I found it and got it on you as soon as I could."

Huw's heart stopped as he heard what Murfee was actually saying.

"It's a wondrous balm, Jaky. You're a lucky man. I took care of you as soon as you told me about it. Someone values you highly to give you such a gift," Murfee's soft voice confirmed his fears. "You're going to be scarred up pretty badly, but I think you'll be able to play your lute. Your hand is healing even as we speak." Huw could see Murfee's own questions went unasked. "You'll keep your eye."

"Do you know who I am, then?" Huw asked, knowing he'd given himself away when he'd told

Murfee to look in his bags. There was no going back now, and he'd have died without the medicine.

"I do. I recognized that lute. Only one man I know plays a bowed-lute, though the bow seems to be missing. Only one like that exists in all of Waldeyn, made of cherry and inlaid with rosewood and abalone. The sound is deeper and richer than any other lute in the land. It's the most beautiful and unique instrument I've ever seen, and I know very well who the man was who made it for his journeyman's piece." Murfee chuckled wryly. "With your disguise as Ugly-Jak, I didn't recognize you, so maybe no one else will. You changed the way you speak and besides, when you were posted in Clythe, you had the beard and all that long hair. I sure didn't recognize who you were even this morning, so maybe the others won't. You managed to tell me the truth without telling me anything, and that's a bard's skill if ever there was one." He paused as if he had something else to say but had to think about it. "My brother is first mate on a Weyllyn ship, did you know? For House Alenmor, the very house Murfee's Merchandise does business with. Verle's wife, Orla, is a potter, and she lived in the Artists' Quarter."

Huw's heart sank, but he nodded, fearing he knew where this conversation was going.

"The Dolphin had just docked in port one day last March. Verle stopped to buy some flowers on his way home to see his wife and kiddies, from the old lady on the corner of Bards' Street. As he walked, Verle saw something that bothers him to this day. Two men he recognized were hung there like common thieves." Murfee sighed. "This happened just before the guild hall mysteriously caught fire, killing every last bard and taking the city with it. I'll keep your secret, don't fear. You've more than earned that from me." He looked Huw in the eye, and Huw saw trust and respect there.

"Murfee, I've tried to tell the truth all along as well as I could, but I have to protect someone I care about, so how I made it all the way to Clythe will have to remain a secret. My grandfather was born a tinker, as was my father. I am a tinker's son. It was our heritage that shaped the Bards' Guild, though for obvious reasons we never made that known. After all, tinkers are the lowest of the low, used by everyone and respected by no one. With their stigma, tinkers have no chance to own property. Oh yes, we're wanted to mend broken pots or play a sweet tune. The bully-boys abuse our wives and mothers as if they were common whores and then run us out of town. God forbid we should ask for proper payment for our work.

"The minute a tinker's family walks into town, chickens begin to vanish. It never occurs to the irate owners there's little place to hide ten stolen chickens when all you own in the world is on your back. Where the chickens disappear to is always a mystery, but, of course, tinkers pay the price for someone else's stolen dinner. 'Tinkers in town' is the perfect opportunity for the local thugs and villains to get away with any sort of mayhem, including murder. After all, lynching tinker men, women and children is a favorite pastime for bullies and Crows nowadays. Just look at the abuses the traveling people have suffered since the mess in Ludwellyn. The murder of a tinker is considered to be no great loss." Huw couldn't disguise the bitterness in his voice. "Were you ever told how tinkers became traveling people, homeless and scorned by all?"

Murfee shook his head. "No. They've just always been, haven't they?"

"No, there have only been tinkers since the years just before the joining, when the great houses were jockeying for position and trying desperately to cement their own boundaries and alliances. Those wanderers you know as tinkers were once the teachers and scholars of the great Library of Eyn."

Understanding dawned on Murfee's face, and he said, "The great library…hundreds of years ago the old Grefyn grew angry at the scholars who spoke out against his alliance with the Lanques. It's said he discovered they were spreading dangerous knowledge, though what that could be, I have no idea. He seized their lands and possessions, and burned the university to the ground along with the great library, so their 'dangerous knowledge' wouldn't contaminate Eyn. Then the Crows whipped their leaders. After that, Grefyn's Crows turned their dogs on them, driving them into the wilds. He branded them as traitors and forbade anyone to offer them food or shelter. No one knows what happened to them."

"All knowledge is dangerous to those who clutch at their power, Murfee. This is why the nobility of both clans in the valley encourage illiteracy and ignorance. Those teachers and scholars were shunned and run out of every town and village. Still, Aubryn Owyn, the last Master of the Library, not only survived the terrible whipping they gave him, he saw a way to get even. He determined he'd have his revenge by spreading the knowledge and history of Eyn, despite the taint and difficulties of the scholars' new, unfamiliar lives. He gathered the survivors and their families together, telling them that since they were no longer allowed to settle and own property, they'd embrace the traveling life. They'd use the fact they were never allowed to stay in one place as a way to keep the knowledge they had alive. He'd accomplish this by putting the truth to simple songs and ditties. Aubryn and two other old professors taught the others to play the simple pipes, flutes and bodhráns they were able to craft.

"Using those instruments, Aubryn and the others spread the knowledge they gathered, taking the news from one town to the next in catchy little tunes even the Crows found themselves singing. They carried the culture of Eyn on their backs, in their instruments and their colorful garb and tents, or in the few brightly painted wagons. Since books could be burned, they wrote the sagas and epic tales on scrolls that could be hidden anywhere, but more importantly they were memorized for safekeeping. They put the history of Eyn into rhymes, sonnets and songs with popular tunes anyone with an ear would pick up and sing without knowing the truth behind the music.

"Pushed from town to town, the traveling people survived by making and selling small musical instruments, mending pots and playing music for coins. Soon everyone was playing the bodhráns and flutes sold by tinkers and singing songs that told the true history of Eyn. The old song 'Emmitt Talog's Cornfield Burns' isn't just about the laughable antics of a farmer and a disaster. It's the true account of the torching of a peasant's cornfield. Emmitt Talog refused to allow his liege, Earl Dunnings, to rape his daughter on the night before her wedding, and the earl took action against him. Three hundred years later, children are still singing this song and skipping rope to it, laughing at 'fat old Dunnings who thought he was a lad, when everyone knew he was dirty and bad.'

"As new events unfolded, more songs found their way from village to village. This is how the truth was kept alive. This is what the traveling people live to protect. The bards were the lightning rod, the obvious source that draws attention from the real keepers of the history. Now they're gone, but tinkers are the true guardians of the history of Eyn, and they remain.

"My grandfather was Taryn Owyn. He was a direct descendant of Aubryn Owyn. Taryn saw many sad things on his travels, things he couldn't understand. He wanted to change the valley for the better, to make life less difficult, not just for the Owyns but all the commoners living under the yoke of the nobility. Despite what most people believe, tinkers only want to have some small part of what the rest of the people in the valley have. They desire a home and a chance to live comfortably, but the stigma of being thieves and traitors is more than we as a people can overcome. We know we'll wander forever, but Taryn had an idea.

"All the best entertainers are tinkers, but Taryn wanted to give them respectability—a way to make the nobles welcome them into the highest places. Creating the guild was his way of giving a voice to the common man who has no say in his own future. He chose only the tinker lads who were born with eidetic memory and perfect pitch and educated them in every aspect of musicianship. Tinkers from all over the valley brought their children to the guild to be tested, but the gift of memory is rare and only a few qualified. We've never had more than fifty at a time.

"Those few were taught from the hand-scribed copies of the precious volumes that were saved from the ashes of the library, which was once the glory of Eyn. These special entertainers were to be the voice of the people, without drawing attention to the fact they were spreading the true history in the old sagas. Taryn called the exceptional ones bards after the bards of old. By virtue of having a visible guild hall in Ludwellyn, they separated themselves from the stigma of being tinkers and gained a legitimacy that allowed them entrance to the highest of the nobles' homes. Taryn, in turn, passed the books and the craft down to my father, Balen, who meant to pass them on to me. Now, even those precious few ancient volumes are gone, turned to ash by yet another of Grefyn's greedy, blood-soaked, toadying thugs. There's always fire in payment for us Owyns whenever we reach too high." Huw coughed, wincing as his bruised ribs protested.

"What happened to your mother? Balen had a wife who was a crafter. I remember hearing it." Murfee's expression said he suspected what the answer would be.

"Mum still lived in her old family home outside of Maury. She was murdered." Huw's voice broke. "The Crows nesting around Maury killed her right after the mess in Ludwellyn because she was known to be Balen's wife. Probably all the wives and mothers have met the same fate. The Crows placed the stigma of being traitors on us again, so anyone who takes a dislike to us will abuse us. I don't think my mum knew I survived. The Bear is married to mum's cousin, Mora, and they're all the family I have left. He's as much a father to me as Balen was. When Sinean refused to flee north with me, I was heart-hurt. But the Bear was right about her. She was never the marrying kind." He fell silent as Murfee carefully removed the bandages that covered Huw's arm to check on his burns.

Tsking at the scalded mess the firedrake had made, Murfee said, "He cooked you good, Hu—Jaky, but at least you lived." He carefully looked at the skin from the elbow to the wrist, where it was worst, and then at his upper arm and as much of his shoulder as he could see. From his bicep up, Huw was pink and had a few blisters, but it wasn't too bad. Murfee made Huw drink a poppy-laced tea for the pain and then reapplied balm where he thought it was needed, especially on the wrist. "It's going to leave some terrible scars, but it's already healing. You can practically see the balm working its majik. Your friend's gift saved your hand and maybe your life."

Huw looked at his arm and hand. He was taken aback at what the firedrake had done to his flesh, but he'd known it was bad before he saw it. The memory of the pain was still sharp in his mind. He had to swallow at the thought of the three men he'd only just gotten to know, who didn't make it. He burst out hoarsely, "God, Murfee, it's not fair—Lorne, Grison and Bryce—three good men, gone like that. It's just so wrong."

"Yes. It is that, lad." Murfee was silent for a moment, tears filling his eyes. He lightened the conversation. "The Crows nesting around Maury, they'd be House Doleyn." Huw nodded, and Murfee continued. "You might be interested to know their earl and his sons are all dead. They lost their bid to take the coronet back, and it cost them dearly. Their bones may still decorate the walls of the Grefyn Palace in Ludwellyn, for all I know. Doleyn is no more, and once again a Crow of House Lyndys wears the coronet of Grefyn, this time with twice as much land and gold as he had before."

"The winners take all when the clans battle within themselves, and the women and children pay the price." Tears filled Huw's good eye and ran down his cheek, although he couldn't understand why he was crying for the clan who'd brutally killed his mother. "It's always been that way, but it's barbaric. With the guild dead, there's no one to keep a rein on the nobility now. It's as good a time as any to leave the valley."

"Don't worry, I won't tell anyone what lies hidden in your saddlebags. The lads would keep your secret, but the fewer who know, the less likely you are to be discovered," said Murfee, after he finished checking Huw's arm, smearing a bit more balm on his face and his eyelid and covering his eye again with a fresh bandage. "I understand why you're so desperate to leave the Long Valley. I wouldn't want the Bear to be punished for harboring a bard. He'd be treated harshly, the way things are right now. In fact, I'd say you're likely to be a marked man just for your father's political leanings, even if you personally didn't draw their attention. Balen was known to be a controversial man in some ways."

Huw agreed, nodding, unable to trust himself to speak much beyond a strangled "thank you." He was grateful to know the ones who'd coldly executed his mother had met their own messy end, but thinking of the fates of the women and children of that ill-starred family made him sick. Finally he said, "Justice in the Eynier Valley regularly harms the innocent more than the guilty. I've given up seeking justice. Too many people suffer for it. I say let the winners have the valley." The poppy and the majik of the balm began to work and he yawned, drifting off again. "Fewer people get hurt that way."

Murfee patted Huw's good shoulder, letting him sleep.

The healing balm worked amazingly well and fast, causing Huw to wonder what sort of connections Lackland had that he could so casually give away a pot of such high quality medicine. Even so, four days passed before Huw was able to use his hand completely, and Murfee had been right. It was never going to be pretty. Still, he had the full use of it, and that was what counted. He secretly stretched his fingers and worked them despite the discomfort, knowing if he didn't keep them limber he'd never play the lute again. Now he was impatient to get to a place where he could actually play his instruments, but knew it'd be a week or more. The fact he could still use his hand was a miracle, and he was grateful for that mercy. *Lackland saved my life*, he thought as he finished saddling Blackberry on the morning they finally continued their journey. *I'd have lost my hand or died from the* putrefaction. That's what usually kills folks who've been badly burned. Just the thought made him queasy.

"Can you handle riding tail by yourself?" Bil stood in the doorway. "We've only the three of us and I need Derik to ride center. The drivers are all ready to jump into any fray. That firedrake put the fear of God into them."

"If I can't, I'll be too dead to tell you, but we don't really have a choice," Huw grinned at Bil's expression. "Someone has to do it. Tail is the new lad's job, and I don't mind it."

"It should be pretty simple. Might see some cats or highwaymen now we're coming into the pass," Bil shrugged. "There're no trees to speak of near the road up there. Henri's men keep the few that grow in that sort of altitude cut well back. Those remaining never grow much above head-high. Cats and bears don't have anywhere to hide, so they don't come near the road very often. The highwaymen usually lurk around blind corners and hit the leaders of a caravan when they're forced into working up there. The weather is fierce much of the time at the pass. Only the most desperate will choose the summit for their ambush."

"I think I can handle most anything. My arm's good now - even my wrist and fingers work well enough. I can use the knives with no trouble, and my sword arm was never hurt. Now the black eye is healing, I can see again too." Huw laughed. "I'll be glad to get back on the road."

"Fat Pat's insisting on driving tail, in case you need backup. He's sure you saved us all when you threw

Lorne's sword down the firedrake's throat. " Bil's face broke into a grin. "I know for a fact you saved my life with that little trick, so thank you. I was so beat I could barely lift my sword, and death was staring me in the eye. In some stupid way, I was looking forward to dying, just to be done with the fight."

"It was a lucky throw. I'm glad it worked, but I scarcely knew what I was doing. When I threw it, I hoped to get him in the eye, but missed," replied Huw, elbowing Blackberry in the gut and tightening the girth straps. He turned and looked at Bil solemnly, admitting, "That firedrake was the worst thing I've ever seen in my life. I was terrified, exhausted and certain I was going to die. I don't know how we managed to kill it." He shook his head in wonder.

"They're all still laughing about you refusing to bury the damned thing," Bil's chuckle faded. "Everyone knew you were badly injured, and yet you kept at it. It's what mercs do, see? We just keep hacking away until we kill the beast or it kills us, whichever comes first. You've the makings of a good merc, whatever else you are." Bil turned and walked back into the shelter to make sure nothing had been left behind.

Huw stood wondering what he meant for a moment, then shrugging, led his horse outside.

The rest of the journey was fairly quiet. A pair of squatters from Lanqueshire had taken over the last shelter and had to be run off, but they put up no fight when Murfee told them to go to the nuns at Hyola, and they would be helped. Apparently that happened sometimes. Murfee groused about having to clean up their mess but just got on with it. By the time they rolled into Bekenberg a week later, Huw had grown used to his routine as a mercenary, doing his tasks automatically as if he'd been doing them all his life.

Chapter 16 Bekenberg

The town of Bekenberg was a collection of log huts surrounded by something called a stockade—walls made from tree trunks sunk into the ground like so many giant fence posts set cheek-by-jowl. Armed soldiers swung the enormous doors open as Murfee's caravan approached and stood guard as it entered the village. The gates closed behind them immediately after the last man passed through.

The village straddled the entrance to a large valley, and was situated on steep ground. The town itself was comprised of fifteen or so tiny one-room houses with steep thatched roofs and wide eaves. Glass shone in very few windows but the sturdy shutters were all thrown wide open. Continuing through the stockade on its way east, the trade road passed through the village center, with two manned towers flanking the gate.

Murfee led them past an immense, rundown inn. "The Broken Wheel isn't a good place to stop. Too many mercs from foreign parts stop over here because it's on the crossroads, so there's frequently trouble in the common room. It's cheaper and they don't ask questions, but I wouldn't stop there if it was the only place open in the North. The Raven's Nest is just outside the east gate," Derik told Huw. "Therese, Sara's mum, keeps it open while Sara's out on the road drumming up business, and Matteus St. Coeur maintains order. Matt's another noble with no land to inherit and finds life as a merc agreeable."

Murfee kept on going, driving through the tiny village and out the east gate, receiving nods and hellos from the guards posted there. Soon they pulled into the stable-yard, and the wagons were safely ensconced in an immense barn alongside several others heavily laden with goods. They led the horses to a stable opposite and left them in the care of the ostler, an older woman named Mayme.

"Don't worry, lad," she said, seeing Huw begin to unsaddle Blackberry and recognizing he was a new addition to Murfee's crew. "We'll take good care of your mounts. You go rest up from the road while you can. After you get settled, we've a decent enough bathhouse so you can wash the stink off. Since you're working for Murfee, you get your laundry done for free too," She pointed out the bathhouse and then turned to Murfee saying, "You're a few guards light and several days late, old man. What sort of trouble did you run into?"

Murfee gave her the story of their journey, winding it up by saying, "Three biggies between Clythe and the pass…it was the worst trip of my life. I don't think I can make this journey again, so I most likely won't be back this way. Our lads don't do firedrakes like you Northerners do."

"That's hard. We don't have to deal with them very often, thank God. I've only run into two in my whole time on the road," replied Mayme, grimly. "When you have a little advance warning one is lurking nearby, it's best to let the king's men handle them since they all have those fancy bespelled shields. We can't afford to lose people, and that's what happens when we run into a firedrake." She looked at the number of men he had with him and said, "You boys did well, taking on a firedrake and only losing three." She shrugged. "It's hard losing your mates though."

Murfee simply nodded and then changed the subject to one he was more interested in. "So, Mayme, my lovely flower of the North—are you off the road permanently then? You swore you'd die in the saddle, married to your sword!"

She grinned. "I did swear that, didn't I? I didn't count on living long enough to retire! Still, my scapegrace niece lets me muddle around here, pretending to help her out, so I'm still in the game. Alas, my sword's too slow nowadays for me to be out on the road. Someone could die, and I don't want to be the reason." As Mayme worked, she and Murfee reminisced about old times on the road, and then she shooed them all out of her stable. "I've got work to do, Murf, and flirting with you ain't getting it done! I'll see you at suppertime, so shoo! You can stow your things in my room if you want to bunk with me for old times' sake. You know the way."

"Aye, lass, if you're up for it, I am. You were always the best part of being on the road for me," Murfee replied, with a wicked glint in his eye and a broad smile. He led his crew out of the stable with a lighter step than when he entered it.

They stowed their saddlebags in their respective rooms and went down to the bath house. There were six tubs, each with a bench beside it for clean clothes and toiletries. On one end of the bench rested a rough but clean towel, and a bar of soap. Huw sat on the long bench by the door, waiting for his turn in a tub. An old man scurried about, filling tubs with buckets of water from an immense boiler, and refilling the buckets from a hand pump conveniently placed beside the cistern.

Murfee selected his tub, and began undressing. He stepped into the steaming water, sighing with relief as he did so. "Ahhh, that's good."

Two more hopeful bathers entered and sat on the bench beside Huw. Fortunately, everyone washed quickly out of courtesy to those who waited, and the old man was nimble, quickly rinsing out the tubs and refilling them. While Huw didn't get to loll in the water as he'd have liked, he did feel immensely better, and the feeling of wearing clean clothes was indescribable.

The Raven's Nest was an older inn and quite different from those of the Eynier Valley, being built of logs like the rest of the village. What the Southerners called the tap room was known as the common room. Huw entered it and sat with Murfee. "Where are the others?"

"Getting reacquainted with old friends. Most of my lads have worked with the Ravens at one time or another. They'll be here soon." Grinning and sliding a mug of ale toward him, Murfee said, "This one's on me. I know you'll be leaving us here." There were mugs waiting for the others, too. "My lads and I will stay here until the next caravan east leaves. It could be tomorrow or the next day, judging by the number of wagons in the barn. That'll get us to the high pass at

Wister. There we'll join a new caravan down into Vyennes. Where are you headed from here?"

"Castleton, I think," replied Huw. "I've a friend who's working for some mercs out of a town near there, and he said I'd be welcomed by his captain. He's the one who gave me the medicine."

"How do you plan to do this? Traveling gets rougher the further north you go until you get to Somber Flats. The condition of the road makes it nearly impossible to go with any speed between there and Castleton. I'd say it's a good week of travel to Somber Flats if you have good weather and a group to protect you. Who knows how long if the weather turns sour or you try to make it alone."

Huw's heart sank. He couldn't imagine how the road could be any worse than what he'd already been through. "Sara gave me a letter to give to her lieutenant," he said. "I hope to work my way north, if he'll let me."

"Well, that's what you should do then." He clasped Huw's shoulder. "You'd have made a good addition to my crew, but...."

"It's better this way," Huw smiled. "I'll let the Bear know where I end up, so you'll know I'm not wasting my life away when you worked so hard to save it."

"You'll land on your feet wherever you go, lad. You can make your way as an entertainer up here, you know. No one needs to know your past. In fact, you could play here tonight, if you've a mind to. Nothing fancy, just some songs anyone would know. The lads figured your story out even though I didn't tell them. It dawned on them where they knew you from when they saw you working your fingers, stretching them and trying to make sure you could still use that hand once you healed. They have your back, Huw. They won't tell anyone in the South you still live, so you may as well just be who you are."

Huw was silent. A lump in his throat threatened to become tears of gratitude, but all he said was, "I'll do it if you all join with me like we do at the Green Man. I haven't played a note since the day I left Ludwellyn in March. I don't know if I remember how to play my lute anymore. I think I could manage the pipes."

"Some things you never forget," said Fat Pat, dropping into a chair beside Huw. "Even when you were pretending to be Ugly-Jak, we noticed you can't keep still when everyone else is making music. You're one of the best as ever passed through Clythe, Huw. Let's have some real music tonight and maybe one of your tales, eh? We all agreed you should have your disguise for as long as you thought you needed it, but you're safe now. You can be Huw Owyn from here on out, and no one will care. The troubles in the valley don't matter up here."

The ale was good but different from that brewed in the South. According to Murfee, Sara prepared hers from her father's recipe. The scent of good food permeated the room, and a woman in an apron served them. She was as tall as any man and striking, with a heart-shaped face. Her long blond hair was plaited and coiled about her head like a crown. Something about her caught Huw's attention.

"Therese, this is Huw Owyn," said Murfee. "Therese is Sara's mum. Huw swings a good sword, but for reasons of his own, he's going to Castleton when the next group goes north. He's also quite good with a song or a tale, as you'll hear tonight."

"Ah, and a handsome lad, too!" she winked at Huw, who couldn't help but smile, eyeing her appreciatively. She looked enough like Sara to be her sister. His pulse raced as he gazed on her. "You lads from the South all make such beautiful music. We've been looking forward to you all joining in a chant-dance tonight. When your lads were up here last year, Murf, it was the best music we've ever heard."

"Try to stop us! Music is the heart and soul of Eynier," replied Murfee, laughing. "We don't get to play much on the road, unless we're at an inn or a shelter, and we miss it."

Speechless and smiling like a fool, Huw nodded, wondering what Therese meant. As she moved off, he finally asked what a chant-dance was.

"You saw how poor this village is when we came through. Well, lad, this place is rich in comparison to most other places up here. Life is hard in the North, and comforts are few. Instruments other than simple drums were never really part of their culture until Wald and Eyn were joined, so only one or two of the Ravens play the flute or the lute, and they came from wealthy families. The rest sing though," replied Bil. "What we do at the Green Man with our pipes, harps, and bodhráns, they do with their voices and feet."

"They sing and dance the rhythms, stamping on the floor what we'd drum. It stirs the blood like you'd never believe," added Derik. "You'll be amazed at how much they appreciate music here. They don't get to show it when they go south, but they love it as much as we do."

"You'll hear a lot of songs we don't know down in the Eynier," added Murfee. "Their music isn't sad, as ours is. It's light, about all the beauties of the land and life. A fair amount of their songs are just plain silly, but they're fun and easy to join in with. I'd bet 'Firedrake in the Kitchen' is one of their ditties—that's how their sense of humor works."

"They say the better a man dances, the more likely he is to get a girl. I don't know how true that is, but I've never met a northern man who didn't dance better than a Vyennesk courtesan," offered Fat Pat. "It's like nothing you've ever seen!"

Sure enough, when the southern lads brought out their instruments, the room erupted in whistling and pounding on the tables. This enthusiastic expression of gratitude was distinctly different from the polite applause that signified appreciation in the South, and it startled Huw. By common agreement, they started with "Firedrake in the Kitchen," a country song that now had a great deal of significance to Huw. He played his pipes rather than his lute for most of the evening, as his fingers had lost their calluses and the burns had left them tender.

Huw would never forget the first time he saw the men dancing; the sound of them pounding out the beats in unison traveled through his bones. The sight of them all in a line, making exactly the same steps and tapping and stamping the rhythms awed him. The sound grew and multiplied as if by a hundred drummers. *No wonder the best dancers get the ladies. There's few men could dance like that for hours and still have the strength to make love to a woman!*

During some of the songs, the men and women danced together, weaving flawless, complicated patterns, all of them stepping and tapping to the rhythms perfectly in time with Murfee's bodhrán. Huw was bemused by the sight and the thunderous beats that swept him away. *We Southerners think the valley is the only place in the world for music, because we're so rich compared to these people and even the poorest play the pipes or bodhrán. The South has never witnessed anything like this. Now I've seen it, I'll never be so arrogant about the so-called culture of the South. The music I've always known is tame! These are the same melodies but with their dancing, the music is as wild as the land that surrounds us.*

After an hour or so, everyone's throat was dry. Murfee announced Huw was going to perform a quest tale. "We've been playing the songs you all know, and that everyone down in the Long Valley knows too. But there is among us tonight a man whose talents go far beyond what we poor men know. You've never heard anything until you've heard our lad, Huw, sing the 'Ballad of Merewyn's Sword' the way it's sung in our part of the world. Huw was raised a tinker, and tinkers are the best entertainers. He learned it from his father, who learned it from his father, and now he'll sing it for you." Once again the room erupted in hoots and whistles and more pounding on the tables.

"It's been a while since I've sung it, so forgive me if I stumble," said Huw, as he tuned his lute. "The origins of this tale go back to the days when Wald and Eyn were two separate countries...." He strummed the opening chords and launched into the tale of the young, embattled girl who became a queen.

"Merewyn was a queen, though the girl was but eight. They murdered her father and locked her away. Merewyn grew lovely, Merewyn grew fair; still they ruled her country as if she weren't there. A wedding was planned to the king of the Lanques; an old man was he, with skinny old shanks. Merewyn was beautiful, clever and brave; she vowed to seek vengeance o'er her father's grave. The lass stole a sword and the pirate king's horse; into the night she fled to the North..."

The tale followed the young queen's journey to the wild north country of Wald, hoping to receive help from the elderly king. On her journey there, she fell in love with the barbarian prince. Aelfrid was the heir to the throne of Wald; he gladly helped Merewyn regain her sovereignty, and the two disparate countries were joined.

When Huw finished singing, there was a moment of dead silence. Then the room erupted in thunderous appreciation. Stamping on the floor and pounding on the tables, whistling and shouting for more, the Ravens made their gratitude known. Huw was overcome. In the same way as had frequently happened before when he was at the top of his craft, he'd completely lost himself in the joy of the music and the telling of the tale, and forgotten he had an audience. Tears filled his eyes, and he had to look down, pretending to re-tune his lute. *I was afraid I'd lost the gift. Thank you, God, for letting me keep it.*

Murfee's hand clasped his shoulder, and Huw looked up to see pride in his eyes. "See, lad? You're still the bard, and always will be. No one can sing an epic quest tale like you. You haven't forgotten anything." The others nodded as they too thumped the tables in the northern fashion.

Chapter 17 Matt St. Coeur

Three days later at dawn, Huw watched Murfee and the lads departing on the next part of their journey to Vyennes. He suffered a brief moment of anxiety, but buried it and busied himself assisting Matt and Therese around the inn, much the same as he'd helped the Bear. He was alone now, with no familiar voices, surrounded by northern accents. Still he was able to keep a cheerful face on things, despite the uncertainties in his life.

Huw was drawn to Therese. Whenever he saw her, he had the urge to talk to her, to flirt, and see the sparkle in her eyes that was just for him. He found himself attracted to her in an unexpected way. Frequently, he hung about in the kitchen making a nuisance of himself, but she didn't tell him to leave, so he had hopes.

There was something about Therese he couldn't get out of his mind. She was genteel yet earthy. Her conversation was clever and witty, and she was compassionate, caring deeply for everyone who slept under her roof. Sure, she was older, but her face was unlined and her hair showed little silver. At thirty-eight, Therese was ripe and fine-looking, and he couldn't stop thinking of her. The other ladies tried to capture his attention, but he wasn't as interested in them, though he'd followed Fair Ellen up to her room on his first night there. She was lovely and pleasant, but a shade too hard once he'd gotten to know her. When he left her, he'd found himself wishing it was Therese who'd extended the invitation. Huw slept alone after that night, wanting to be with Therese instead.

He'd just finished taking the chamber pots out to the privy and was at the pump washing them when he saw Matt's shadow looming. Huw had discovered Matt was Sara's business partner and something much more. Matt had put up half of the money so Sara could buy her sisters out when their father died. Matt and Sara took turns leading the long trips with one going on the road while the other minded the home fires and accepted short jobs. They also had a loose romantic arrangement, and shared a room.

Huw suffered terrible pangs of guilt when he saw Matt, as his wild night with Sara loomed large in his mind whenever he thought about starting a conversation with him. He'd not realized she "had a lad," as these Northerners termed it, and wasn't sure Matt would approve of his brief fling with her, although she seemed a woman who conveyed her favors when and where she chose. Thus he kept to himself except for making music and asking for tasks to keep occupied.

"Huw." Matt's voice was a mellow baritone with the unmistakably clipped accent of the northern nobleman. "Why're you killing yourself doing Jimmie's work when you could be taking the short jobs with me? It'll net you a gold coin for the week, and we'll be home for dinner every day." He grinned, a charming smile. "I'm short four Ravens now since I sent them with Murfee. I need at least one more sword for this. Mayme would do it, but she says you need to get out for a bit. It's quite local and simple, only guarding the farmers further down in the Sherman Valley to and from market here in Bekenberg. It's not likely to be too much effort, since we keep the valley cleaned out pretty well. We'll split the take. It could be two weeks or more before anything comes along heading to Castleton, so you may as well make the best of your time here and earn a little something."

"I'd like that," replied Huw, grinning back at him. "I get bored and staying busy keeps me out of trouble."

"I've heard about you," Matt laughed. "Your mates told me you get into no end of trouble with the ladies, and I believe it, having seen the way they swarmed you the other night at closing. It looked like Fair Ellen won out in the end, though. I had my money on her winning the scuffle, and I netted a gold in coins all told, thank you very much! I heard Sara ate you up like so much candy. She and Ellen have the same taste in lads."

Huw choked, and Matt pounded him on the back. "You'll find the ladies up here make the rules. They decide who they dally with, and we lads just hope we have most of their attention. We all get lonely on the road. Nothing is certain in this business."

"Oh. Ah…it's probably the fact I'm the new lad. Or maybe they just like entertainers," Huw laughed self-consciously. He looked at the collection of chamber pots, wondering what he should do.

"I was off on a long job to Vyennes for several weeks and didn't return until the day after Sara left for the South. She gets lonely, and I knew she'd eventually find company on the road. It's just how she is. Neither of us can go without company for too long." He gestured at the chamber pots awaiting a good scrub. "Therese is sending Jimmie out to finish these. He says he's bored, what with you doing all his work," Matt said. "Go get geared up, and I'll meet you in the stable."

Jimmie was Mayme's son. He'd been injured by a highwayman's sword on his third trip out as a Raven. His left side was crippled and he couldn't speak clearly, but could write on the slate he carried. Jimmie had devised ways to do tasks a normal man could do, using a special sled to hold things he would have carried in his arms before. He'd not yet turned twenty, but was as slow as an old man since he had to drag his left leg and could only do each task with his good right arm. Despite his terrible injury, Jimmie was still mentally sharp, regardless of his inability to speak. He was good-hearted, hard-working and an integral part of the Raven's Nest, as were two other former Ravens with crippling injuries. Another code of the mercenaries was they took care of their own, especially if they were wounded so badly they had to leave the road but had no family to care for them.

Huw quickly washed then went up to his room, putting on his clean shirt. He dressed in his mail, strapping on his sword and feeling absurdly like an apprentice.

The Crown paid for those guarding the farmers for the same reason it provided shelters in the high mountains. "We all have to eat, and the king needs this outpost here in the wilds to provision guards on the caravans to Vyennes, so Henri pays us to help the local farmers get the crops into the storehouses this time of year." Matt pointed out how the farms were all protected by stockades and high earthworks and were strung out down the fingers of the winding Sherman Valley. Fed by numerous chill creeks, it was a sheltered, well-watered valley with a small but thriving community.

Huw and Matt rode straight out to the farthest farm and working their way back to Bekenberg, picked up and escorted the growing train of wagons to town, stopping only to add another cart to their impromptu caravan. They made three trips over the course of the morning with five or six wagons each time. Some were driven by nervous farmers and others by people who'd been mercenaries before they'd left the road for good. The ex-mercs were chatty about the "glory days" and often had stories that made Huw and Matt laugh out loud, usually at some poor merchant's expense. At the end of the day, they made the same trips in reverse. Every day after that, Huw rode out with Matt, developing a close friendship with him, and most evenings he played music in the common room.

Huw continued his courtship of Therese. At first she put him off. "You're too young to be chasing me, Huw. Deren and I knew your father, and he was my age! What does a handsome lad like you see in an old dame like me? The young ladies all want you." Therese wasn't a woman who conveyed her favors lightly, as she wasn't ruled by her desires. She'd been a widow for three years and taken no lovers in all that time. However, after five days, Huw's relentless pursuit finally weakened her defenses. Confessing it was against her better judgment, she allowed him into her room. Huw knew he'd worked his way into her heart, even though she knew he was leaving when the next caravan went north. "I won't be leaving Bekenberg, Huw. My life is here with the Ravens and this place, so don't ask me to go with you when you leave. I just can't do it, not even for you."

Now his nights were frequently spent enjoying the company of the lady whose witty, sophisticated conversation and genuine warmth far outweighed the age difference. Therese was a storehouse of knowledge in regard to the mercenary trade, and while she was nearly twenty years his senior, they found great pleasure in each other's company, both in and out of bed.

He was surprised one night when, going back to his room, he passed Matt in the hallway, leaving Alauna's room. They both grinned and kept on walking. Neither man said anything, but Huw felt immensely better knowing Matt wasn't inordinately faithful to Sara.

The next afternoon as they walked back from the stable, Matt confessed he'd like to marry Sara, but knew she'd never settle down. "Last year she fostered our babe with her sister over in Galwye. I admit it was hard to accept, but she's not a motherly sort of woman, and Marlene's never had children of her own, so Bettina is well loved and cared for. Sara will never leave the road. She's just like Mayme. Therese raised Jimmy for her, you know."

"How did you feel about fostering your child?" Huw asked, thinking of a certain noble babe whom he could never claim, or even admit to knowing. "It's hard having no say, but I know it's sometimes unavoidable."

"We agreed I was most likely the girl's father, but who can say? If Sara had left the road and married me as I begged her to do, I'd have claimed her and Bettina would have been mine then with no doubt, because it's the way of it among mercenaries. I feel sure I *am* her father, and both Sara and I send money to Galwye. I've put a bit by for her dowry or gear if she should take up the sword, and she'll be my heir should I die in the saddle." Grinning at Huw's somber expression, Matt elaborated. "These aren't women who were ever suited to be wives, Huw. They *fear* the constraints of motherhood far more than they do a firedrake! Most of them can't cook anything you'd want to eat, though Sara cooks as well as Therese. The difference is Sara helped out here at the Raven's Nest all her childhood. She's unlike most mercenary women in that way. She was raised to the craft, and when her sword slows, she'll take over for her mother here.

"The majority of mercenary ladies are runaways, escaping arranged marriages, or they've been badly abused. Some share a pillow with other ladies and don't care to be with men that way anymore." He shrugged. "Then there's the rule that says noblewomen can't be knights, a silly thing when you think about it, but there you go. A woman with the heart of a knight and who wants to swing a sword must languish tied to a pack of babies and a husband she has no great love for, unless she joins a mercenary company."

"You've given me a lot to think about. From what I've seen, you'd be hard-pressed to fill your jobs without the women in your Ravens," Huw agreed. "At least they find acceptance and respect here. And lads...I've noticed several who'd be murdered out of hand for daring to show their love for another lad, were they in the South."

Now it was Matt whose face held the incredulous expression. Huw continued. "It's a soft land, as far as offering safety from beasts and wild creatures, but it's a harsh land to live in. Not a league passes without some sort of town or village, and even the poorest of them is rich compared to Bekenberg. The sheer number of farms and houses on every back road and lane would surprise you. It's why it was so difficult to make my way north unnoticed by the Crows. I was a wanted man, and anyone who helped me would just as easily have sold me to them had he known my true identity, because the nobility has all the say.

"They enforce the rules with their armed men, and anyone caught going against them pays the price by losing his property or his life." Huw shrugged. "No one resists them, at least not openly. The Eynier Valley is an easy land, but it's hard for anyone who doesn't fit in because they have what we refer to as a 'stigma.' Lads who love other lads, ladies who want to swing a sword, tinkers and traveling people—anyone different is treated harshly."

"I've heard society is stern there," Matt nodded his understanding. "Henri wants to tame the North and ease the plight of the commoners in the South, but he's only now emerging from the shadow of his mother's regency, and he's still limited in his power. Wald is the last wild land and was a wilderness until St. Aelfrid built Castleton and created the knighthood. He unified the tribes here and formed the Brothers of St. Aelfrid. Before him, we were really just like Fornost and Lournes, very tribal and quite barbaric. When you Southerners refer to us as barbarians, you're not far off the track." Matt laughed at Huw's shocked expression.

Feeling a bit affronted, Huw said abruptly, "I've always found it offensive to refer to half of our country as barbarian and will *never* stoop so low. It's an insult and undeserved. You and everyone I've met here, even the lowest farmers, are the most well-educated and civilized of people. In the South, to be born with light hair and eyes makes you a barbarian and is a stigma. *Anything* that makes you different is a stigma. It can get a lad killed at the gentle hands of his friends. Yet it's no disgrace down there to be ignorant and narrow-minded. It is, instead, an honor and a duty!" Huw's tone was sharper than he intended, and he smiled self-deprecatingly, trying to take the sting out of his words. "I'm done with the South and their stigmas."

Matt had taken no offense. "Well, it's what we call ourselves, Huw. At the time of St. Aelfrid, we were nothing but simple, forest-dwelling barbarians, hunting in roving tribes. Our knowledge and lore were written on scrolls, and they were the greatest treasures we had to offer, more valuable than the precious metals, furs, and hides we traded with you Southerners. Quarrels and inter-clan wars over the best hunting grounds, mines and forests were frequent. Many of the nobility were still that way at the time of St. Aelfrid's grandson, King Aelfrid III, whose marriage to Merewyn the Warrior Queen saw the joining of Wald and Eyn. Even today, many of the wilder parts of the Northwest out by Galwye and the East to Fornost and Vyennes are still that isolated.

"It was St. Aelfrid, the first high king of Wald, who over three hundred years ago unified us and began the great change by gaining control of the majik. Before his intervention, majik-wielders were demon-controllers and witches as often as they were kindly healers and weapons-smiths. They were frequently more trouble than the majikal beasts. Now if they don't serve the people through being bound to the church, the ability to sense majik is taken from them by the Mother Church."

Huw said, "To be born with majik is a stigma in the South, and children with the gift often disappear, never to be seen again, unless they're found by the Brotherhood or Sisters of Anan first. Wise parents try to smuggle them north if they can. Everyone turns a blind eye to this heinous murder, believing it must be done so they won't grow up to be witches. And yet our people pay fabulous sums for majik amulets and healing potions made by the very friars and sisters they'd have murdered had they met them as children. But in a way, this gross absurdity is logical because of the lack of knowledge nurtured by the nobility. You see, most folks think those children will go the way of the Lournesque witches if they're allowed to live. It never seems to occur to them they're killing off the very people whom they expect to majikally protect or heal them."

"The witches of Lournes are very dangerous, it's true. I've a story or two to tell you about them," Matt's bright blue eyes twinkled. "But anyway, our land is now fairly civilized in the far North, beyond Castleton. Bunder and those parts of the country are mostly protected—at least there are very few reports of the *big* beasts there. But the further south from Castleton you travel the more chance you have of running into trouble. It's been three hundred years of struggle to get the northernmost parts of Wald safely civilized, and that's where our population mostly live. Henri has declared he'll have the entire land safe in his lifetime, all the way to the sea."

"I wish the king well in his efforts. I doubt it'll happen, but it would be good if he could do it. No wonder few people travel unguarded here. How can one lone traveler deal with creatures such as I've seen between here and Clythe? They can't. Even without the beasts, you have to deal with the Lanque highwaymen," said Huw.

"We usually don't run into them one after another the way you lads did on your way here, thank God. Besides, you'd be amazed, Huw. Many people journey alone. Of course, we take poor travelers with us for free if they happen along when we're headed their direction." Matt shrugged. "The Friars of St. Aelfrid ride alone and they make useful amulets for the rest of us, including ones that cast a sleeping spell on most of the baddies. The Sisters of Anan travel alone also as do many who can't afford to hire mercs. Dealing with the big beasts isn't really too bad once you know what to look for and how to avoid them. The dangerous ones are the sort you ran into, creatures that shouldn't have been down by the road at all."

Thus Huw passed the time, loving Therese and forging a lifelong friendship with Matt St. Coeur and the Ravens, waiting for a caravan to go north to Castleton.

Chapter 18 All the King's Men

Most evenings Huw sat on a stool and played the pipes, harp and lute, wondering when a caravan going to Castleton would arrive. He knew he had to continue going north, but didn't want to. Therese and the Ravens had a hold on him, and he knew he would feel the loss keenly. Idly playing his melodies, he watched the crowd as Therese and Matt tended to the guests. As always, he played the songs any traveling entertainer might, but never sang unless the others joined in. The Ravens who were in and around the place knew why he didn't pull out his best music when strangers who might be from the South were in the house. He wore a Raven's armband, so as far as anyone else knew, he was one.

Huw made small, simple instruments for a few of the Ravens who requested them, showing them how to play. They received the little flutes and bodhráns as if they were princely gifts, with the most musically inclined learning simple melodies quite quickly. "Now our chant-dances will be much livelier, and Jimmie can be part of them again," Mayme told Therese as she watched Huw coaching Jimmie in playing his flute. "He missed it badly, now he can't dance." Jimmie mastered the flute rather quickly despite his disability and could often be heard playing when he'd finished his chores.

Huw told Therese that once he was settled in the north, he would make Jimmie a set of pipes and send them down when the Rowdies came through Bekenberg next. "I've been teaching him on mine, and he has the knack. He'd make a good apprentice, if you can spare him once I've a place. I think he has the ability to make some small instruments, albeit slowly. I'd send him back after half a year or so."

"Yes! This is exactly what Jimmie needs, Huw. You've no idea how hard it is for him now he can't speak his thoughts anymore." Her joy was palpable.

"He doesn't need to be able to sing to express himself, and his mind is a sponge, soaking up every melody." Huw smiled in the dark, smugly satisfied he'd delighted her. He knew their time was short and wanted to do as much as he could to please her before he had to leave. Therese's family was everything to her, so Huw did what he was able to make their lives happier. "Tomorrow Jimmie and I'll play together, the two of us, and you'll see. With Stevy on the bodhrán, it'll be fun."

On the eighth evening of Huw's sojourn with the Ravens, the door to the common room swung open. A rather pudgy knight wearing a suit of plate-armor stood, blinking. As his vision adjusted, he hurried over to Matt. "St. Coeur! Just the man I wanted to see." The knight looked familiar, yet he was sure he'd never seen the man before.

"Oh, look. It's old 'Sir Pouty,' Morty De Portiers. What the hell do *you* want?" Matt's disgruntled reaction to the odd-looking noble intrigued Huw, who continued to play quietly as he observed the interaction. To his knowledge, Matt had never behaved so rudely to anyone, which perplexed Huw. Even more interesting was the nobleman's pained reaction.

"It's *Sir Mortimer*, St. Coeur, not 'Morty.' I'm here on the king's behalf, with some business for you." The knight's tone of voice was almost that of a whining adolescent. "Your pocket will benefit so pretend to have some gratitude."

"Well, then, *you* can call me *Lord* St. Coeur since we're going to be all formal about this! I don't have to toady to you, De Portiers. I outrank you on every level. You can kiss my noble arse." Matt started to walk away. "I don't need your money, and I certainly don't need you."

"But Henri sent me! Well, not him personally. He's taken the fleet south, but our cousin, John De Portiers, did. He's Henri's Lord Dog-Walker now old Squash is dead. You've no idea the horrors my men and I've endured getting here." Now Sir Mortimer was pleading. "John sent me with a packet for your people to carry south, to…." He looked over his shoulder at Huw and the others in the room and lowered his voice. "To *you know who*. She needs to know he's sending help." He held out the packet to Matt, who looked at it distrustfully.

"Old Squash is dead? Well, John's a smart man, right for the job. Why did he send you and not a real knight? Someone like your brother." Matt's voice was suspicious. "It just seems odd he sent you. I'd have thought an important jackass like you would be far too busy fairy-bothering to take on a task a mere messenger could have handled with less trouble."

"Everyone's gone south, and Julian is busy too. Wait—what do you mean by that? I'm as good a knight as anyone, especially my brother." Young Sir Mortimer's voice rose indignantly. "Why does everyone think Julian is such a great knight? It's always Lackland this, Lackland that! Oh, too bad *I'm* the firstborn. *He's* a landless nobody and *I'm* a bloody baron, but he gets all the attention. It's not fair!" Huffing indignantly, his lower lip stuck out like a spoiled child; his sulky expression ludicrous on a man in armor.

Huw hid his grin. Apparently Morty had never got past being a dull boy with a slightly younger but much better looking, more talented sibling, who shone like the sun in comparison to his own less-than-handsome features and lackluster presence.

"Stuff it, Morty. Next to your brother you're naught but a turd in a tin can," replied Matt, his eyes hard as slate. "And don't get all huffy. You're not allowed to handle sharp objects and you know it, so don't try to pretend you're in Lackland's class. You aren't fit to wipe his arse." He glared at the would-be knight who fumed resentfully and inarticulately. "All right, I'll accept the packet since John De Portiers was so desperate to get it here he sent *you* with it. A caravan is leaving for the South tomorrow. Fair Ellen will ensure the duchess gets it." He pointedly turned his back on the knight and busied himself behind the bar.

"Um…." There was a slight clanking as Sir Mortimer shifted from one foot to the other.

"What is it now?" Matt's voice was muffled as he bent down to reach the lower shelves. "The privy is out back."

"Well, my men and I need rooms for the night," replied Morty. "You can't imagine what we've suffered, the creatures we fought. It was dreadful, and we'd like a bit of a rest and hot baths before we return to Castleton."

"Well, it smells to me like you fought a skunk. I've half a mind to send you and your pathetic arse to the Broken Wheel," replied Matt. "But I do have four rooms available at the reduced Crown rate of three coppers each, plus a copper for stabling each of your horses. Supper will be another copper per man, but you each get a mug of ale with your meal. Every mug after that is one copper each. If you have your usual lads with you, that'll be twelve coppers for the rooms and four for the horses." He held out his hand expectantly. "Now."

"Skunks are vicious killers," spluttered the knight, his face turning an ugly shade of purple in his outrage. "It was a close battle. And this is highway robbery! I won't pay it."

"Fine! They've plenty of room for you lot at the Broken Wheel." Matt gestured toward the door. "If *I* have to put up with your nonsense, you'll pay me to do it. Otherwise, move on. I'm giving you the Crown rate as it is. I can get five coppers for each room from the mercenaries who travel through here and three for the meals."

Reluctantly, Sir Mortimer produced a purse and counted out fifteen coppers. "We've only three horses. My horse...," the knight turned red and looked at the floor.

"You lost your horse again, didn't you," laughed Matt as he accepted the coins. "What's your excuse this time?"

"Highwaymen stole it," Morty muttered, "while we were sleeping."

"I somehow doubt that. As I recall, your most recent mare was a fat old lady with a slight sway to her back from carrying heavily armored nincompoops and was possessed of no initiative whatsoever. She was perfect for you. What really happened?" Matt glared at him expectantly.

"Don't look at me like that," replied the knight, scowling back. "You wouldn't believe the truth anyway, so I'm not saying."

Huw's ears perked up. He smelled a tale, and now knew what his evening's entertainment was to be. He'd become Sir Mortimer De Portiers's close friend and confidant, at least for the evening. Grinning, he set his harp down, and walking over, put a coin on the bar.

Matt looked up, nonplussed and confused by the light in Huw's eyes.

"I'd like to buy this man a mug of ale, Matt. I'm sure this brave knight will have a tale or two to tell a poor wounded merc such as I," Huw said, letting his sleeve fall back, exposing the rough red welts of his badly scarred arm. "It's hard being crippled in my sword-arm and unable to go on the road when you all do. I miss it so."

The pathetic expression on Huw's face was ludicrous, but Matt managed not to gape at him. "I don't know what you're up to, but it's your ear will pay the price. He can't shut up once he's had a glass or two." Matt took the coin and dutifully poured Morty an ale.

Sir Mortimer glared at him and turning to Huw, said stiffly, "Thank you, good sir. This cur was raised with better manners, but he's forgotten them." He accepted the mug. "At least *some* folks appreciate a poor knight's suffering."

Matt snorted and made a rude gesture. "Damned right I forgot them. I don't have to put up with jackasses whose only redeeming quality is they were born first. Terrible shame, that."

Huw hid his grin behind his own mug of ale, which he pretended to sip. He intended to get as much information about Lackland as he could from his envious brother and knew just how to go about it. Huw was curious to know why the king was sailing past the pirate-infested city of Port Lanque instead of taking the trade road south and avoiding it completely. *We have the Crown Port at Ludwellyn, so we don't have to sail past the bloody Lanques just to get our goods to Vyennes. I hope Henri's got some sort of a plan.*

Later that night, after the common room was closed, Matt met Huw in his room to discuss what they'd gleaned from both Morty and his men.

"It appears the king is taking the entire fleet down to Lanqueshire to stop them interfering in Waldeyn's politics once and for all. Sir Morty was quite in awe of Henri's new cannons," said Huw. "They sound like fearsome weapons, but I've heard they aren't effective if the enemy has a friar or lightning-witch on their side."

"That's true," agreed Matt. "According to my father who was there, Henri's father, King Herrold, had a hot young friar on our side whose lightning majik blew the old King of Lournes clear to hell along with all his cannons when they were settling the issue of where the northern border actually is. That was thirteen years ago, just before Herrold died." Matt laughed low. "It surprised *them* mightily! Henri is going to fire his cannons on the fleet in Port Lanque on his way to Ludwellyn. The rebel clan in the Long Valley will be made to kneel to him, or he'll turn his cannons on their cliff-top palaces next! He's got several Brothers of St. Aelfrid on every ship and some Sisters of Anan, casting spells to obscure the fleet from the witches among the Lanque pirates. It won't stop them for long, it never does—but at least Henri will be sneaking up on them this time.

"Of course, you know it was most likely Lackland who actually planned this on Henri's behalf. There's a serious lack of ability right now at court, but God forbid we allow a landless knight to lead us to war. None of the current firstborns has enough military expertise to fight his way out of a well-made bed. This generation of knights is pathetic. Those of us with the ability to wage war aren't the ones able to supply the gold to fund a conflict or the armsmen to fight it."

Huw agreed. "Yes.... If I recall correctly, it's why our king is married to Morganna of Lournes, though in the Eynier Valley she is frequently suspected of conspiring against him, throwing her support behind the Grefyns. Their betrothal as children helped to settle the dispute. Henri inherited a mess, having to keep incompetent men in positions of importance. But the king is a canny man." Huw was off and running on one of his favorite topics. "He sees a way to work around the silly constraints and ensures your abilities are available to him when he needs them, by letting you all get situated as mercenaries. All of this is accomplished at no cost to his empty treasury because you pay your own way.

"He's made the feudal laws work for him by ensuring good knights of strength and ability are not only out doing the real work of protecting the countryside, but you're fully trained, kitted out, and right where he needs you. And believe me, the king is going to want *all* of you in the next year or two, because this little foray down to Port Lanque with the fleet will escalate into another Ten-Years War with Lanqueshire, just like in our grandfathers' day."

A look of surprised consternation crossed Matt's genial face. He said, "I never thought about it that way. That actually *is* quite smart on Henri's part! You seem to know an awful lot about politics for a mere tinker-lad." His grin faded. "My amiable, good-hearted brother, Arturus, hasn't had all the brains bred out of him like some we could mention, but he's certainly not a tactician. He'd be the first to tell you Lackland is the finest strategist, but he has no position at court. Arturus is Lord Admiral of the Fleet only because *he* has the dukedom, the title, the soldiers and the money. As the fourth son of a minor northern duke I've been given a pointless title, Lord of the Northern Marches, and no real position at court. This makes me fit to be married off to a wealthy merchant's daughter or that of a lesser noble looking to climb the social ladder. John De Portiers is in much the same position, but he qualified to inherit his father's position as the king's Dog-Walker."

"I meant to ask you. What is this Dog-Walker? I've never heard of such a thing." Huw mentally took notes. "And who was old Squash?"

"Well, King Herrold had the same trouble getting good help as Henri has. Lord John De Portiers is Lackland's cousin, so he is of house De Portiers just as Lackland is. John's father, William, was known as Old Squash for reasons I never knew, and he was a genius at organizing things. Herrold invented the title of Lord Dog-Walker so he could have Old Squash's services without putting the real nobles' noses out of joint. It's as useful a title as Lord of the Northern Marches, for the love of God, but the landed nobles pretty much do as he suggests. John De Portiers is very good at keeping Henri organized. The court would fall apart without his capabilities."

"Ah. I'm not familiar with the Northern Marches," Huw admitted.

"I'd be surprised if you were! The Northern Marches is a wood-wraith infested swamp covering about fifty frozen leagues in the high country on the northern sea, nearly in Lournes. It's part of my brother's dukedom that has no useful purpose other than to give me a social standing to impress the commoners. I've a rundown hunting lodge there, but I don't get up to it very often. It may have fallen in on itself by now for all I know." Matt was silent for a moment, and then he said, "Our system of government is wrong. The king shouldn't have to resort to subterfuge to get his work done properly." He realized he'd grown a bit loud, and tempered his voice. "But it's the system we've always had, so it's unlikely to change any time soon. Fortunately, Henri has Lackland close at hand to give him the plans he needs, and since Henri wears the crown, the fools our king is forced to suffer listen to him and do as he says."

Huw said, "It's much the same way for the nobles in the South, only more so. The younger ones either become glorified clerks in the family's shipping business, bowing and scraping to their brother, or they're sent off to sea to keep them out of the way. Frequently they meet with accidents before they can develop notions of sitting in their brother's seat," Huw grinned as he sipped his wine. "Speaking of delusions of grandeur, Amstyce Lyndys, the new Grand Duke Grefyn, is going to be rather surprised when the king shows up and puts him in his place. I can't say I'm sorry to hear it. Lyndys's captains and lieutenants have a slight accent to their speech reminiscent of Lanqueshire. They're happy to bully and murder the weak and the poor in the name of the Grefyn! I'm glad to see Henri is aware of the danger Amstyce Lyndys's close ties to Lanqueshire present." He thought for a moment. "Sir Morty's brother, Lackland, was trained in the knightly arts by one of the friars. He told me so when I met him down in the South. The Brothers of St. Aelfrid are amazing in battle, so I've heard."

"Lackland is something special." Matt laughed and said, "Of course, he's also completely mad, but you can't have everything!"

For a while, they sat before the fire in Huw's room in companionable silence. Something about Matt made Huw feel as comfortable as he had in the company of both Lackland and Davey Llewellyn.

"Did you ever find out what really happened to Mortimer's horse?" Huw had been unable to get a straight answer from Morty or his men, no matter how much ale he plied them with.

"No," replied Matt, a twinkle in his eyes. "The others shushed young Sir Ricard De Ponte when he mumbled something about fairies, but he'd said nothing that made any sense. They were all hiding something. I suspect Sir Pouty and his men accidentally ate some of those vision-inducing mushrooms by mistake when they were foraging for dinner." Both men grinned knowingly. "They aren't very clever, though they pride themselves on being able to live off the land. Morty probably didn't picket the poor old thing properly and it wandered off. The horse may have been taken by a bear or something. It really is gone."

"How will he get home?" Huw was curious because the knight's men had been unhappy at Morty's having to ride double with them, feeling it was undignified.

"His men will figure it out. He might be able to buy a horse at the Broken Wheel," replied Matt, rolling his eyes. "I assure you, Mayme won't sell him one of our spares because we've none he can safely manage. He's a terrible horseman, being what our old armsmaster used to call 'round-bottomed.' What Sir Pouty really needs is a tired old pony, but with all that plate he insists on wearing, none could possibly carry him. An elderly, gelded war-horse long past his glory days or a good old mare on her last legs was all he could handle when we were lads at court." Both men chuckled, and Matt began to reveal all sorts of hilarious, juicy tidbits at the expense of the "real" nobility as they talked far into the night.

Sir Mortimer and his men were shown the door early the next morning, and Huw settled in again to wait for a caravan. Morty had offered to escort him to Castleton, loudly averring it was his knightly duty to protect crippled mercenaries as well as damsels in distress.

"Thank you, your lordship," Huw flattered him outrageously, "but no, I think I'll stay and see if my wounds heal a bit better. I'll give it a few more weeks. I may get my sword arm back, and if I do, I'll stay on here."

The common room was quiet again, and Huw sat with his sleeves rolled up, sharpening his knives and running an oiled rag over his sword. Watching the bard honing his blades, Matt suddenly realized Huw had been showing Morty his left arm and saying his wounds had crippled his sword-arm, when he was actually right-handed. "You sneaky bastard! I was feeling quite sorry for you myself!"

Huw just laughed wickedly.

Chapter 19 The Road North

Huw and Matt again rode beside a wagon full of turnips, escorting another farmer to market. Matt mock-innocently asked Huw why he'd refused so generous an offer of an escort to Castleton by the Royal Guard.

"Hah! The last thing I want is to run up against a firedrake with only Sir Mortimer and his pleasant but naïve young companions to back me up," Huw replied, shuddering.

Matt laughed uproariously at the look on his face. "Sadly, it'll be highwaymen those four need to worry about," he said after he calmed down. "And those babes-in-the-woods really *are* in danger from highwaymen. Firedrakes generally stay up in the mountains the further north from the pass you get, unless they've been run off by a bigger one and are looking for easy kills."

"Matt," Huw said, at last confessing his deepest fear. "I don't know if I'm really cut out to be a mercenary. The road here was so far beyond my skills, and it was only luck I survived the journey. I don't have the desire to save the world like you and Lackland do. I don't think I could die to save someone else. I just want to be a bard and tell the tales of *your* heroic deeds! It's all I've ever known and all I want."

"Maybe so, but maybe not. I think you haven't been fully tested, so how would you know? Life will test you and you'll pass the trials, just as you already have. You may doubt yourself, but I know you and your fancy knives would be right there at my back, doing what any good merc would do, saving my sorry arse," replied Matt, clasping Huw's shoulder. "You have the heart of a knight, whether you believe it or not."

As soon as he was able, Huw spent two days crafting a proper bow for his lute. He found the perfect wood growing just outside the front porch of the Raven's Nest. It was simple enough to do. Mayme let him use her tools and workbench, and Therese found him the gut he needed to make the strings. The first night he played the proper melodies to accompany his tales, everyone was amazed. Few of them had seen a lute before, and none had ever heard of a bowed-lute. The dancing was merry as he played his favorite reels and jigs. Matt just grinned as Huw politely declined the invitations of several of the ladies.

"Why're you being so coy? They just want to have fun," Matt asked him later as they once again sat before the fire in Huw's room.

"I thought you knew! I've had an arrangement with Therese since the first week I was here, temporary though it may be," replied Huw, his grin fading to a sad smile. "It will cut me to the heart, leaving her, but I have to go further north. Mercs from the South regularly pass through here, and it's not safe for me. Besides, I'm no butterfly like some I could mention!"

"Therese is a woman who doesn't take lovers casually, so you must be something special to her. I don't know how I missed that." Matt laughed again, saying, "I've as much as I'll ever have of the woman I love by not caging her. I can't change Sara, and don't dwell on it. We're just made differently, you and I. I believe in seizing the moment, because death waits around every corner for a merc. 'Live every day like it's your last' is my motto!"

After three weeks absence, Sara returned to the Raven's Nest. Huw couldn't help himself—he watched Matt and Sara, with interest. When they were together, it was obvious they cared deeply for each other. They were of one mind in everything. Yet, he knew firsthand neither was faithful to the other, and they made no pretense about it. It seemed to be an accepted part of mercenary culture, one of many things radically different from the principles of the South. For the most part, the lack of social strictures regarding who a person found comfort with was refreshing.

Nevertheless, to his surprise, Huw was taken aback by the acceptance of casual promiscuity that was the hallmark of mercenary culture. *I've become a prissy old man. What happened to the lad who had no embarrassment regarding infidelity in his own life? I wasn't faithful to Sinean, or she to me, so what's happened to change my point of view? Maybe only that I've learned how important it is to have one person in your life, someone who values you above all else. Maybe losing everything and everyone has changed me.*

The Ravens all demonstrated an understanding of loneliness and personal frailties, and this, along with the lack of jealousy displayed, was remarkable. Still, Huw wondered how people felt underneath the surface. He sensed a deeply buried unhappiness in Matt with regard to Sara, one Matt himself didn't acknowledge. Huw did know this much—now he knew Therese as a lover and Matt as a friend, there'd never be another night with Sara for him, no matter what the circumstance. He had to live with his own conscience.

Huw's relationship with Therese went far beyond the simple slaking of their lust. He cared deeply about her, and leaving her behind would create a hole in his heart. The softness of her cheek and the way she tilted her head when she was interested in what he was saying captivated him. The curve of her hip never failed to arouse him, and he loved brushing her thick, golden hair, letting it slip though his fingers and enjoying the way the candlelight played upon it. In the first days of their love, he wrote a tender ballad for her. *The Fairest Rose of Bekenberg* was immediately hailed as a moving, beautiful, romantic love song, and many who passed through the common room wondered for whom he'd written it.

At last, a caravan heading north rolled into the stable yard at the Raven's Nest, and with some trepidation, Huw made preparations to leave. Waking in Therese's bed in the wee hours on his last morning in Bekenberg, he held her, knowing if they ever saw each other again, things would have changed between them and the time he'd spent with her would just be a beautiful memory. Tears burned his eyes at the thought.

"Thank you for letting me into your heart," Huw told her, as he gently brushed her hair in the candlelight one last time. "You didn't have to since you knew I was leaving. You've changed me for the better."

"Be happy and well, Huw," she told him. "It's a rough life here in the North, but I know you'll do wonderfully in the Rowdies. Write some happy songs, my love. I know we'll hear your tales when you pass this way again." They embraced, reluctant to part, yet each knew their time together was over. "It's getting late, nearly dawn. I have work to do, or folks will go hungry." He followed her down to the kitchen, where he watched her preparing breakfast one last time, lifting the heavy porridge-pot off the hearth for her, and stealing kisses every chance he had.

Voices in the common-room alerted him to the fact Matt was up and about, and getting ready to depart. "Go, love. You need to be out there with the crew. I won't watch you leave—just be safe." Tears filled her eyes as Therese turned away from him, working her bread dough with vigor, as if it would make her feel better.

"I love you." Huw picked up his saddlebags and opened the kitchen door.

"I know. I love you too." Therese's whisper floated through behind him, lodging in his heart, making him smile despite the fact that once again he was leaving someone he loved. He stepped into the common room, where Matt was seated with the guards, assigning positions, laughing and joking as if it was just another day.

All told, he'd been at the Raven's Nest five weeks. Leaving Therese behind was painful, and he very nearly changed his mind, but logic overruled desire and he mounted up, riding tail as he had with Murfee's crew. When at last they departed Bekenberg, Huw was edgy, feeling as much anxiety as he had on leaving the Green Man. This time he was embarking with clear knowledge of the beasts and such that lurked in the wilderness of the North. He wondered what lay before him, given the terrible journey from Clythe to the pass itself. He'd been serious when he told Matt he was unsure he could handle the job.

Despite Huw's apprehension, the journey to the place called Somber Flats was long but uneventful. No big beasts, no little beasts even. They were well enough armed even the highwaymen avoided the caravan.

The northerners were a fascinating people to Huw, with an amazing culture and appreciation of life unmatched by any he'd ever met. They embraced life with all their hearts, accepting the bad as it came along with the good, seeing it not as evil but as simply a result of living. Instead of fearing and viewing it with superstition, they gave it a name and made it a part of them, thereby bending it to their will. Lackland, Billy Ninefingers, Somber Flats—all names pointing out something that would have been a disgrace in the South and which was worn like a badge of honor. That ability to live every aspect of life to the fullest was what Huw had lacked and he knew without doubt he was no longer a man of the Long Valley. He'd never return to live there even if he outlived his "dishonor."

The road was long and exceedingly lonely. There were no towns, although the valleys held the occasional cluster of farms. They camped along the road, as Henri hadn't yet managed to find the money to build shelters on the northern leg of the trade road. The southern end was much more important because of the caravans back and forth between Vyennes and Ludwellyn. The regular campsites were well marked with logs drawn up around good firepits and wide grassy areas for picketing the animals. They found wood stacked near the fire and replenished the pile before they left.

Still, whenever it rained, as it did almost daily, the road was nearly impassable in some places, and it could take hours getting the teams and wagons through those stretches. Because the rain had made a quagmire of the track, nearly two weeks passed before they arrived at the line of steep hills and fertile valleys that marked the last descent to the swiftly running River Limpwater.

Every time they crossed the winding river on a shaky bridge or attempted a deep ford, Huw was aghast at how different this torrent was from the lazy thing that graced the South even in the flooding season. He found it hard to believe it was the same stream. This young version of the river swept over many rapids and waterfalls, carving its way through a landscape both astonishingly beautiful and incredibly vast. The wilderness stretched further than the eye could see, over the snowcapped mountains of the Coastal Range to the west, and the towering, snowy reaches of the high countries of Harlynde and Fornost to the east.

Indeed, Huw could understand why the northern road was considered to be so rough. In terms of distance, it wasn't too long. However, the road ran through the most remote wilderness, characterized by narrow defiles, with thick virgin forests obscuring the trail as it wound up, down, and around a low string of hills Huw would once have called mountains. He knew what he was crossing now was merely a steep ridge, one of the many they'd climbed since leaving Bekenberg. In fact, the entire northern trade road was naught but a narrow, muddy trail that twisted along the Limpwater River through constricted, blind gorges, except where the river was impassable, at which point it wound along slender crests and dangerous cliffs. He'd remarked on it the first evening on the road. "The land is so steep, it's no wonder northern towns are so few and far between," he told Matt. "Even Bekenberg is more up-and-down than flat."

Matt laughed uproariously. "We're more than half mountain goat up here! You'll get the hang of it soon, you soft lowlander. The real trick is to not fall off the *up*!"

Huw liked that turn of phrase so much he immediately made it into a song, which soon had them all laughing and singing around the fire.

Eventually, they crested the final line of ridges. From there, the road sharply fell to a vast, flat marshland along a wide, deceptively calm stretch of the sparkling river. Small farmsteads began to dot the valleys more regularly, surrounded by stockades and berms of earth.

Matt dropped back and rode beside Huw. "Be cautious in Somber Flats, the town we're approaching. You can't see it from here—it's around this bend in the river. The rumors are bad right now. Folks who've lived here all their lives are leaving town and fleeing north to the settled country with whatever they can carry. Percy St. John told me Bloody Bryan is in charge of the Wolves now. He's always been an evil bastard, and now he's even more so. We have to decide whether to stay at the Powder Keg tonight or camp on the road. If we stay here for the night, he's likely to cheat us for lodging, and if we don't, he's likely to confront us. It just depends on which way the wind is blowing in his head at the time."

Huw nodded, and Matt rode back to the front. It turned out no decision was necessary. William De Vayne, the merchant whose wagons they were guarding, firmly refused to stop in Somber Flats. Apparently he'd had enough of Bloody Bryan on his trip southeast to Vyennes, so they followed the trade road through the stockade and passed the sad, rundown string of buildings perched on rickety stilts that comprised the town. Several burned-out structures lay just within the stockade, buildings that looked to have been homes, barns, and what were now weed-infested gardens. The town had definitely seen better days.

The caravan kept traveling without incident, past a low rise in the center of town. A large wooden building stood there, surrounded by a collection of grey, shuttered huts. A peeling sign swung over the front door, depicting a keg with a burning fuse. *Miners use blasting powder. Maybe there's a mine here*, Huw thought.

"It used to be a mining town. We dug out copper, but there's nothing of value in the ground here anymore, not since my grandfather's day. That's the Powder Keg," said Una, the older lady Raven who rode tail beside him. Her harsh tones were a surprise. She'd been a pleasant, quiet companion in the common room at the Raven's Nest, and was a lean, handsome woman somewhere near his mother's age. Una wasn't over-bold, preferring to sit by the fire with a book when there was no music or dancing in the evenings. "The Wolves work out of here." She looked at Huw out of the corner of her eye. "I used to be a Wolf, but Bastard John took over for Mad Marien when she died, and everything changed for the worse. Billy Ninefingers's dad, Eddie MacNess, formed the Rowdies and went north. I should have gone with him, but I stayed on with the Bastard because he was married to my sister, Elma, and good old Mad Marien was his mum. Still, I couldn't take his drinking, so when my contract was up, I went south to the Ravens and I'm glad I did.

"Bastard John disappeared one night early last spring right after he attacked Billy MacNess for no good reason. Bloody Bryan took over the Wolves by bullying his way to the top. Everything's gone downhill since then. No ladies will work for him, and none of the lads-who-like-other-lads will either." Her low voice was scathing, full of deep, private anger. "Bryan is a beast."

"You sound like it's personal," replied Huw, interested in what could cause such scathing comments from a normally quiet and competent woman.

"It is. I've not heard from my sister since May. But when I passed through Wister, Tom Saunders told me Elma passed away in her sleep one night." She looked at the sky, gazing at the grey clouds lowering ominously. "She was only thirty-two! Bloody Bryan never even sent me a letter, and he knew we were close. I don't know what Elma died from. Bryan told Tom he'd kill me if I set foot inside the Powder Keg, and I believe it." She raised her dark eyes to meet Huw's, and they were as hard as slate. "But I know this. Bryan is dangerous to have around little girls and boys alike, see? He tried to force himself on me one night, but my long-knife said he should back off. I know in my heart he killed my sister."

Huw understood exactly what she was saying. Suddenly the face of the tinker lad he'd rescued, Ned Wells, and his broken spirit rose in Huw's mind, blinding him with the rage that always accompanied the memory. He fought the nausea...his knife slashing Dwyn's throat...the blood spraying...he could feel it hot on his hands....

Suddenly Huw was aware of Una looking at him oddly. "I'm sorry for your loss." His comment sounded lame even to him.

She grinned. "By the look of you, I'd say you've suffered some hurts of your own," she sympathized. Privately, Una thought Huw handsome, despite the sadness etched into his face. The sudden murderous look in his pretty blue eyes startled her but didn't put her off. "Don't worry. All mercs are full of secrets most folks are better off not knowing."

"I'll hold your hand if you'll hold mine," he quipped, all traces of his momentary mental lapse buried under an easy grin as if it never happened. "A burden shared is easier to bear." The Eynierish proverb rolled off his tongue as he winked at her.

Completely charmed, she laughed and said, "You're a rogue, lad!"

Chapter 20 Billy's Revenge

The next day they began what Matt warned Huw was the most dangerous leg of the journey. "Highwaymen love the lay of the road through here, so stay sharp. This is ambush country. Many good mercs have met their end here."

They travelled along the top of the aptly named Windy Ridge. It was unsettling the way both sides of the narrow track fell so sharply down to the gullies far below. The famous Rainbow Canyon glittered on the west side of the ridge, the rainbows created by the waterfalls and rapids clearly visible in the morning sun. If Huw hadn't been so terrified it would have been breathtakingly beautiful.

The Limpwater was supposedly navigable by barges north of the canyon, but the river was dangerous even in the safer stretches. Only things too big to be carried by wagon were transported by barge; the villages this far south were too small to justify the expense.

Huw's heart pounded as he followed the caravan across the barren ridge, clenching his teeth so they wouldn't chatter, and thinking it was like walking a tightrope. The travelers were buffeted by heavy wind gusts coming from the East, but at last began another descent. Now a chasm dropped on one side of him, and a rock wall rose on the other. He let out the breath he didn't realize he'd been holding. *A stiff breeze up there could blow you to an early death*, he thought.

His musings were confirmed when they stopped at a ford to water the teams. Matt said, "We were lucky today. Usually the wind is a lot brisker up there. It's been known to gust so hard unwary travelers have been blown down into the Rainbow Canyon, wagons and all."

Once the horses were watered, they were back on the narrow, winding road that cut through a defile barely wide enough for the caravan to pass through. At several places, the walls came close to touching the sides of the wagons. Looking up, the sky was a ragged slash of blue, so high above the narrow passage was bathed in an eternal twilight. Making things worse, the canyon curved to the west, so even those riding point couldn't see too far ahead.

Just when it seemed to Huw they were completely lost with no chance of being found, they emerged from the forested hills and canyons onto a wide, rocky steppe that was the Broad Valley. When they crested the higher knolls, he could see small, solitary farms interspersed with thick stands of sweet-maple, forests of fir, and hemlock. Down near the river were groves of white-barked birch. Even though it was only early September, the maples were already beginning to turn gold and fiery orange, a full month earlier than in the South. Huw was lulled into a near trance by the beauty of the scenery.

Suddenly he heard shouting toward the front of the caravan. Wondering what could be going on, Huw unsheathed his sword and rode quickly to the front, prepared to fight whatever had attacked them.

Matt was sheathing his sword as he arrived, and giving orders to back the wagons up to a safe distance. Once he had everyone doing as he asked, Matt looked at Huw and said, "See this?" He pointed to a mound of dirt, rocks, and sticks that looked unnatural, as if someone or something had built it. It stood at the edge of the road.

Huw saw a great many small creatures that looked a bit like hairless chipmunks with skinny, rat tails. They were kind of charming in a way, and their metallic, coppery skin gleamed wetly in the sun. They went about their business as if they had nothing to fear, moving pebbles and sticks, paying no attention to the Ravens now gathered about them planning their demise. As Huw was to discover, nothing could eat them, so they had no natural predators.

"It's a nest of firesprites, a new one. Firesprites are a nuisance because they're poisonous to the touch. Even the weeds around the nest will have their poison clinging where they have brushed against them. See how the foliage is shriveling and dying? We can't just leave them here, or they'll build a nest further out on the road, and someone's horse will stumble into it and die a painful death. Cleaning your sword after you've killed them is tricky, as you really don't want to get the poison on you. We'll need a bit of majik since none of us are as mad as Lackland." Matt rolled his eyes. "He claims it's not a fair fight if you use an amulet." Turning back Matt called, "Una! How's your amulet? I've a sleep charm with me, but I've used it twice. I was going to have the Fat Friar restore it for me in Limpwater. I doubt it'll knock out this nest. There's about eighteen or so firesprites."

Una fished inside her mail and held something up. "I've used it once, so be prepared to use yours if it doesn't do the job completely."

Matt agreed and pulled his own amulet out just to have it handy. He turned back to Huw. "Now we need to herd them to the center of the nest and get them bunched into as tight a group as we can. Don't touch them whatever you do. The slime on their skin will burn you like the hottest fire, and there's no stopping it from eating your flesh away. That's why they're called firesprites. The wounds keep putrefying, and amputation is the only remedy. Water helps but only if you get it on the affected area immediately before the poison has done too much damage. I'm talking minutes here, and you have to really sluice the wounds to get it off. Sadly, they never seem to nest near water."

Una said, "They like to nest along roads because there's not so much foliage and they get more sun there. The sun heats their nests and hatches their eggs."

"They don't look much like a sprite, do they?" Huw said, thinking they were interesting but not really fairy-like. "At least, not what I always thought a sprite should look like."

"I think it's because when they're looking for grubs and such all you see is a little flash of copper as they disappear into the brush," Una replied. "I've always wondered about that too."

"You still have fairies up here, don't you?" Huw's naïve question made her laugh.

"Yes, fairies live in most flower gardens. They sip nectar and don't bother anything. They seem to be attracted to houses with flower gardens, so they live in towns more than in the wild. They're creatures of majik, like wood-wraiths and such. All the old majik creatures still live here in the North, although many of them are becoming rare, thankfully." Una chuckled and said, "Fairy-bothering is an activity twelve-year-old boys seem to be drawn to."

Going back along the road, they cut young branches that were too high for the firesprite poison to have touched. Matt gestured to Huw and the others to spread out around the low mounded nest. "Don't let your legs or cloaks touch the foliage." Huw was careful to stay a distance from the contaminated shrubbery. Fortunately, the creatures were rather easy to redirect. Just a slight nudge of the branch would get them moving in the direction Matt wanted them to go.

Una held her amulet up and said the words that unleashed the majik, and soon the tiny creatures were all sleeping soundly. Matt quickly killed them, cutting their little heads off.

"I can't sheath my blade this way, or it'll taint the scabbard. So this is how you clean it." Holding his sword carefully, pointed toward the grass, he poured water over both sides of the blade, using all the water in his canteen. Then he put on his gauntlets and used his bandanna to wipe down his blade. "Now, Huw, we'll do it again. If you'll be so good as to pour your water over it, I'll need your bandanna." Once he was done, both rags were buried. With the situation resolved the Ravens walked back to their horses. The caravan began to move forward, rolling down the trade road as if nothing had slowed them.

The Ravens didn't seem to think the firesprites were anything out of the ordinary. They were just a pest to be dealt with, not even a hitch in the day's plans. *A nuisance, Matt called them. Things with poison skin that burns like fire, eats your flesh away, and they're only nuisances? I wonder what they consider dangerous here. You're in over your head, Huw Owyn, but it's too late to turn back now.* He was silent as he rode, wondering what new horror lurked in the deceptively beautiful forest.

At mid-afternoon, they passed an even less frequently traveled crossroad, graced by a signpost that proclaimed "Dervy—3 Hours" to the west, "Hyola—2 Days" to the east, "Castleton—1 Day" to the north, and "Somber Flats—1 Day" to the south. Beneath the arm for Castleton, an obviously new sign read "Limpwater—Ahead."

"We're nearly there," said Eron Smithson, the driver whose wagon Huw rode tail beside. "Fortunately, the trail between Somber Flats and Limpwater isn't too long a leg as journeys go. Now we're finally in the Broad Valley, the hard part is done for today. The road gets really difficult the further north you go."

"I noticed the wagons can't go very quickly in the hills," agreed Huw. "I thought the road out of Clythe was bad, but the trail out of Bekenberg isn't really even a track."

Eron laughed. "You Southerners are spoiled, with all the flat land you have. Roads up here are notoriously hard to build and even harder to maintain. The weather destroys them as soon as we get them built. The Crown has chain-gangs working on them nine months out of the year, and the repairs will last for about a month once the rains really hit in the winter. Two good long caravans and the road turns to mush."

A league further on, at a signpost that read "Limpwater," they left the narrow, rutted trade road, turning down a wide, well-maintained, newly-graveled street that obviously led somewhere important. Winding around a low hill, the street ended at a crossroad. Another newly painted signpost read "Limpwater Market District—South" and "Factory Quarter—North." Arrows pointed in the appropriate directions. A small sign underneath them read "Tannery" with an arrow pointing to the Factory Quarter.

They turned south on a broad, graveled avenue closely lined with small plots of land staked and marked for sale. Many were sold and had houses in various stages of construction. Tents provided temporary housing on most of the plots while buildings were being raised. They neared the center of the newborn town and began to find lots occupied by stone cottages with thatched roofs. After passing several tidy houses with small gardens, the caravan turned a corner and entered the wide center square with boardwalks along the front of the shops. Bright, newly-painted signs advertised a tailor, a bakery, and a general merchandise store, all with workmen hovering about them, though they were open for business. These shops stood opposite the grand façade of a fine, new, stone building that encompassed one whole side of the square. A large, rather lurid sign swung over the inn's door. A bloody knife proclaimed this was "Billy's Revenge."

They rode to the rear of the inn and entered the immense stable yard. "Billy has the best of everything for us here," said Matt. "He has the finest bathhouse I've ever seen. You'll be extremely well cared for. I'll give your letter to Billy. He'll have a place for you, I'm sure, even if you don't see yourself as a real merc."

The largest stable Huw had ever seen was run by a cheerful, grizzled, old ex-merc known as Cob John, who took their horses. A graveled path led from the stables to a smithy from which the sounds of hammers rose. Beyond that, a large log cabin was visible through trees; the path led to the wide front porch. An immense, heavily fenced vegetable garden and an equally well penned run filled with many chickens lay between the stable and the wagon barn. The steeply sloping land between the inn and the river was enclosed pasture, and several horses munched grass in the meadow.

The Ravens paused at an outbuilding where a small, sinewy old man wearing an apron and a bandanna tied about his forehead stood on a stool, skinning a pair of freshly killed bucks that hung in the doorway. "Hey, Mick! How's things?" called Matt. "This is Huw Owyn." He turned to Huw, saying, "This is Chicken Mickey, the best provisioner in the business. It figures Billy snagged him. Knowing our Mick, he probably runs everything here in Limpwater. No doubt the whole town would starve without him."

"Nice to meet you, Huw. Now, Matt, you know it's Billy as keeps this place afloat," replied the old man, his knife flashing as he deftly worked. "Young Lackland and One-Shot George brought us a nice pair of bucks for tomorrow's dinner, so if you don't mind, I'll just finish this. You boys look knackered, and your horses don't look any better. Was it a hard trip?"

"No more than usual. We had moderately good weather and some fairly dry roads, although Huw here probably thinks it was bad. He's never been this far north so he doesn't know what normal is yet. We got lucky this morning. Windy Ridge was nothing too exciting. We didn't stay in Somber Flats. We camped outside the stockade, so we've been on the road sixteen days, what with the muddy passes and all. Bryan must be out on the road—he didn't bother us," Matt replied. "What's going on in Somber Flats? Una ran into several Wolves up in Wister, but they weren't merry at all. Tom Saunders was upset. He said Elma passed away in her sleep, which doesn't sound right to me at all." His sharp eyes probed the old man's face.

Mick's knife paused for a moment. "Well, it *ain't* right—we all know that. Bryan murdered the Bastard and we all know *that*, too. And he hid the body where we'll never find it, so we can't prove it. Bryan got Tom and several others too drunk to know which end was up and tricked them into signing contracts with him, so now they're stuck for another year. Johnny Malone is a Rowdy now, and Stella One-Eye. Johnny says the Wolves all think Bryan done Elma so as he could lay claim to the Wolves with no interference from her. You know Elma handled the business for them when the Bastard got to be such a drunk he couldn't manage things, so they were doing well enough." He shrugged, looking at Matt, who just nodded.

Mickey and his knife went back to work, deftly skinning the buck. "It's a good thing Bryan ran me and Cob John out of town last April when he first took over." He paused and turned his old eyes to Matt. "With things so bad in Somber Flats, folks are pulling up stakes and fleeing here. Two or three families arrive every day hoping to find work, and Billy doesn't turn anyone away. He's hard-pressed to feed and shelter everyone until they get their shops up and running, but he manages to do it. Things *are* good here, and crippled hand or not, young Billy's proving himself to be a real leader. He cares about folks."

Matt shook his head as he and Huw walked around to the front of the inn, entering the common room. "Billy's town is going to be a proper city and soon. It'll be the first real city south of Castleton. The next big place is Clythe, and now you know firsthand how much wilderness lies between here and there."

Matt led Huw to the bar where a portly friar stood sipping a mug of ale. "Friar Robert De Bolt, this is Huw Owyn. Robert here is a dab hand at making amulets and casting spells. He swings a good sword too, though he'll deny it because he's too lazy to get out and use it, hence the moniker 'Fat Friar.'"

"Nice to meet you, Friar Robert." Huw shook the man's hand, noticing the strength and hard callouses of a sword-master. *This man is a Brother of St. Aelfrid,* thought Huw in awe. *But why's he pretending to be slightly drunk? He's as sober as I am, and that's muscle under those robes, not fat.*

"Pleased to meet you, Huw, but you can call me Robert or Fat Friar, everyone else does. And that's entirely true, St. Coeur. Ale before bloodshed, I always say," replied the friar with a drunken grin, toasting Matt with his mug. "Besides, someone has to keep Billy in business."

A huge, blond man with a ruddy, youthful face and massive biceps entered from the kitchen, carrying a wooden keg on his immense shoulder, one arm wrapped around it. He was taller and more muscular than anyone Huw had ever seen, towering over Matt by a good six inches, and Matt was quite tall. "I'll be with you in a moment, Matt," he said cheerfully. "I have just enough rooms for your group, but if I run out of ale, Robert will keel over from thirst, and we can't have that."

Finally the big, blond man sat down and Huw was introduced to Billy "Ninefingers" MacNess. "Billy," Matt said, "I've a lad here who needs to be scarce in the South for a while, so the Ravens really won't do for him, as we go that way too often. Huw's a good man with the knives, and he's got a merc's heart, but he's a tinker and entertainer by trade. Still, he killed a mountain lion with his sword and took down a wood-wraith with a knife to the eye." Billy's eyes widened. "He came north with Younger Murfee and fought a firedrake near the High Falls. Murfee recommends him."

"I could use another lad for some of the smaller jobs, and if *you* say he's good, it's all the reference I need," replied Billy, grinning and spitting in his maimed palm and holding it out to Huw. He did the same, and Billy clasped it in a surprisingly strong grip, considering how damaged his hand was. Now Huw was a Rowdy. "A tinker, you say. I've been thinking an entertainer would lend a bit of class to the place." He stood up. "I'll show you your rooms," he said to all the Ravens, and turning to Huw, he said, "This is your home for as long as you want it. Your room is on the Rowdies' floor." Billy's open smile made Huw feel as if he'd come home, and for a moment, he was overcome with emotion. "Oh, and you should all get your baths now. The Rowdies will be back soon and you'll want to get in there before they return."

Soon Huw was in his own room, a place Billy said he could call home. He looked out his window at the town that grew before his eyes, absorbing the beauty of the afternoon sun shining through the autumn foliage. A fleeting wish that Therese was there to enjoy it with him passed through his mind, and a poignant smile crossed his face. Following on the heels of that was the memory of the promise he'd made to her that he'd start rebuilding his craft as soon as he was settled.

I'll start looking for wood for my new harp tomorrow, he thought, watching the workmen trying to get as much done as they could before dusk fell. *There's bound to be plenty of scrap wood from the furniture crafter. The strings are what'll be difficult, but maybe Chicken Mickey can help me find what I'll need. I'd bet he'll help me get tools and a place for a workshop. I'll make her as large as My Lady was. I wonder if abalone shells are available up here for the inlays.*

For the last two nights, Huw had noticed something he'd never seen in the South, but heard about. Frost sparkled in the high hills the last two mornings and there was a slight chill in the air. This meant he really appreciated the fine, warm bathhouse Billy provided.

Huw met Matt on the stairwell, and the two went down together. He found it was every bit as opulent as he'd been told, with separate sides for the men and women. On each side were large dressing rooms with full-length mirrors and washbasins plumbed with hot and cold running water, four hammered-copper tubs, and six flushing toilets, which meant no smelly privy. Marble tiles covered the walls and floors. Large gilt mirrors hung over the washbasins, all combined to make the most opulent bathhouse he'd ever seen. *Even House Dwyn isn't as rich as this,* Huw thought as he looked around in stunned silence. *I wonder who keeps all of this so shiny and clean? Probably there's a maid.* The faint scents of vinegar and salt bore testament to the daily polishing of the fixtures.

Huw undressed and settled into his steaming tub, letting the hot water soak away the aches of the road. He and Matt relaxed in companionable silence until he could restrain his curiosity no longer. "How on earth do they keep this place looking so fine? It's one thing to polish a few copper pots every day, but this…." He gestured around the room, which seemed to glow in the afternoon light that came through the high windows. "And the ladies' side must be every bit as lavish."

"It's larger, so the ladies tell me. The widowed mother of one of Billy's Rowdies keeps this place looking new. We'll rinse out the tubs when we're done, as is only right, but she'll be in after us to make sure everything looks bright for the next lucky bathers. Billy takes care of his own just like the Ravens do," replied Matt. "I suspect there's more work than there are hands to do it in a place like this. I don't envy Billy his task. To have so many souls depending on him must weigh heavy at times."

Shaving with hot water seemed luxurious to Huw after all the days of traveling. As he trimmed his hair, he gazed at his reflection in the mirror. The man who stared back looked renewed, as if the troubles and sorrows of the past months had washed down the drain with the dust and dirt of the road. Clean and feeling rested for the first time since leaving Bekenberg, Huw returned to his room to finish putting his things away and think about the latest turn his life had taken.

Billy provided room and board and arranged for work, sending each Rowdy out on a rotating basis. He kept twenty percent of the take and was considered by all to be the most reasonable captain in the business to work for. From what Huw could see, Billy was a special sort of person. *There's a story here,* he thought. *Billy and Bess aren't ordinary people. He's the kind of man who makes things happen.*

Bess, Billy's pregnant lady, explained to Huw that she brought up a change of sheets on Mondays and said

Edythe, the maid who did laundry and cleaned the paying guests' rooms, would change the bed if she was asked. The Rowdies each gave her a copper a week for her extra services, as she was a widow with four strapping sons to feed. Myrtle, the bathhouse attendant, also received a copper a week from each of the Rowdies.

He put away the few clothes he owned and placed the framed portrait of his family on the mantel. The sets of embroidered pieces that were his mum's last creations he laid on the table. *Tomorrow I'll have the tailor make me some shirts with these sewn into them. I'll never wear a bard's robes again, but I'll still be dressed well.* Then he laid the small tapestry he'd saved on the bed. *I'll ask Mickey to help me hang this and my dad's harp,* he thought. He looked at his room with a sense of wonder, touching each of the possessions he'd struggled to save, the bits of his parents' lives which were all that remained to connect him with them.

Finally Huw unpacked all his instruments and went downstairs to the common room, where he selected a stool from which he could see everything. He set each instrument where he could reach it with ease and began playing his pipes quietly, his soft melodies providing a sweet backdrop to the conversations that went on in small groups and corners. Soon he was lost in his thoughts and music.

Suddenly he was grabbed in a bear hug, and a familiar voice shouted, "Jak! Jak the tinker's son! You've cut your hair. I knew I'd see you again!" Lackland was over the moon with joy. "Billy! Mags! Everyone! This is the very tinker-lad who rescued me from the cage in the haunted village and saved Farroll from a miserable death!" He hugged Huw enthusiastically again. "And what are you calling yourself *now*, Jak? Will we know your real name? I knew you were no scholar."

"I am Huw Owyn, and yes, it's my true name. Sadly, I am *most* definitely a scholar as are all of my people," laughed Huw as he and Lackland sat at a table with a beautiful lady with flashing dark eyes and burnished mahogany hair. "You must be the lovely Lady Mags, about whom my exuberant friend here waxed so poetic, while he regained his health after his ordeal in the South."

"I'm pleased to meet you! None of these louts believed my poor Lackland when he told them he was held captive in a haunted village," she laughed. "He's known to be a bit imaginative, but even Julian couldn't hallucinate a haunted town and gibbet cage."

Matt sat down with them, saying, "Huw! You never told me *you* are the famous tinker who rescued the Great Knight! Everyone's heard Lackland's story, but now we'll hear what really happened."

"And so you will. I've made it into a ballad," replied Huw, his eyes sparkling with mischief. "I hoped I'd have the chance to play it here first since it *is* Lackland's story."

As he tuned his lute, Huw looked around the room, full of friendly faces. The warmth and genuine acceptance from Billy Ninefingers and plump Bess, the camaraderie of the Rowdies as they entered the common room and greeted their friends, the Ravens from Bekenberg, and the sincere welcome from various merchants, all of whom were retired mercenaries who dined there—all these feelings made his heart swell to bursting with a myriad of emotions Huw never thought he'd ever feel again.

Home, he thought, feeling a joy so sharp it was nearly pain. *I've come home, and I'll never have to leave again.*

>>><<<

unique electronic & print books
United States   United Kingdom   Australia

ABOUT THE AUTHOR

Connie J Jasperson lives and writes in Olympia, Washington. A vegan, she and her husband share five children, eleven grandchildren and a love of good food and great music. She is active in local writing groups, and is the Olympia area municipal liaison for NaNoWriMo. Music and food dominate her waking moments and when not writing or blogging she can be found with her Kindle, reading avidly.

You can find her blogging at: Life in the Realm of Fantasy http://conniejjasperson.wordpress.com

Tower of Bones Series – Book I, Tower of Bones takes the reader to the world of Neveyah, where the Gods are at war and one man holds the key to winning that battle. Book II, Forbidden Road is the follow-up, and picks up the story six years after the end of Book I, Tower of Bones.

Tales from the Dreamtime, a novella of fairytales consisting of two short stories and one novella.

Billy's Revenge Series – Huw, the Bard takes you to the world of Waldeyn, and a medieval alternate reality. Fleeing a burning city, everything he ever loved in ashes behind him, penniless and hunted, Huw the Bard must somehow survive.

MYRDDIN PUBLISHING GROUP
Book List
WWW.MYRDDINPUBLISHING.COM

URBAN FANTASY ~ PARANORMAL ~ ROMANCE

YUM by Nicole Antonia Carson (YA)
Can Jim and his great-granddaughter Emily stop the carnage?

Brawn Stroker's Dragula: The Journal of Dee Flaytable by
Nicole Antonia Carro (Mature Readers)
When the Vampire Queens battle, who will win? Dragula is pure smut.
Enjoy!

HEART SEARCH SERIES by Carlie M.A. Cullen (New Adult)
HEART SEARCH, book one: Lost, HEART SEARCH, book two:
Found
One bite starts it all. . .Fate toys with mortals and immortals alike, as
two hearts torn apart by darkness face ordeals which test them to
their limits.

THE GUARDIAN SERIES by Joan Hazel (New Adult)
Book I THE LAST GUARDIAN, Book II BURDENS OF A
SAINT
Delta Pack is an elite force of shape-shifters charged with
maintaining order in both the shifter and human communities. High
adventure and sizzling romance!

HIRED BY A DEMON by Gypsy Madden (YA)
A simple babysitting position goes terribly awry for Vara…Urban fantasy at its best!

SCIENCE FICTION

LAND OF NOD SERIES by Gary Hoover (Appropriate for all ages)
Book I—The Artifact,
Book II - The Prophet
Jeff Browning has been haunted by terrifying dreams since the mysterious disappearance of his father (a renowned physicist). But when he finds a portal in his father's office, he must overcome his fears in an attempt to find him.

THE DREAM LAND Series BY Stephen Swartz
Book I Long Distance Voyager,
The Dream Land 2 - Dreams of Futures Past,
The Dream Land 3 - Diaspora
An epic of interdimensional intrigue, alien romance, and world domination by a couple of high school nerds mashed with psychological thriller and time travel.

~~~

STEAMPUNK

THE CROWN PHOENIX SERIES by Alison DeLuca (Teen)
The Night Watchman Express
Devil's Kitchen
The Lamplighter's Special
The South Sea Bubble
A magic typewriter, time-travel, a mysterious train—high adventure written with Edwardian flair!

The Infinity Bridge (The Nu-Knights) by Ross M. Kitson (Teen)
Three teenagers are propelled into an action-packed race against time, involving alternate realities, airships, clockwork killers.... and Merlin.

~~~

LITERARY FICTION

AFTER ILIUM by Stephen Swartz (Mature readers)
Seduction and betrayal on the road to Ilium. An epic of interdimensional intrigue, alien romance, and world domination by a couple of high school nerds mashed with psychological thriller and time travel.

TALES FROM THE DREAMTIME by Connie J. Jasperson (Literary Fantasy, Mature Readers)
Three grownup Tales from the Dreamtime in one novella....A conversation with Galahad, a prince on a quest and a goddess in mourning, a stolen kingdom and the Fractal Mirror. Three tales of wonder and great deeds, three tales of heroes and villains.

~~~

EPIC FANTASY

HUW THE BARD by Connie J. Jasperson (Medieval Fantasy, Mature Readers)

Fleeing a burning city, everything he ever loved in ashes behind him, penniless and hunted, no place is safe. Abandoned and alone, Huw the Bard must somehow survive.

TOWER OF BONES SERIES by Connie J Jasperson (Epic Fantasy, Mature Readers)

Book I, Tower of Bones

Book II Forbidden Road

The Gods are at war, and Neveyah is the battleground.

PRISM SERIES by Ross M. Kitson (Epic Fantasy, Mature Readers)

Darkness Rising 1 – Chained

Darkness Rising 2 – Quest

Darkness Rising 3 – Secrets

Darkness Rising 4 – Loss

Bravery is measured in moments. The forces of darkness are rising—and tragedy awaits even the most heroic.

unique electronic & print books

United States   United Kingdom   Australia